VOO

RUSH

Chris Manno

White Bird Publications
P.O. Box 90145
Austin, Texas 78709
http://www.whitebirdpublications.com

Cover design by Mark Banzhoff

ISBN: 978-1-63363-205-9
LCCN: 2016955703

PRINTED IN THE UNITED STATES OF AMERICA

“We all have our demons and weaknesses,” Avery said,
“And when they find each other, which they always do,
there’s hell to pay.”

Visit Chris
At:

http://ChrisManno.net

Amazon: http://goo.gl/jie9cD

https://www.facebook.com/chris.manno

https://twitter.com/search?q=chris_manno

https://www.linkedin.com/in/chris-manno-09566312

VOODOO RUSH

White Bird
Publications

Chapter One

"The croc," droned Big Lou, "Has no overbite. Teeth match up," he said, "one for one on a narrow pointy nose." Gawd, there he'd go again.

"Not like the alligator, which has an overbite."

Though Lou's Cajun accent, the last word sounded like "Ova bide," which left half of his sweltering passengers mystified.

The flat-bottomed, tin roof-covered skiff glided into the waterway, motor grumbling idly, gargling muddy sad greenish swamp water as Big Lou backed us out, trying to engage the pasty, high falutin' touristas with marsh saga. I tuned out.

I was there for one thing, and one thing only—to not be there. And there, in this case, was one small, dank crumbly shop in *da kawta*. No, not Dakota— The Quarter, the French Quarter. It was complicated.

Big Lou swung the boat around, urging his captive tourists to take a panoramic shot as he did. Nada. Lou worked hard, if only to control his normal profanity stream and mercurial temper, but nobody got it. Except me, knowing Big Lou as I did. He was short; Big Lou was built compact, swarthy, Cajun and mean. His older brother—also a sawed off boatman—did time in the state pen for his first years of meanness. He'd get his second set, probably with a death sentence, when he finished the first. Still, I'd bet on Lou to get to Death Row first.

But if I was with Big Lou, he wasn't dead—nor was I. I needed to be offshore, deep in the Lafitte Swamp, at least until late afternoon. Laugh if you want, but that was the simple harshness of life on that day, that bayou, that swamp. The ass end—stern, Big Lou would correct me, stern goddamit—rotated starboard to port, counterclockwise, and Lou gave me a squinty one-eyed stare. I got it, Lou. I got it.

This signal biz could have been so much easier, but Lou was old school. He ran a boat to the cargo pier twice a week, and carried back a mental manifest of illegal drugs or worse, destined for The Tombs here in the LaFitte swamp, waiting aboard ships in the harbor. Kind of a switchman in the rail yard, signaling which track would carry what railcars. Only his cars were basically crammed with felonious cargo.

Technology? Sure, you could accomplish the communications signaled so clumsily by Lou's bow and stern turned instantly by text or smartphone app. But those could be hacked, could be intercepted, decoded, cached, and ultimately, played in court. Instead, it was me and my warm body and sharp eyes reading the silent, unspoken semiotics, then passing them along.

A graveyard, bone-white with arched tombs, bleached, cracked dry by years of bayou sun, lay over my shoulder ashore as the stern—ass end, eff Lou—challenged the touristas to rise from their bench seats and snap a shot or two. That boded well for Lou's tip jar. You looked at the graveyard, the reedy shoreline, the marsh, the moss-draped, low-slung trees and you'd think, for god's sake, how did they get there, bury stuff, raise monuments? But I knew.

A buzz boat snarled by—that's what I called the airboats with stadium-seated, ear-protected, and slack-jawed touristas riding the wooden prop driven skiffs—as Big Lou motored us into the swamp. The noise, gawd, the raggedy, chainsaw noise, covered a multitude of sins. Lou and I knew this, and we waited. Uptown, I repeated to myself, confirming Lou's deliberate swing of the ass end. Uptown.

Last night at original *Masperos*, early, Boucane appeared like smoke in the dusk, coming together out of nothing, swirling, then visible in the mirror over the bar, seated on a barstool to my left—mahogany bar and Boucane, both burnished by time and tide; he swirled two fingers of dark Bourbon in a clear glass. He stared straight ahead at the mirror over the bar. I did likewise.

"You know," he said, his voice at once a growl and a purr, "You know we're at a turning point."

Heard that before; scary, then and now. Without missing a beat, I slugged back a boiling shot and nodded, clearing my throat to speak as the fire burns lower. Boucane raised a hand. "No."

No? His eyes widened, observing me in the shadowy old mirror edged with a jagged mountain range of booze bottles on the bottom and an etched, smoke-stained silhouette of St. Charles Cathedral on the top. "You be gone tomorrow." He meant afloat, I know. That's a bad sign, but I said nothing. "Gone" normally meant "offshore," but sometimes, too, it meant dead.

Ancient *Masperos* was a sanctuary, for us, so I forced a calm that didn't fit the dread I felt and held my breath, hoping Boucane didn't notice in the mirror. Amédée studiously avoided my eyes, refilled my glass, and then vanished.

"Listen carefully," Boucane formed the words deliberately. "If things go uptown, you get gone. Hear me, mon?"

We locked eyes in the mirror above the bar. Slowly, noncommittal, I nodded. Then still looking directly at each other, watching hands in the mirror, we raised glasses, then drank.

"I hear you, my friend," the words came from my mouth but sounded like a distant audio track, whiskey-scratched and breathy. "And now we're even."

Boucane faced me, his eyes crinkled narrow, almost amused. "No," he said, "No. Now you owe me."

A freaky tropical storm zigzagged over the Gulf of Mexico, took one look at the Crescent City, and then zagged west, leaving *Nawlins* under a ridge of high pressure that kept it uncommonly rainless, even at noon, with a languid high anchored over the Mississippi, shooing the storm west. A light breeze, scented with reedy grasses and burnt oil from somewhere, blew over the marsh, blessedly cool in the noonday sun as Big Lou motored us deep into the swamp.

"We gon' see a gatuh' up close an' puhsonul," Big Lou promised the rather sparse boatload. How could this be? Summer, tourist season and a half full boat? Half empty, Lou would say with a scowl. And yet, the real purpose of the swamp was served—or being served; besides what was shown but left unsaid, we could talk under cover of the nuisance airboats, far from listening devices or prying lenses.

I owed Lou nothing, really, but I tried to scrawl a debt on his ledger: "B says get gone tonight." I let that hang in the air, as still and unwavering as the Spanish moss draped on sagging branches on both sides of the inlet we slid through.

"Smoke and mirrors bullshit," Lou grunted. "Smokey's a false prophet." I cringed at even Boucane's nickname said aloud, indiscreetly. Ahead, a ridged black mound rose to reveal stubby legs, then glided from the shore to the water, swimming our way. Touristas seemed not to notice.

"Do what you want. Just passing the word," I said as Lou altered course a couple of degrees toward the gator wriggling smoothly our way. Lou grunted again, his look darkening. Pepe, a smallish gator, maybe four feet long, did his duty, swimming alongside as Lou throttled back and tossed two fat marshmallows into the murky water.

"Gators can't eat underwater," Lou lectured the touristas. "So you see him raise up, tail up too, wid every bite."

Would have been more dramatic if Pepe had snapped at the bobbing marshmallows, but he just let each float into his mouth in turn, then barely tossed them back. Lazy.

But that meager spectacle got the touristas to the rail, snapping away with cell phones. I'd kept an eye on them, always hoping to witness an iPhone slipping out of a sweaty hand, then *kerplop*. Not today; at least not yet.

"Look," I said quietly, "You want something from Meng or doncha?" I'm not from the bayou; I don't talk like they do and only barely understand the vernacular. But he damn well knew what I meant.

Lou slapped a disposable phone into my palm then spun the wheel left, easing us toward a sprawling, moss-draped tree. I worried about snakes hanging from the scraggly tree limbs more than gators swimming bored below. Touristas snapped pics of Pepe swimming away.

"Yeah," Lou muttered under his breath. "You tell her my price just went up."

That's nothing you "tell" Meng. A tourista MILF caught a glimpse of Big Lou's ginormous bayonet only barely hidden behind the boat wheel. She seemed rattled, and I smirked in spite of myself. For a second, then back to business.

"Jeezuz, Lou—"

"You tell her, podna."

I pocketed the phone and nodded, resigned. After all, I

was just a courier. The phone had deets that I was supposed to blindly pass along. Lou grabbed his gun-metal bayonet and stabbed a shrink-wrapped package of hot dogs, splitting it wide open. Big gator show next: The Admiral, a six-foot, shiny black gator surfaced out of the murk, knowing exactly where and when hot dogs would appear on the calm surface. Five, maybe six years old? A little over five feet nose to tail, but slim nonetheless.

"That's uh-baht-a six-foot gay-tuh," Lou told the rapt touristas. "At least six hundred pounds and mean. I'll show ya how ta feed a big gay-tuh."

Boucane wasn't the only lying sombitch. I took the opportunity to slide back on the metal bench and prop myself against the aft bulkhead, resting. I would take the blue sky, the light breeze, Big Lou's growly drone for the touristas; the freedom of a gliding skiff in the Lafitte Swamp, going nowhere, going slow. The mahogany man of smoke, promises of doom, the handoff to Meng, and inevitably, raven-haired Avery's nut-brown eyes probing my own, asking, "What have you gotten yourself into, perfesser; what this time?"

I had about two hours to figure out an answer, then stay alive after I did. That, I'd soon find out, would not be enough time.

Chapter Two

"Can't believe I let you drag me onto this stupid tourist trap," Avery sighed. Meaning, being a resident of the French Quarter, the old restored paddle wheeler was culturally below her threshold of interest.

"Look, your last name's O'Toole," I wanted tell her, "so drop the Cajun facade, wouldja?" Of course I didn't say a word, but I filed all of this away. Because if I undercut her outward identity, I might have to back away from my own.

How would that go? Yeah, the "Doc" in "Doc Mosby," which everyone called me, referred to my doctorate in Critical Analysis and Applied Logic. And "Mosby" is a name I chose, a sly nod to "The Grey Ghost," General Mosby, who appeared out of nowhere on the Civil War battlefield, kicked ass—then vanished just as quickly. At least, that's been my strategy for as long as I've been in this shady business.

But Avery's Cajun facade came with a side order of concern I sensed instinctively; who is she really? But until I was in a position to answer that question asked of myself, I decided I'd hold it in abeyance for her. But back to her gripe.

"Why are we on this ridiculous tub?" she asked again.

What could I have said? "I'm heeding the *Masperos* warning, being offshore? And want you to be safe, too, even though I can't figure out—yet—what is "unsafe" about you?"

"I have all these drink coupons that expire this week," I answered, only stretching the truth a bit; they will expire "this week" of next month. The *Natchez* swung into the breeze and away from the pier. Avery remained inscrutable behind her sunglasses, but she seemed at least placated for the moment, with our drinks lined two deep against the deck rail.

"Free drinks at *The Saint*," she sighed.

"Yeah, when you're working. And for me, not you."

Her silence confirmed what I already knew; the wait staff all drank on the job. And Avery, it seemed, drank the most. Too much, I'd say, and too often. But that was beside the point.

"I just wanted to get you out of the quarter and see how you look," I said.

Avery had fire just below the surface—I'd seen it before—and, if anything could shift focus from why we were really easing out into the Mississippi on an antique steamship, that rude, sexist question would do it. Then, the both of our dark sides could remain, well, in the dark.

Red had started working that darkness about ten years ago, as frontman for as a small think-tank, intel operation doing outsourced grunt work for larger corporations. I came onboard early on as an analyst, recruited from my university's doctoral program because the fledgling Tactical Analysis Group, or "TAG," as we were known, needed cerebral nerds with the ability to crunch complex data arrays into actionable results. The ginormous data arrays and readable, useable results were essentially what a Ph.D. dissertation was, right? Add to that my military service background and you had the ideal TAG operative.

Red miraculously wrangled a few DARPA contracts—Defense Advanced Research Projects Agency—and promised exactly what they needed—cheap, accurate intelligence. And he produced amazing work, predicting the Argentinian elections (I'd gotten arrested in Buenos Aires, plus an epic battle with E-coli, in the process, but still) to within two percent among eleven candidates, and predicted an assassination in Malaysia accurate to within a day.

But really, TAG, Red, me, and the entire staff were mostly a fortunate coincidence of the new economic reality; congressional intelligence appropriations were slashed. Demands remained unchanged and, in post-9/11 America, expectations ran higher than ever among congressional big mouths demanding results from traditionally bloated government agencies like the CIA, DIA, DEA, and the FBI. Also, along came the Department of Homeland Security, a huge, inexperienced juggernaut, nonetheless charged with enormous responsibilities. Red was there on the spot, in the right place at the right time, and cost effective. We didn't take federal holidays, didn't stay home when it snowed in DC, and maybe most importantly, we didn't have the federal leash on our necks as we bloodhounded our prey; no probable cause, warrants, or judicial review—just answers.

In the process, we had no powers of arrest, no weapons authorization, no military backup. We also had no rules of legal oversight, no Inspector General, and really zero authority. Which left little power to abuse, barely any supervision (it was in our contract that our clients would deny any knowledge of us) and nothing, save our consistently wily operatives, and our secret support teams, on our side. That last—support teams—were a throwback to the old NASA manned space program; we had a boiler room staff of experts I could call on from out in the field to get me answers, pronto. But our real power was in our invisibility; we'd get the results, then vanish. Mosby, remember? I'm a ghost. I made a note to toss my support team Avery O'Toole's identity, to see what they'd uncover. But a part of me held that in reserve. I just wanted her to be there on the deck of the *Natchez*, at least until I needed to know more.

And she needed to chew my ass, then and there.

"See how I look? Let's see how *you* look when I heave you overboard."

That's my girl. Anger is such a powerful distraction—something I never forgot. A cool breeze swept off the muddy water and circled around the stern rail. The sun eased itself lower and spilled a golden tint atop the receding skyline. We sailed upriver.

Earlier in the day, mid-afternoon to be exact, I'd left Big Lou to the rest of his duties—both official and "off the books." I'd trudged down Royal; a couple of rights, a left, another block; Pirate's Alley. Around the corner, a narrow alleyway, a barber pole mounted over a heavy door. A crude bell rigged over the door clanged as I entered, and I took a minute to let my eyes adjust from sunlight to the dimmer, yellowy fluorescents overhead.

Meng motioned me to a barber chair. "You're late, asshole," she growled in a raggedy smoker's rasp.

You had to back her down. "Bullshit," I snapped back.

Like Lou, Meng's another old-school criminal, acting as a traffic control supervisor for the criminal exchanges at The Tombs, she sorted out drops and deliveries, keeping rivals apart, letting the bad guys do business without bloodshed. That was the good and bad of The Tombs, which moved the criminal exchange out of the Crescent City, but let it explode in the swamp, brokered by the likes of gruff, chain-smoking Meng.

She laughed, then coughed a thick, rumbly smoker's cough. "Sonofabitch." She whipped a large barber's cloth over me like a matador swinging a cape in a bullfight. The cape fluttered noisily, perfectly around me and the chair, and she clipped it snugly around my neck. Underneath, I'd palmed the cell phone Big Lou had passed to me in the swamp and with a catlike motion, Meng's rough hand then snatched the phone without a sound. Nice job—absolutely no way that transfer could make it into any unwanted digital or audio recording. On the phone, I knew, were the details of whatever exchange was to occur at the Tombs, the graveyard Big Lou had motored us by that afternoon. Almost done.

"So where you headed, 'Doc Disaster'?" Meng asked. I let the question float in the air like the dust motes buoyed in the jaundiced light pouring down on the old school barbershop. I liked that she always had a new, insulting name to pair with "Doc." She fluttered away behind me with pointy scissors, skimming the back of my head.

I forced a yawn, but just thinking about yawning made me actually yawn. Epic performance for the three guys lining the wall, ostensibly reading newspapers, the two other bored-looking barbers, one of whom had a familiar client in his chair. Fuck you all; my yawn had been intended to say. "Uptown."

The scissors stopped for a heartbeat, then resumed. The air in the room clotted thick and dead, for a moment. Uptown meant upscale, big time exchange at the tombs, some high value, highly illegal, and probably dangerous exchange rather than the typical swap of coke for cash between bayou drug gangs.

"Well, you're not going anywhere till I say you look presentable," Meng growled at last.

I distinctly heard, couldn't ignore, a slight strain in her voice. I needed to see her face to be sure, but she stayed behind me, snipping away. I'm paid to detect nuances and anomalies and as importantly, to see patterns in their convergence. "Uptown" was Boucane's warning— "If things go uptown, you get gone"—and apparently the word sent an electric charge through Meng and her shop, too. Boucane's warning, Lou's demand, Meng's reticence. Sweep the floor, Red always said; see what's there and as importantly, what's not.

"Boatman sends his regards," I offered the bait casually. She knew I meant Big Lou.

That drew an instant, raggedly laugh from Meng. "Yeah, I bet he does. You know, I'm gonna miss that fucker."

Quietly, quickly, I did the math; Meng aside, Lou was a survivor; I weighed that and intrinsically knew that Big Lou's gone—but only for now. Meng had written him off when she heard the "uptown cue," but he saw that as leverage. Boucane had warned us that we were on the brink of disaster; I dumped the cell phone contents to my support team before I got to the barbershop. That data I could retrieve when I got a safe, secure line. The rest of the answers would be offshore, where Boucane had urged me to be. Even Boucane finally made sense, too; he was testing me. If I were law enforcement, I'd have to spring the trap, raid The Tombs Big Lou pointed out, signaled, as in play today.

If I were to remain offshore, then he'd know I'm not law enforcement, and he'd have just saved my ass from whatever was actually going down at The Tombs. I knew what was supposed to happen, so I could deduce what actually did. Come to think of it, I really did owe Smokey.

And beyond intel, I had one other mandate hanging over my head—containment. That's how we at TAG maintained our invisibility, which is how we made it in and out alive.

The ship channel. "Look for The Devil," Red had warned in the last secure data package. The channel.

"Paging Doctor Mosby," Avery yelled to no one in particular. We motored upstream as the shrinking skyline over the quarter perfected itself against the bluing sunset and growing distance. Pay attention.

"Huh? Yeah. Let's operate." She gave me that squinty-eyed look that meant either she doesn't wholly believe me—or she was getting drunk. I made a note to reconsider, later, the logical possibility of both.

"Let's go forward," she said, taking my arm. Fine. We walked uphill from the ass end (nod to Big Lou) as the Destrehan Plantation brooded below the scrubby tree line in the waning sun. The boat was full but hardly seemed so. That why I always liked the sunset cruise. That and tonight, being offshore in a good way—in the way that meant, for Boucane, not dead.

Still, there was a missing piece to the puzzle, but as in most intelligence conundrums, the answer was often staring you in the face, if you could only take a step back. So I did.

"So is this so bad for a night off?" I asked.

"Three days off." She squinted into the gathering dusk as the old sternwheeler began a sweeping starboard turn. "Remember?"

We'd return to Nawlins via the far side of the channel. Freighters anchored there in a neat line, awaiting Customs. As they waited, a ferry service brought them food, supplies, and amenities from shore. That was Big Lou's other job, officially. Unofficially, Lou ferried contraband from certain freighters to the graveyard. That's what TAG had predicted and on site, I'd verified; a South American connection; bricks in, cash out. DEA hadn't more than an inkling but outsourced us a contract to find out the reality. Within two months, I was at the core. But tonight, clearly, things had changed.

The paddleboat splashed through the inner channel between the anchored freighters and the land. Four similar hulks in a row weathervaned in the tide, silent and barely lit, waiting.

Maybe it's an intel fetish, but at ground zero in a drugs for cash op, I needed to know who was anchored there. First, the *Cosmo*; rusty, quiet, waiting. She'd been there all week. Two similar ships rested at anchor ahead. But the fourth stood out. Unfamiliar. More onboard lights maybe? Who was she?

"I've got a few days off too, actually," I mentioned, squinting into the dusk. A few days between summer sessions at Tulane, where I was expected to teach a class as an adjunct. Worry about that next week. Who was the goddam fourth ship?

We motored lazily past her port side, the lettering on the stern fuzzy but legible in the gathering night; *Teufel,* Monrovia. Red's warning rang in my ears; look for The Devil. *Teufel*, the German word for devil, and from my own support team work up before I was embedded, that meant The Big One; not drugs for money, but drugs for arms. There'd be a trail of dead bodies in the switch. That was the "uptown" warning that spooked Meng—and me—as well.

"Ever been up the Cane?" Avery asked. The Cane River. Cajun backroads. Plantation Alley.

I fixed my gaze on the *Teuful* as we motored past. She just looked sinister, brooding at anchor, a few yellow lights glowing on her bridge. Whatever arms they'd brought from Haiti were already on their way to the swamp. "No." I turned to her. "Should I have been?"

She silenced her own phone, which buzzed with yet another text. "Maybe you should. We should."

The *Natchez* cruised past downtown, then swung a graceful one-eighty, and prepared to dock. Just Avery saying "should," and the emphasis she placed on the word, telegraphed a concern that I knew I'd best heed.

"I'm in," I said nonchalantly.

"Fine. I'll drive."

That didn't necessarily seem like a good idea, given how much she'd had to drink, but going north, letting things settle, then getting a secure connection with TAG did.

"Sounds like a plan, Ms. O'Toole."

She tossed me a withering look as the *Natchez* came alongside the pier. And so it was settled; putting distance between us and Nawlins seemed like a good idea.

On the other hand, heading north one on one with Ms. O'Toole, who I wasn't really sure I knew honestly, was a calculated risk, offset only by my well-practiced ability to vanish into thin air easily and at a moment's notice. Odds were, I knew, that I'd have to do just that. As it turned out, I'd pretty much underestimated the risk, but there was no alternative. We marched down the gangplank together, and into the night.

Chapter Three

I drove while Avery snored against the passenger side door. Darkness, midnight, by the time we got her stuff and my gear and headed for Baton Rouge and beyond. Seemed as if the rest of the world had decided to crawl into a giant hermit crab shell, asleep, so that headlights and tail lights were scarce on the highway.

I'd known only a few people like her, who slept without any movement, and so quickly, too. By the time we'd hit the ever ker-thunking Louisiana slab highway over the black marsh below, she was snoring quietly, motionless.

Until about fifty miles south of Baton Rouge. She stirred.

"Where are we?"

Well, you could always just look at the moving map; it's your car. I didn't say that.

"Still south of Baton Rouge."

"Okay." She tapped a few buttons on the dash. Thought I saw "Previous Destinations" pop up, then scroll forward. She selected one.

An automated voice spoke from the dash. "Okay. Continue to follow the road for...eighteen miles." The map highlighted an angular route.

"Really?" I glanced at Avery, already snuggling back against the passenger side door.

"Trust me," she said, eyes once again slammed shut. "Okay?"

We motored on. For a moment, the sky yawned wide; a moon slice reflected off the gun-metal gray water between stumpy trees, and the thump of the wheels on the concrete highway beat a steady tattoo that lulled me with a blanket of peacefulness. For a mesmerizing moment, I could actually forget why we were fleeing north, maybe not speculate on the death toll of the ugly Tombs transaction, plus our own uncertain position in the conflict.

I thought I did a good thing, the right thing, by getting Avery out of there. I knew I did a good thing getting away myself. The rest was complicated, but time and distance would make that clear, eventually.

I pictured Meng, or at least heard her croaky voice, laughing about what she had to know meant certain death for several people she knew, like Big Lou. But she didn't know him as well as I did. I'd bet my left nut Lou sidestepped whatever went down in the swamp.

To find out who did or didn't survive, I needed a secure hookup with my support team at TAG, then maybe a talk with Red. Where was the DEA, our clients, on this, both after and maybe, more importantly, before? Why didn't they see this coming, and if they did, why didn't they warn us, pull us out? They had people in there—they might sustain casualties, too.

A red line materialized on the dash screen, then a dispassionate voice instructed, "Take the next exit..."

Avery sat up and ran her fingers through her hair, tossing her head as if to shake out the cobwebs of sleep.

"Brace yourself, perfesser," she breathed. "You're about to tangle with The Irish Sisterhood."

I looked at her pointedly, waiting for an explanation but none was forthcoming as she studied her face in the vanity mirror. "I look like I slept in a car all night."

"Much of it," I said, mostly to myself. The barest glow of a grudging dawn picked at the eastern horizon. I followed the map display to a well-lit one-story cinder-block building with a parking lot surprisingly full for that hour of the morning. But then, that was their business, morning, dawn; *Coffee Call*. Cafe au Lait, rich with chicory and cream, stand a spoon up in it, pry your sleepy eyes open from the inside. And too-hot-to-eat beignets (don't let that stop you) that explode in a blizzard of powdered sugar with every bite. Smart woman, Avery. Now, what was this "Sisterhood—Irish Sisterhood" thing?

I held the door for her, then stepped into the bright lights and a provocative cloud of rich coffee smell and—probably just my imagination—the air carried the flavor of frying dough. But what struck me next seemed like an imaginary image, a mirage, yet it was all too real; a carbon copy of Avery, face to face.

"I warned you, didn't I?" Avery's voice came from my left side, but an exact duplicate, face-to-face, grinned her same patented "I like that I make you nervous" grin.

"He really doesn't look like a professor," the apparition spoke, glancing at her double standing beside me.

"He says he is," Avery answered. Uncanny, even the voice, the inflection, tone—a carbon copy. "Although I've never seen him on a campus. So what does he look like?"

"I don't know," the apparition mused. "Insurance salesman? High school band teacher?"

Avery furrowed her brow. "I could see that. He's pretty geeky."

"Anyone care to introduce me here?" I asked. The Irish Sisterhood; twins. Unless god forbid, triplets.

"Audrey, Mosby; Mosby, Audrey. He has a first name, but that's what everyone calls him."

Speaking of geeky, Audrey was the tamed version of Avery, wearing business attire rather that Avery's more edgy wardrobe. She looked like she could be a high school principal.

"Audrey practices law in Baton Rouge," Avery offered.

"Call me Jay," I said, offering my hand. "Everyone else does."

Uncanny, it was, that she had the exact same smirk as her sister. Avery shook her head. "Mosby. Jay is a really nerdy name."

"I gotta find the men's room," I said, trying to extricate myself. "Been driving a few hours straight."

"We pulled over an hour ago," Avery tossed over her shoulder. "I figured that was what you were doing on the side of the road." She took Audrey's arm and headed to the seating area.

And I'd thought she was asleep the whole time. I made a note of that for future reference. "Just order me the usual, wouldja?" She smiled that squinty-eyed smile that means she's really happy.

As I headed for the men's room on the far side of the restaurant, words scrolled across the bottom of a newscast droning from a wall-mounted television; "Louisiana State Police investigating four bodies discovered in Lafitte graveyard..."

Damn. Didn't break stride, but felt the wind go out of my sails; four bodies likely meant more than that dead, some of whom I probably knew. If some of the fatalities were DEA, there'd be a major war, but if that were the case, TAG would quietly disappear from the conflict. That's way out of our league.

I splashed cold water on my face in the men's room,

then dried off with a coarse paper towel. Yes, I had stopped an hour south of Baton Rouge, for the reason Avery expected, or at least partly. I'd called Red from a burner phone with one hand while I watered a fire ant mound on the side of the road with the other. She probably hadn't noticed that part.

"Really?" Red's voice barely disguised his annoyance, "Five in the morning."

Four-forty-five actually, and I'm still on the case, I wanted to say but didn't. And I didn't want to talk to the On Duty TAG coordinator who couldn't answer my questions anyway. Just Red.

"Side door. Sent the flowers." That was unspeak for I'd had to make a quick exit and that I'd dumped the cellphone data Big Lou had passed me for Meng.

Red sighed. "You with Alpha now?"

I glanced back at the car. "Yup." The ants were pouring out of the mound, pissed off. Or on, really.

"She's gone rogue," he said, tonelessly. "Delta, and outside the law. Was at the Tombs last night; eight morts."

He let that sink in; "Delta" meant DEA. And rogue? My blood began to boil; no, she was with me. On the *Natchez*. But DEA? And eight fatalities—morts—rather than the four reported in the press?

Think. Even Red could be wrong; was wrong, I was with her, but how and why and from whom had he gotten bad intel? Who wanted Avery "rogue?" The answer was either on the cell phone dump, which I couldn't access until Tu'u, my backroom honcho, signed in to TAG, or the DEA? Hard enough to believe Avery was DEA, but rogue? Turned? Blamed for eight murders?

"We need a secure conference," Red said flatly. Meaning, encryption. Like the "cone of silence" in the old Don Adams "Get Smart" television spy spoof. Red wouldn't pass anything further until we had a secure, encrypted channel.

"Noonish, best guess," I answered, telling him when I

figured I could make that happen. I had a feeling that Baton Rouge wouldn't be our last stop.

"Good," Red answered, then added, "Be careful, Ghost; this one's burning hot."

What to say? I knew? In fact, I knew what you don't, can't know? That's the problem with running dark ops from a distance, as Red had to do; it was like looking through a straw, seeing but a fraction of the picture.

"Will do," I answered with no particular inflection. At least I hoped there was none, because Red was so good at the intel biz that sometimes it seemed he could read minds. At this point, I didn't want him reading mine, at least till I'd sorted it out for myself.

We'd marked Avery for a player, but we just didn't know whose team she played on. If she was DEA, that had to piss Red off; why were they, the client, spooking us—me—while we did their outsourced dark work?

I took a deep breath, cursed the dark circles under my eyes in the wall-length mirror, and stepped out of the men's room and into the unrelenting overhead lights of the dining area. I waited in line, ordered three *au laits* and three orders of "donuts," as they call beignets, and then headed back to the corner table where the Irish sisterhood chattered like it wasn't just barely the dark ass crack of dawn.

Both women clammed up when I sat down, eyeing me with an uncannily familiar version of each other's pasted-on smile. On Avery, at least, that meant once again she was either really happy or really pissed, hard to tell which. Had to assume the same for Audrey, at least to be on the safe side.

"Tell me, perfesser," Audrey said, head cocked and eyes squinty with the dangerous smile her sister had perfected. Really didn't need a second one aimed at me this early, "How many hours do you have to teach?"

"I'm just an adjunct," I answered automatically, "So usually only six. But this being a summer session, only three."

"That sounds like a pretty good gig," Audrey answered, seemingly sincere. "Is there a decent enrollment cap?"

"Twenty, but I can add two more from the waiting list if I want to."

Avery stood. "My turn for the powder room. You two get acquainted."

Audrey gave her a cute little wave and a smile, then watched her march down the hall and into the ladies room. She turned to me.

"You *sonofabitch*." Her face was stone.

"Wha—"

"You sonofabitch, what have you gotten her into?" I wondered what kind of law she practiced. The scowl said more Assistant District Attorney than patent lawyer. I tried to make my face a blank. This wasn't exactly my first hostile interrogation.

"You're going to have to give me a hint," I answered carefully, "Because I have no idea what we're talking about."

'We're talking about,' I'd said, as if to defuse a little of the 'me versus you' context. The ADA look relaxed a bare fraction. Bet she didn't want me to notice that. In fact, bet she didn't know that I had.

"Here she is risking everything to save yet another stupid sonofabitch's ass," she fairly spat the words. "And I'm not letting her take the hit again."

Again? Another? I assumed I was the latter sonofabitch. Ironic, too, that I'd actually just risked everything for her sister. How much did Audrey know? I thought back to the deck of the Natchez, with Avery's phone buzzing with texts like a beehive at sunrise, knowing now of her DEA connection and the Tombs disaster playing out as we sailed. I'd been up all night, so it was just too hard to put that together and still handle the cross-examination by the very cross ADA. I filed it away to analyze later.

"Look," I held my palms up, and half shrugged, "I just

met you, and I'm not sure what sonofabitch we're talking about..." I paused for a two-count, then began again deliberately, as if struggling for words. "But I've been up all night, driving her away from whatever it was she's afraid of, which I don't completely understand in the first place."

Audrey dropped her gaze to the Formica tabletop. She let her breath out slowly but said nothing, picking at a chip in the scuffed surface. Out of the corner of my eye, I spotted Avery walking our way.

"I don't trust you, Mosby, or whatever your name is." Bad memory? Or disbelief—her face gave no hint. "If you do her any harm, or mean her any harm, I will track you down and make you pay, so help me—" She stopped talking a heartbeat before Avery sat down.

When Avery sat down, the sisterhood reconvened. I concentrated on my hot, golden beignets and the blessed, soothing, creamy warmth of the coffee. I'm not sure if Audrey avoided my eyes or I hers, but we never shared a look directly. She'd returned to her previously placid, pleasant self in conversation with her twin.

I've always been a two-beignet guy. The first one is amazing, hot, doughy, erupting with powdered sugar at the touch. The second was an encore, but almost too rich to finish. The third? That's just showing off, wretched excess. I always left it sitting there, willing to stop eating before just shy of the beignet bloat. The sisters showed no sign of slowing down. I stood and glanced at my hands. "Gonna wash off a little glaze."

They seemed not to care. So, back to the men's room for some hot water to rinse off the stickiness. When I returned, both women were standing, waiting.

"C'mon," Avery said, "Let's get your shit out of my car." I raised an eyebrow. Audrey's mouth was drawn into a tight line. I'd seen that look before too, and this was beginning to get interesting; Audrey telegraphed what Avery was probably thinking. Nervous, unsettled, maybe worried? Avery revealed nothing, but I knew that was just a pose and now if my hunch was right, I knew what lay beneath.

"And let's get mine, too. We're swapping cars." Avery walked briskly ahead, and Audrey shot me a dark look, as if this was my fault. If only I knew what "this" was. Avery popped the trunk with the remote and ducked her head in, rummaging.

Audrey scrawled a number on the back of a business card and handed it to me. "When she needs me, you call," she ordered as if giving instructions to a child. Did she have one, maybe? I took the card but said nothing.

Audrey put one fist on her hip and cocked her head expectantly. Finally, she asked, "How do I get ahold of you?"

I gave her my best imitation of the smug smile she and her sister had bestowed on me when we met. "Just dial 1-800-sonofabitch," I said pleasantly, then walked toward the yawning trunk to collect my two handbags of "my shit."

Avery handed her key fob to Audrey. "Thanks, I owe you."

Audrey sighed. "Yes, you do."

"One minute." Avery held up a finger to me, as I opened the driver side door. I tossed my bags into the back seat, then slipped behind the wheel, watching her in the side view mirror. On the row of cars parked cars behind ours, a U-Haul sat hitched to a pickup truck with Utah plates. She wedged what looked like a cell phone between the ball mount and receiver hitch.

Audrey shook her head and looked away. A bare moon slice faded against a rosy-fingered dawn striping the eastern sky. The sisters hugged, then Avery slid into the passenger seat. Her eyes were bright, happy almost. That made no sense.

I couldn't ignore the signs; swapping cars. Ditching her cell phone, a DEA cell phone, no doubt. The only reason to avoid being tracked is because...you're being tracked.

"North, Mosby," she whispered, for no reason I could

figure. "Just drive north, and I'll tell you when to stop."

A sixth sense, borne of too many split-second decisions gone awry, urged me to open the door, step out, and walk away. In fact, every instinct I'd cultivated during many years of dark work screamed *you'd better vanish into a safe nowhere, right now*.

I turned the key, and the engine purred to life. "This better be good, Miss O'Toole."

"Oh, trust me, Mosby," she smiled what seemed like a brave, yet at the same time, less than confident smile. "This will be epic."

I eased us out of the lot and onto the main road.

Chapter Four

"You gotta *hapax* here, brah."

I didn't need to hear that. Okay, I did need to hear it but didn't want to, especially from my support team.

"Hit me, Tu'u." *Hapax legomenon*; a curious one-time happenstance. Leave it to Tu'u to find the exact word for the perfect conundrum presenting itself as the Irish Sisterhood. Locked in the filthy one toilet men's room in "Tommy's Gas and Meat" in Krotz Springs, Louisiana, I'd passed him the plates on Audrey's car.

"She's an attorney, but the name's not O'Toole," Tu'u growled, not meaning to, but he was a bear of a man, Samoan to be exact, standing about six-six and weighing about two-fifty. "I've got Alpha" —Avery, in TAG-speak— "separated from her in grade-school, and no paper trail between them since."

There wasn't time for me to get Tu'u to run Avery; plus I wasn't sure I was ready to know her full story even if he could reliably unearth any details. Rather, paste-up some Bakhtinian dialogic; define her in terms of her twin, thereby learning about both.

"Thirty-seven, divorced three years, private practice criminal law after five years as an assistant district attorney..."

Ah, the prosecutor who'd chewed my ass in Baton Rouge. But so far, nothing noteworthy. And I was running out of time.

"And?"

"Here's the thing, brah," Tu'u spoke quietly, as if reluctantly. "Their parents were original BNND. Killed on assignment in the Carib. I'm digging, but that's a dead end now."

Bureau of Narcotics and Dangerous Drugs—the forerunner of the DEA. Orphans? Separated? Caribbean? *Hapax logomenon*. My previous resolve began to crumble.

"Red says Alpha's rogue." Avery—I needed answers.

After a pause, Tu'u sighed. "I know. But I don't think it's that simple."

"What did you get off the pass?" Meaning, the Big Lou phone pass to Meng back in the barbershop.

"Nothing. It was totally corrupted."

If Tu'u was being circumspect, that meant someone might be listening. After being awake for nearly twenty-four hours, I wasn't going to piece that together. Another puzzle to file away for later.

"Wipe yer ass, and get out!" a growly voice yelled from beyond the locked men's room door. Tommy's Meat and Gas was a sort of melting pot; I'd guess. A fist banged on the door.

"I'm pulling from DEA now," Tu'u continued. "Gimme a day or two."

I didn't have a day or two. I needed to decide exactly what and even who Avery was before I could decide what

I'd tell her about myself.

"Okay, just ping me, Tu'u. I'm running low on comms." At least secure phone, chips, and SIM cards. I pulled the SIM card out of the phone slot and stowed it back in the heel of my shoe. I crushed the phone, ground it into the filthy tile, then scooped the plastic shards into the toilet with a paper towel and flushed. The jaundiced tide rose and swirled, threatening to boil over, as I opened the men's room door.

"Whew," I sighed, fanning the air, "Sorry, cracklings always shoot right through me."

A tall, rawboned man in a gimme cap scowled at me and scrambled into the men's room, bolting the door. A tattoo on the side of his neck; did I see that? Couldn't be sure, he flashed by so fast but suddenly, something seemed deeply wrong. I grabbed a package of Voodoo chips on my way to the front of the store as curses, and the splattering sounds of a deluge drifted out of the bathroom.

"Chips?" Avery's voice drifted from one aisle over. "You big wuss."

"I like these," I said. "Not the super-hot kind."

Our paths converged at the aisle end cap festooned with flyswatters and dangling cardboard room deodorizers. She held out a small, grease-soaked paper bag.

"Boudin," she said quietly. "You will eat some."

"Why will I eat some?"

"Because you want to look like you fit in, perfesser."

Organ meat; lips and beaks and hooves, rolled in dough, deep-fried. On top of beignets. I grabbed a hot, doughy ball and took a bite. Nasty.

"Chew, swallow, walk," she said in the same low tone, as if a supervisor was coaching a new field agent. DEA. A chilling thought. If the good guys were really the bad guys...

"Just the chips," I said to the dish-faced woman at the register twirling her split ends with one hand. Her eyes narrowed. This seemed like a good time for cash. Which I didn't have.

"Dear?" I looked at Avery; she rolled her eyes, slapped some bills in my hand, and flounced out the door, clanging the bell rudely.

"She's a little cranky this morning," I said to the cashier, watching her eyes that though narrowed, were no longer watching mine. Behind me. I figured I had a pace or two head start on something or someone, at least till her eyes widened.

"Keep the change," I tossed the bills onto the counter and took a stride toward a video game rather than the door Avery had just rudely shoved open. As if I was going to stay, which would make someone's job, something or someone, behind me easier.

Then I whirled clockwise—odds are anyone trying to coldcock you will be right handed, that's just the way of the world—so at least I'd be moving away from and not into whatever fist or worse was flying at my face. I kept my puffy bag of chips to the inside, because come what may, I didn't want smashed Voodoo chips; they're no good that way.

Ah, tall, wizened, pissed off toilet guy. I smiled. "Did you wash your hands?"

He lunged; I ducked, then darted out the door into a steamy, sunlit parking lot, figuring I had about two seconds till—

The door banged open; toilet guy stomped out, legs akimbo like some kind of gunslinger. Then he pulled a Baretta out of the waistband of his dungarees, just before Avery's boot swung up between his legs from behind, into his baggy-panted nut sack. As he lifted up on his toes in pain, she kicked her left leg under and in front of his, kneed his right leg from behind, and he went down, gun clattering. She dropped a knee onto his back harder than necessary, wrenched his right arm back at a nasty angle and pinned it, then hit the back of his skull with the butt of what looked like 320mm so hard his forehead bounced off the pavement.

She pressed the muzzle under his left ear.

"I'm sure your momma told you; it's all fun and games till someone loses an eye," Avery whispered into his ear. He groaned but didn't struggle. "Sure, the muzzle is just a girlie 320. But if I pull the trigger, it shoots a girlie slug through your skull and comes out your right eye."

I grabbed his 9mm and purely following reflex, patted him down, pulling another handgun out of his boot, plus a stiletto with a carved ivory handle.

"Can he keep the knife?" I asked her, adding my own knee and full weight to his back. "It seems like a family heirloom or something."

Avery gave me a wilting look, still whispering into toilet guy's ear. "Should listen to your momma, don't you think?" She bounced his head off the pavement one more time, then stood. I eased away, concealing his handguns and knife. What we really didn't need was a crowd now.

Avery's handgun had vanished. She pointed at the curled up bathroom guy. "Write this down so you can remember," she said. "You tell Hefe that Molly Hatchet is alive and well."

"Molly Hatchet?" I asked. Again, she gave me that "shut up" look. "Too soon?" I added as we moved quickly towards Audrey's car. I had the feeling that I too could lose an eye, so I shut up.

We slammed the doors; I cranked the engine, put the car in gear, and eased us carefully out of the lot, onto the road, and into a very pregnant silence.

I cleared my throat. "Maybe," I said carefully, "Maybe we should talk." I glanced right, but Avery was staring straight ahead.

She took a deep breath, let it out, and then turned to me with that dangerous smile.

"Okay, Ghost," she said pleasantly. "Let's talk."

Chapter Five

Avery gave a few left, right, left again directions as I drove and soon we wound east on a small two lane road. I tried to restore my inner calm, but knowing that she had a gun—so did I, come to think of it—somehow changed the game in a way I hadn't anticipated. We were no longer the professor and the waitress he was dating. Sure, I always knew we were more than that facade, but suddenly we were living the real deal, contract spook, and undercover DEA agent. On the run.

"Well, how's this for starters," I offered carefully. "What the hell happened back there?"

She let out a long breath. "I really want to trust you, Mosby."

"Same here." The words hung in the air like a thick fog. I tapped the temp selector down a few degrees. As the sun climbed higher, the humidity seemed to rise with it.

The usual cat and mouse intel game from here would be me trying to deduce how much I could get away with not telling her, based mostly on how much I determined she might already know. But she'd called me Ghost. And we were both swinging in the wind; if Tu'u says Red's written her off as rogue, and I knew damn well she wasn't ...

"Okay," I said. "I'll go first. I'm a contract embed working intel data out of a drug exchange. It's a DARPA subcontract to DEA, which my boss reports to. Field work, a nine-month contract which..." I paused, but what the hell, "seems to have blown up down in Lafitte last night."

She turned to me, looking at me intently but showing no emotion.

"This is where you talk," I said. "And maybe start with the angry toilet guy with the gun. There was toilet paper in there when I left. I think."

"Creed," she said quietly. "He's Creed. He runs with your buddy, Possum."

The tattoo on his neck; the swamp gang with roots in the Louisiana penitentiary. I did see that after all. But my buddy, "Possum?" There's only one guy I know with that same tat, a certain sawed-off, foul-tempered boatman in the Lafitte Swamp. Pieces were coming together.

"Lou?"

She raised a hand. "We call him Possum—he plays dead when it's convenient."

"He's a very talented guy. But he's small time, running low-value stuff offshore."

She set her jaw and stared straight ahead once again, melting the tint clean off Audrey's windshield. "He's in way over his head. If he's still alive."

"I'd bet my left nut he is," I said, glancing at Avery out of the corner of my eye. "Lou's a survivor." And we might need him going forward, I thought but didn't say.

"Never mind Possum," Avery said, sounding a bit less dark. "You and me." She sighed. "We're on the same side."

Not surprising; when we started pulling serious crime intel out of the swamp, suddenly there's a government agency wondering why they'd outsourced pay dirt to TAG.

"And I'm here because I fucked my boss," she said quietly. "This is payback."

"Payback how?" We'll get to that "fucked her boss" thing later.

"He's got me linked with you, and you tagged with murder at The Tombs."

I wrenched the wheel left and slammed on the brakes; we did a one-eighty with tires squealing, dust flying, and ended up parallel-parked neatly on the right shoulder as if I'd intended to do just that. I kind of had, actually.

"Okay, Miss O'Toole," I said as casually as I could. "You've got my attention. What's this 'murder' thing?"

She brushed her hair back with one hand, calmly, as if I'd just eased us off to the side of the road. "Last night. They have a facial recognition software hit on you at The Tombs."

"How? No, not how—why?"

"Back up," she said quietly, almost sadly. I put the car in reverse; then she gave me that wilting look again. A grackle flapped down from an oak tree and landed on the hood, eyeing us suspiciously first with one eye, then the other.

"When you were on the swamp boat the other day, you got the handoff from Possum."

I eased us back onto the road, and as soon as we moved, the grackle flew off.

"Big Lou," I answered. "Yes. And I passed it to Meng. You familiar with her?"

"Middleman, broker," Avery dismissed her with a wave. "Small time. What was in the pass?"

I thought back to the morning on Lou's boat. "Just that the drop was uptown. Then I carried the phone to Meng. I don't know what was on the phone because it was encrypted." I thought back to Tu'us words; totally corrupted. Someone, somewhere, didn't want anyone in the swamp to know what was coming. "Tell me why that matters."

"Because your boss says you did that on your own."

"Meaning what?"

"Meaning you knew the Haitians were moving guns and that the Creed swapping smack would get lost in the crossfire. And they did—but it gets worse."

"I don't believe my boss said that. But go on."

"My division chief is missing. And so is a lot of DEA money."

I stared at the road. This was more dangerous—burning white hot—as Red had warned me, and much worse than I'd imagined only a night before watching the New Orleans skyline slide by as the Natchez cruised. The *Teufel* must have been the gun runner. Big Lou knew, that's why his price went up with Meng. And she wrote him off as dead.

But more immediately, if there were DEA money missing from within the DEA, no doubt, the scapegoat would come from outside the agency. *They got a facial recognition hit on you at the Tombs*. Of course, they did. So I had to ask.

"Where's your partner in all this?"

She waved a hand, then stared out the side window. "He's out of the picture."

"What the hell?"

"Alcohol rehab." She sighed.

I tried to keep my composure. "Are you *shitting* me? You're on a major op without a partner? *Solo*?"

She nodded, still staring out the side window. "Hiring freeze. We're undermanned."

"And your division Chief is *missing*?"

She turned to me. "So is yours," she shot back, glaring.

True enough, but I knew why Red was missing. We were so fucked. Speaking of which... I took a deep breath. "What was that 'I fucked my boss' thing?"

"I slept with him," she whispered. "Once. It didn't mean anything."

"You slept with me too. Twice." That slipped out. "It meant something."

"Once."

"Twice."

"We were both drunk," she all but yelled.

"It still mattered to me."

"It mattered to me, too."

I shook my head. "So, your boss sent you to the Russian front."

"He's married and in line for a major promotion."

"And he sent you without a partner," I finished my thought. "Into a guns-for-drugs deal gone bad."

She nodded. "Looks like."

"That's about the worst—your partner, your boss, both just left you hanging in the wind."

She stared out the window. "We all have our demons and weaknesses; and when they find each other, which they always do, there's hell to pay."

The road wound under deep magnolias that split the sunlight into shafts that fanned the asphalt. The relentless sun boiled the sky into towers of clouds, brooding to the north, where we were headed. There would be storms, lightning, wind, and rain. You could feel it in the air.

"Molly Hatchet?" I didn't want to ask but felt we'd better get it all out.

"It was a band, a song."

"I know that. I have the CD."

"Of course you do. Dork. I was undercover with Creed; that was my nickname. Somebody," she paused, "and I'm pretty sure…I know who gave me up."

Great. Wanted dead by Creed, in the middle of a Haitian massacre, and now they'd want payback. And TAG gone dark. At least part of TAG, anyway.

"How about you drive," I said, sounding more tired than I wanted to. But that much was true; I was eye-crossing exhausted.

"What?"

"You drive. You know where we're going." I paused a moment, then figured what the hell. "I trust you. And I need sleep." I eased us onto the shoulder and put the car into park.

"Okay," she answered. "Okay. I'll drive."

I popped the driver's door open and stepped out onto crumbly gravel. The air hung thick and still, wet. Avery walked around the hood and slipped behind the wheel.

Somewhere deep inside I hoped maybe she'd speed off and in fact, I made sure I stood clear of the rear fender in case she fishtailed when she did. I'm not sure I wouldn't have done so myself if our situations were reversed.

The car waited, idling. I opened the back door and crawled in, reclining against the passenger door.

"Okay, Avs," I said. I'd never called her that before; it sounded like "Aivs" when I said it. Somehow, that fit. "You and me against the world."

She smiled. "You don't know the half of it, perfesser."

We both laughed. She drove. In a moment, I slept.

Chapter Six

I woke gradually to the sound of wind, rustling leaves, and birds. All the windows were down, and a cool, wet breeze drifted through the car. I tried to figure how long I'd slept. Trees masked the sun, but the angle was much lower than it had been at Tommy's. My neck felt stiff, my spine twisted from sleeping half reclined against the passenger door.

Outside, Avery sat in front of a double-wide trailer on a lawn chair, her feet propped on another. Between the chairs, a sawed-off shotgun leaned against an open cooler.

"Happy hour, perfesser," Avery called across the dirt driveway. She held up a dark-glass Voodoo beer bottle. The driveway ran downhill and disappeared into a thicket of trees. I sensed running water somewhere—the scent, maybe even the sound. The Cane? I popped the car door open and stood.

Avery moved her feet as I walked up. She nodded at the chair. "Have a seat."

I glanced at the shotgun. "That's way illegal," I said, plopping down in the chair. "I'll need to report this to the proper authorities."

She laughed. "Best perimeter defense I know of. Don't even have to aim."

I pulled a beer out of the cooler. Warm.

"Why is this in a cooler if it's not on ice?" I twisted the cap off.

She waved a hand. "Power's on, but the water's off. Easier to carry. You looked like you needed the sleep, so I just let you."

That I did. "Where are we?"

"Natchitoches. Sort of."

I reached for my smartphone, but she cut me off.

"Really? You go for Google maps, and I'll punch you in the throat."

"Then gimme deets. What's 'sort of?'"

She nodded. "This was my uncle's fishing camp. We're upstream a few miles from Natchitoches. Pretty well secluded, which seems like a good idea for us right about now."

Two squirrels chased each other up a tree, climbing the trunk as if it were a circular staircase, round and round, disappearing into the deep, green canopy. Magnolias, maybe?

"Who knows we're here?" Warm beer was better than no beer, but still.

"You, me, and Audrey," Avery said flatly. "For now."

"Yeah. Time is not our friend."

She shook her head.

"All right," I said, standing. I chugged the warm beer till the bottle was empty. "Point me at the men's room, then let's sit down and make a plan."

Avery pointed at the thicket behind the trailer.

"Seriously?" I dropped the empty into the cooler.

"I told you—no water. Don't be such a wuss."

"I'll call a plumber," I said, headed for the tree line.

"Wuss."

Whatever. We needed a plumber, and she'd find out why soon enough.

Inside the trailer, Avery sat at a chrome and Formica built-in bar. I tossed my duffel onto the sofa and unzipped it.

"Okay," I said, "How about you humor me for a minute?"

She crossed her arms. "Here we go. Big budget intel consultant with a dog and pony show? We have them too; smart boards, hyperlinks, spreadsheets—"

I tossed her a pad of Post-It-Notes, and grabbed one for myself.

"Nope. That's the bloated government agency methodology. Humor me. Write down everything you can think of that you know as fact about this case, a note for each. I'll do the same. Then we'll start sorting and see what patterns of meaning we can extract when we put our heads together."

"Post-It-Notes? How quaint."

"Like pissing in the woods." I shut out the stale-smelling trailer and even Avery, who seemed to be writing something, which was a start. Red had gone dark, taking down the organization for safety's sake; he could, and probably would return to the grid, but most likely, he was protecting us all from whatever leverage the DEA might be trying to apply. Back channels still worked, but that resource needed to be used sparingly.

Avery had done exactly what I'd done; we'd each ignored the op plan to protect the other. In doing so, we both knew that while we were at the center of the problem, we weren't really the problem, as both TAG and DEA were saying. But why?

As darkness fell, we both stopped writing.

"Okay," I said. "Ready?"

She folded her arms again, giving me that dangerous smile.

I stuck one yellow note on the wall by the door. "I know you're in the clear; saw you on the *Natchez* when TAG says you were at The Tombs."

"Same here," Avery stood and posted her note next to mine. "You were set up by someone in the DEA with a fake facial recognition hit. You were protecting me by dragging me onto the tub, and I was protecting you by going."

"Now, I have Big Lou—Possum—as the backwater conduit for drugs going back and forth from the channel to Creed drop offs. He's a bit player—didn't know what was being dropped at the Tombs, just that it would go hot."

Avery posted another note. "DEA makes him as mid-level Creed, climbing. Takes orders from his brother in Angola doing a murder rap."

"We didn't know—or rather, I wasn't told that there were guns in the Tombs deal," Avery offered. "And we have to assume Big Lou didn't either, or he'd have cleared the Creed out."

I posted the name "Benjamin Lucia."

"Who's that?" Avery asked.

I sighed. "An SOI, Source Of Info. I'm not sure how reliable he is, but he's in and out of the Haitian gun runners, and he might be useful for us."

Avery wrote "Lurch" on a note and put it on the wall next to Big Lou.

"Toilet guy?" I guessed.

She nodded. "Real name is Raymond Marcheaux. He drives the first leg of the smack pipeline north. A big, dumbass courier; another Angola alum on the Creed payroll."

I stuck another note on the wall. "My boss went off the grid, dark, a few hours ago. My guess is he's taking TAG down to eliminate any law enforcement leverage. Waiting for subpoenas and warrants."

"Or he's letting you take the fall," Avery suggested.

"That's not how we work." I stared at the wall. "Even if he was going to do that, he'd tell me." I tried to maintain confidence in that. "Besides, the missing cash is on your side. How much?"

Avery sighed. "Three million that I know of for sure. But likely more." She posted that note on the wall.

"I put Meng down as unknown—not sure how much she knows, but she figured there'd be fatalities, so she knows something beyond simple dates and times."

Avery tore off another note. "My last briefing came with a sideways warning from the special ops office. Something cliché like 'beware of smoke, there follows fire.'"

Boucane. Could someone at DEA have a connection to Smokey? I put a hand on her arm.

"Who told you that?" I asked. Avery looked startled.

"Just a trusted friend. A GS-9, a clerical sort. She looks out for me."

"Say more."

Avery sat down heavily, staring at the wall. "She's an older black woman, Caribbean. Sweet lady, always checks in on me as she passes plans."

"What's her name?"

"Lourdes. Lourdes Lafimen."

I wrote that down on a yellow note and stuck it to the wall next to "Boucane."

Avery held up her palms. "What's the connection?"

"Boucane. He's my primary and most reliable SOI. Hard to explain, but his answers are always spot on. I'm not sure if he's real or about half illusion."

"That's a stretch."

"I know." I surveyed the wall. "Just collecting data, looking for patterns."

"Is this the kind of voodoo my agency is paying tax dollars for?"

I nodded, still concentrating. "Yup. Except normally we have about a dozen people locked in a conference room doing this at once."

"That's crazy."

"No," I said. "That's centrifugal thinking. At TAG, we look outward. Most law enforcement agencies start with a theory and concentrate on what reinforces what they already believe. That's centripetal thinking, looks inward, and discards anything that doesn't conform. We're the opposite; we want everything, then we'll sort it all out, find what matters. If real answers match preconceived notions, that's a coincidence."

Avery seemed to consider that. Meanwhile, patterns. Money, people, actors, those with no ability to act; relationships, connections, barriers.

"This shows we don't know much," she said finally. 'Or much that makes sense."

I stared at the wall, which now looked like a littered bulletin board. "It's a good start. Sleep on it, see what gels."

"Before we do, one more ugly deet for your collage, perfesser." Avery scribbled another note and pasted to the wall. I squinted at the note.

"A trooper? Dead?"

She nodded. "On my news feed while you were sleeping."

"Why was he at The Tombs?" And why didn't TAG know he was there, I wanted to ask but didn't, at least not out loud. That would be a question for Tu'u tomorrow.

"They weren't supposed to be," Avery said. "We tried to keep them out, but their agency is nutso about local versus federal jurisdiction."

Instinctively, I saw that as a plus; the DEA now had more than just TAG to worry about. Now the Louisiana State Police, as well as the state attorney general, would demand real answers.

"Leverage," I said, mostly to myself.

"No shit." I hadn't noticed that Avery was standing by my side, but she was. "We may live through this after all, perfesser."

I stood back and looked at the wall, trying to perceive any symmetry and connections.

"Is this where you draw lines between notes like a serial killer?" Avery asked.

"You watch too much TV. No, we let it stand and hit it again in the morning." With a third set of eyes, I didn't say, but held out hope. "We burn all this before we leave, too."

She laughed. "Your methodology is a cross between *Law and Order* and *Revenge of the Nerds*."

"Yeah, it is," I said, still staring at the wall. There was more we didn't know than we did, which was good, I decided. So far, everything on the goddam wall—except the fact that we were true to each other—was very bad news. That left room for good news, for leverage, for a way to outthink the bad news.

"Projects always start out like this," I said. "Looks like a hopeless mess. But trust me, it'll shape up." It had too; I thought but didn't say.

"So, this is a 'project?'"

"To me, it's a puzzle, a code we have to break. There's always a best alternative, a chance to out-think the problem," I said, staring at the wall littered with yellow notes. "We just have to be smarter than the puzzle."

"Nerdy, but fine. We have little choice, no matter what you call it."

I nodded, only half-listening.

"You want half a full-sized bed?" Avery offered. Of course I did. I wanted her, too. But not as the last chapter of my life.

"You go ahead," I said. "I'll sleep on this sofa with your sawed-off friend."

She cocked her head, as if considering an alternative, then nodded. "Okay. I'm in for the night, so if that door opens, don't ask questions."

"Won't even need to aim," I finished the thought. She disappeared into the back of the trailer. I killed the lights, but stared at the wall in the moonlight; the scattered notes looking like peeling bark on a cedar tree. The answers were there, as always, and maybe even in the blank spaces, which often turned out to be even more important than the details we knew for sure.

Finally, I slept.

Chapter Seven

"We've got company," Avery's voice cut into my sleep. I sat up and grabbed the shotgun. Slats of sunlight fell across the floor from the mini-blinds on the front door. I covered the two steps to the door still half-awake, and pulled one blind down—nada.

Avery stood beside me. I turned to her.

"What company?"

She peered out the window, wearing just a denim shirt and work boots, holding her 9mm.

She nodded toward the bedroom. "Closed circuit TV on the driveway and main road."

"Really? For a fishing camp?"

"I've added a few upgrades. You should be grateful."

"I am." I nodded. "Very stylish outfit, too, I might add."

"Shut up, perfesser."

Sure enough, the throaty sound of a truck engine and tires crunching gravel drifted in through the open jalousies. First, the grill, then a full-sized one-ton cargo truck emerged from the thicket and onto the driveway. Across the side, "A-1 Plumbing" in faded red letters arched over a barely readable toll-free number.

"What the hell," Avery breathed.

"I told you I was calling a plumber. Mosquitos nearly ate me alive out at 'the men's room' last night."

She put the safety back on with a click. "You've got to be shitting me, Mosby."

The driver's door popped open, and a bear of a man jumped out, holding an oversized iron monkey wrench, and landed heavily on both feet. A plump, white poodle scampered out after him. I opened the trailer door.

"Where's the main shutoff?" he asked in a surprisingly melodic, quiet voice.

I stood outside on the door stoop. "Around the back, near the electrical box," Avery said in a hushed tone, still inside.

"She says it's around back near the breakers," I said, nodding at Avery inside. "And bill her for the service call."

He nodded and walked off behind the trailer. The poodle bounded up the steps, into the trailer, and started sniffing Avery's knees.

She stooped down, petting the dog. "Explain, Mosby—*now*."

"He's TAG."

"And a plumber?"

"Yup. He's my support crew." I walked down the three steps and met the giant as he rounded the corner.

He wrapped me in a one-armed hug, the wrench dangling from the other. "Main shutoff was off."

The sound of water gushing from a faucet drifted out the door.

Avery stood on the steps, shaking her head. "I don't

get any of this." The dog sat next to her, quietly.

"Avery, Tu'u," I said. "Tu'u, Avery." He reached into the cab of the truck and pulled out a paper bag. Breakfast. I smiled.

"C'mon in, amigo," I said, leading him up the steps. "We need your brain power as much as your plumbing skills."

We sat around the Formica bar pulling apart hot, moist biscuits, laying the halves on paper plates then passing around a Styrofoam container of thick gravy. A coffeemaker scowled and sputtered in the background, nearly finished brewing.

"You want to run this for me, brah?" Tu'u asked quietly, pointing to the note-festooned wall with the blunt end of his fork. The dog sat quietly at his feet.

I glanced at Avery. She concentrated on a steaming biscuit.

"Sure." I ran through our list of knowns and unknowns, people, topics—everything we'd thrown on the board and what we'd discussed. Then, silence, as the big man considered the yellow collage.

"Lots of binaries," I said at last.

"I don't speak geek," Avery snapped. "What are you talking about?"

Tu'u smiled. "I like this woman."

"Lots of either-or combinations. Money missing, people missing. Actors, and those acted on."

"Us," Avery pointing her fork at me.

I nodded. "Yes. We're inside this mess, but we're not sure exactly what the mess is."

She cocked her head. "Not sure?"

"Warrants," Tu'u said with a sigh. "Still no warrants, which means only one thing."

"I don't follow," I said.

"I do," Avery stated flatly. "They don't issue arrest warrants for dead people."

Tu'u nodded. The weight of that realization chilled me

to the bone. The inaccurate number of fatalities at The Tombs could be revised to include the rogue DEA agent and a DARPA subcontractor.

"So," Tu'u said at last. "We need to know who's calling the shots at DEA now."

"Raton," Avery said, pulling the coffee urn out of the coffeemaker. "He's acting division chief while Fuego is out."

"Out where?" I asked.

She shrugged. "No one's saying."

"How can they just not say?" I sipped the coffee.

"HIPPA," she answered. "Privacy laws."

I threw up my hands. "Oh, for god's sake."

"We'll find him," Tu'u said. He stood. "Let me show you what we've got so far."

"Okay," I said. "And can we maybe bring Red in?"

Tu'u nodded, holding his steaming coffee mug. "I'll give you a minute to prep her. "C'mon out when you're ready."

The dog jumped up and followed him out the door.

"Mosby, I swear," Avery said, shaking her head. "What in God's name is all this TAG crap?"

"Our best friend," I answered. "In fact, our only friend. TAG has assets, and you and I need answers. Just the fact that Tu'u is here means my boss hasn't hung us out to dry."

"Yet," she added.

I ignored that. "Tu'u will hook us up, and we'll have a secure conference with TAG. But I need to warn you."

I let that hang in the air a moment, studying her face. She seemed focused, not dismissive. A good sign.

"Everything you say to Red, or that Red hears, is intel. In short, he'll be intelligencing *you*."

She drew her mouth into a tight line. "How did 'intelligence' become a verb?"

"A gerund, actually." Avery rolled her eyes; I poured another half mug of coffee. "Just be forewarned—Red's not talking with us, he's interrogating us. The guy practically reads minds, so be as clear and concise as possible."

Her brow furrowed.

"Red's a behavioral psychologist, and *everything* to him has meaning. So don't say anything you can't live with down the road. Facts, period."

She nodded. I stood.

"Alright, let's visit the plumber."

"What, his truck? An intelligence conference in a plumbing truck?"

I nodded. "C'mon."

Chapter Eight

Outside, we crossed the drive to the A-1 truck, circling to the bobtail. Avery grabbed the handrail and stepped into the dimly lit back end; I followed, brushing aside a jungle of hoses and plumbing apparatus dangling in front of a smaller, open door. "Ladies first."

We ducked into the brightly lit and well-air-conditioned interior of a spotless computer center, walls lined with racked equipment, cooling fans purring. A bank of LCDs lined the bulkhead near the driver's cab. Tu'u bolted the sliding door shut behind us.

"On second thought," Avery breathed, looking around, then at Tu'u, "Give Mosby the plumbing bill."

The dog sat at Avery's feet, growling subtly.

"She doesn't like anyone in her seat," Tu'u said quietly. Avery picked up the poodle and put her in her lap.

The dog laid down.

Tu'u clattered away on a keyboard. "I think we're in a clearing wide enough, but I've been having trouble with the SatCom this week. I may have to move the truck—"

The largest screen blossomed to life, blurred, then focused. A pudgy, pasty-skinned man with a thin head of hair and tortoise-shell glasses on his baby-face appeared. He looked tired.

"Ghost, Tu'u," the man said matter-of-factly. Red—never one for extended pleasantries. "May I assume that's Miss O'Toole seated next to you?"

"Yes," she answered before I could. I glanced at her. Her face was blank.

"Okay," Red sighed. "We convened a stasis session here. No definitive conclusion yet."

I turned to Avery. "That's the think-tank I told you about. 'Stasis' means the point of matched forces, where neither side can move. That's where we determine the optimum counter-move."

Avery nodded, her face still blank. That was unsettling. Normally, there'd be a smartassed "perfesser" remark and some type of putdown. She stared at the screen.

"So," Red continued, "connecting the dots so far…we believe someone inside the DEA op set up the switch from a dope deal to an arms deal in order to grab $3.8 million in bait money, then blame it all on a couple of dead operatives in the field."

He paused a second to that cold reality sink in, but he needn't have. Avery and I were well aware of who he was talking about as "dead operatives." It went without saying that we'd ruined the plot just by being alive.

"We believe you have about three, maybe four days at most to link the missing DEA money to Fuego before they shift from saying you're possibly among the dead to issuing warrants for your arrest."

I glanced at Tu'u. He nodded.

"Miss O'Toole, we need a few things from you."

"What do you need?" Avery answered quietly.

"For starters, Fuego's internet server account."

"I have a few email addresses, but the DEA server is layered in security."

"Maybe," Red said, holding up one hand, which held a stylus. "But we've got a pretty good profile on him from both open and closed-sources. We're after his private server."

That made sense; knowing the DEA server was monitored and wrapped in security, why would Fuego use it for anything that might land him in prison?

"He uses a Yahoo account, never sending covert emails, just saving drafts."

"Which certain designated users then access," Red nodded, scribbling with his stylus on a tablet. Oldest trick in the book, really. "If you would please share with Dr. Fa'aola whatever accounts and logins you recall."

Avery turned to me. "Who?"

I tilted my head towards Tu'u. "Doctorate in theoretical physics from CalTech."

"Now," Red continued. "What do you have for me, Ghost?"

"She's got a connection inside DEA that pairs proximately with Boucane. She has a sister with history in the Baton Rouge DA's office."

I don't think Red could see on his screen, but a muscle flinched on Avery's jaw. I figured she'd be protective of her sister, but if a trooper was involved in The Tombs massacre, we'd need to use state leverage. I'd pay for that later, I figured, but for now, Avery remained composed.

"Everything else," I added, "I believe you have, but I'll send our Post-It wall when we're done here."

Red steepled his fingers for a long moment, but said nothing.

"Alright," he said at last. "Dr. Fa'aola will work with whatever we can extract from Mr. Fuego's various cloud drives."

"RATs won't work," Avery said quietly. "Agency internal cyber-security will root them out during their hourly sweep."

RATs; Random Access Trojans. They'd give access to files and as important, audio and video from individual DEA offices through laptops and desktops. I was impressed that Avery was that cyber-savvy.

Red took off his glasses, rubbed his eyes, and then put them back on before speaking.

"We did a fairly deep profile on Mr. Fuego before we took this contract," Red said matter-of-factly. That was an understatement—they'd combed open and closed source information sources, even some black info sources, and knew every nuance of Fuego's private life, including his preference for boxers over briefs from his credit card statements. That fine-grained awareness raised the "I fucked my boss" specter, and I wanted to glance at Avery to see how she was maintaining her poker face, but I dared not let Red see me doing so.

"Like most men his age," Red continued, "He knows very little about digital technology. In fact, he relied on his teenaged daughter to set up everything on his private laptop and tablet."

I hoped Avery was following the trail Red was laying out.

"So now, Mr. Fuego's laptop, tablet, and smartphone have both Periscope and Meerkat installed, plus Snapchat."

"Audio and video streaming apps," Tu'u added for Avery's benefit. "Accounts for each."

"I applaud government agencies spending gazillions on RAT's and RAT counter-measures," Red said, smiling thinly. "Keeps them busy while we gather intel through free apps, with slightly modified coding."

Avery looked at Tu'u. He allowed himself a shy smile.

"Mr. Fuego doesn't even know he has a Twitter account. And everyone's blocked—except for one user account."

A Twitter page appeared, with Tu'u's dog on the profile picture.

"So whatever video Mr. Fuego shares with Spike, we cache," Red concluded.

Avery looked down at the dog in her lap. "Spike? This pretty girl is named Spike?"

The dog looked up expectantly. I was relieved to see the old Avery still inside the icy countenance.

"Problem is, for two weeks we've had no location on Fuego," Tu'u said, "And no Periscope or Meerkat."

"I assume you have assets looking for him?" Avery said to Red. Tu'u and I laughed quietly.

"That's how big government agencies play it," Red answered, shaking his head. "In fact, right now the DEA has several teams scouring central Utah for you two as we speak."

"Your phone," I said quietly, picturing in my mind Avery wedging her DEA phone into the trailer hitch in the *Coffee Call* parking lot in Baton Rouge.

"You saw that?" she asked. I didn't answer. Again, we use empty space—the unsaid, the unknown—at TAG to induce conclusions. She'd come over to the egghead side, eventually. If we both lived.

"No, we'll wait for him to come to us, digitally speaking," Red answered. "We don't give a damn where he is physically. Just need access to his bank records, which we can retrieve once we hack his internet accounts."

"You're still confined to your law enforcement centripetal thinking," I said to Avery. "You Feds picture slapping handcuffs on a perp and work backwards from there. We go for his digital footprints and work forward."

"Then we can bring up the cameras and audio," Tu'u added.

"Which we need to nail Fuego," I finished the thought.

"Let me be clear, Miss O'Toole," Red said, staring out from the screen. "You're a sworn law enforcement officer; we accept that. I ask only that you hold that sworn duty in abeyance until such time as said law enforcement agency stops trying to kill you."

And me, it would have been nice if Red had said, but he didn't. After a moment, Avery nodded slowly. "Agreed."

"If you need to leave TAG cover, now or going forward, tell us and we'll stand aside," Red continued, "But while you're part of our team, I ask that you work *with* us, as we work for all of our sakes. We're not your typical government agency; we don't work in the process model or hierarchy you're used to. But I can promise you, we'll make it through this gauntlet, and then you can return to your federal agency, if you choose."

I suppressed a smile. I wondered if Avery saw the hint of an invitation in that.

"Ghost, anything else for me or the stasis group?" Red asked, nudging our video conference to a close.

I thought for a moment, then against my normal instincts, I spoke. "Just this. Avery has put her life on the line for mine. And really, for all of ours." That was only half true—if she'd been eliminated at The Tombs as Fuego had planned—and I'd disrupted—TAG would have simply vanished, intact. But truly, she'd tried to save my life, even as I was trying to save hers. And going forward from that, we all knew it was a matter of dominos falling—first Avery and me, then TAG key players one by one—indictments, or worse.

"I trust her completely," I continued. "And we all need to."

After a moment, Red nodded. "Duly noted," he said curtly, and that little muscle in Avery's jaw flinched again, but she remained silent.

Red looked toward Tu'u. "You and Ghost sanitize your present location. Then Ghost and Miss O'Toole, get yourselves to Ain't Bee's."

Tu'u and I both groaned as if on cue. Ain't Bee; total reboot. Painfully.

Avery looked at me quizzically. I shook my head—I'd

explain later.

"And get that car back to Baton Rouge," Red added. "The last thing we need is the sister driving around in Miss O'Toole's car."

"I'll tow it," Tu'u said, "While you two head for Ain't Bee's."

"One last thing," Red added. "Why can't we find your partner, Miss O'Toole?"

"HIPPA," Avery said flatly.

"Why?"

"Substance abuse rehab," she answered.

Red smiled. "That's all we needed to know."

Simple matter to find the facility paid for by standard government healthcare policy. There were at least a dozen possibilities in the DEA Headquarters area, but finding the right one was just a question of time. We had about forty-eight hours, probably more since Red always gave conservative estimates. Which still wasn't much.

"After Ain't Bee's, you two work from The Quarter inward toward Fuego. Miss O'Toole," Red paused. "If you're willing, press the Creed as well. We need to blow Fuego out of the water with a full spectrum of evidence if we're to exonerate ourselves."

Avery nodded, scratching Spike under the chin.

"Tell me about this 'Boucane," Avery said to Red.

He shrugged. "He belongs to Ghost. What you all call a 'CI.'"

She gave me a concerned look but said nothing.

"Tu'u," Red continued. "Be sure Ghost has the Doomsday codes."

Tu'u nodded; Avery stopped scratching Spike and looked up. Again, something I'd have to explain later.

After a moment of silence, Red continued. "All right. Secure comms only from here on out. Let's get to work."

The screen went blank.

Tu'u tapped a few keys, then said, "We're clear."

"I don't want my sister in this," Avery snapped. "Any

of this."

"I'm afraid she already is," Tu'u said, stroking Spike's head, her ears flattened back expectantly.

"DEA doesn't know about her," Avery said flatly.

"How, if I may ask," Tu'u said gently, "can the DEA *not* know about your sister?"

"I didn't even know I had a sister, until seven years ago. She found me."

"So you never ran her through any law enforcement databases?" I asked.

"Not DEA. Ever. So they have no idea."

"Well, we'd best keep it that way," I said, thinking ahead to future possibilities. "But if you believe your doppelganger circulating in Creed territory isn't risky, never mind the DEA plastering your identical faces everywhere, you're underestimating the threat. Why do you two have this safe house in the first place?"

"She put a lot of bad people into Angola as an assistant district attorney," Avery answered, looking down.

"Her past," I said, "And Molly Hatchet just put her in the line of fire again."

"Just one more thing I'll have to answer for," Avery said, looking me in the eye.

"Look," I said. "Taking care of her means taking care of you. Let's fight this. Together."

"I'm in it for her. I'm in it for you," Avery said. "I'm in it for all of us."

"I'll bring your sister the car and some secure comms," Tu'u said quietly. "If you wouldn't mind prepping her for that."

"Sure," Avery said with a shrug. I could tell she wasn't happy, probably thinking of her sister in the middle of this mess. But that was just something she'd have to get used to.

"Well," Tu'u said, tapping commands into a keyboard that lowered the SatComm antenna with a humming sound. "You heard the man. Let's get to work."

Chapter Nine

I always liked the feel of a small boat, the chug of a two-stroke engine, even the smell of the oil-tinged exhaust drifting lazily aft as we motored smoothly forward across the glassy Cane. The ride, the sense of being afloat in a small aluminum boat recalled simpler days of fishing and motoring around local lakes in a previous life.

Avery sat at the stern, holding the tiller of the small outboard, steering us close along the shoreline of the river. Tackle, fishing gear—the works, propped across the bow—painted a picture of a couple doing a little fishing rather than a pair of hunted, marked subjects. I put that thought aside.

Tu'u had just set off to Baton Rouge with Audrey's car in tow, Spike gazing plaintively out the window at Avery as they eased away from the trailer. Once they were out of sight, we had taken up our lawn chair positions again outside the trailer as storm clouds piled up to the west.

"Where to start," Avery mused. "How about the 'Doomsday Codes,' perfesser?"

I nodded. "The Twitter feed Tu'u created of Fuego's Meerkat and Periscope auto-play videos are preloaded to a stream hashtagged DEA, US Attorney General, and Department of Justice. The stream will include every major news organization's Twitter handle. Within minutes, everything we have will auto-publish worldwide."

"Lord." Avery shook her head. "You guys are diabolical."

"We'd rather use that threat as leverage, but if any of us go down, we pull the trigger. With a few simple lines of code."

"Why not do that right now?"

"It's not enough. We don't have the smoking gun, like Fuego's bank records, or audio and video of him discussing The Tombs hit."

"That's what we're supposed to drag out of Nawlins. After," she raised a hand, "Aunt Bea? Who's that?"

"First off, you say it 'Ain't Bee' or she'll be offended. Second, she'll give us a digital footprint scrub, plus a new identity, maybe two, depending on what Red decides we need between now and tomorrow when we get there."

"A digital scrub?"

"Remove any credit card, wifi, or most other digital footprints," I answered. "It's not one hundred percent effective, but it will make our last two weeks nearly invisible for anyone looking for us in cyber-space."

"I guess the bloodhounds are off sniffing around in Utah. For now."

"When that trail goes cold, they won't find much else. Now, tell me about your partner," I asked. "I can't fathom someone leaving you solo. And I can't fathom a federal agency leaving you solo in this undercover mess."

She shook her head, staring off into the distance. Gusts of cool wind from the gathered clouds off to the west promised rain.

"He's a good man," she said. "Big guy. Jesse Romero. Believes in what we do. Dedicated father, good husband."

I waited, smart enough to not say anything.

"His husband is a school teacher." She brushed hair out of her eyes. "Both of them are good people."

"What's with the substance rehab?"

"I have no idea. Took me by surprise—one day, he's just gone."

We exchanged a look. I filed that away, figuring we hadn't heard the last of this loose end.

"Now that I know about Fuego, I kind of get Audrey," I broached the subject. "Her hostility makes sense; she sees me as another rescue project and you going down in flames with me as a result."

"She's watched this play out before." Avery sighed. "I suppose I could talk to her, dial back the hostility."

I shook my head. "No, don't. That edge will serve her better in this mess—trust no one, stay defensive."

"Kick Mosby's ass," she finished the thought.

"I'm a big boy." I shrugged. "I'd rather see her stay tough, be guarded, suspect everyone. At least until we've disarmed this time bomb."

Funds had been transferred through PayPal to secure a used car that we hoped would hold together at least as far as the small town in central Mississippi where Ain't Bee waited. Now, we just needed to pick up the car in Natchitoches. Then, at dawn, head north. So, we took the boat and set off upriver for town.

Ponderous oaks, magnolias, and cypress trees with long, gnarled branches that arched out over the water and hung low lined the shore as we eased by. The lower sun angle washed the eastern riverbank with a golden tint and cypress roots like weathered old knees jutted up from the shallows so close that I let my hand slide across their water-burnished, cool smoothness.

Avery twisted the throttle, slowing the boat, and eased

us to a dock.

"I would say I want you to experience some authentic Louisiana cuisine," she said. "But you TAG people seem to unravel everyone's white lies."

"So, what's the truth?"

"The truth is," she said, chopping the motor, "I won't leave Natchitoches without a dose of Bayou soul food—shrimp and grits. Nor will you."

We drifted gently toward the dock, which I caught with one hand. Avery knotted a rope around a cleat, pulled the outboard up, and it tipped forward out of the water.

"More organ meat and intestinal fire?" I asked, picturing the grease-soaked Boudin bag back in Krotz Springs.

"You don't know as much as you think you do, Perfesser." She bounded onto the dock. A set of winding stairs climbed the steep riverbank up to a patio by a single-story restaurant whose awning proclaimed "Maglieaux's" with an empty cedar deck extended over the side of the bank. A quiet, weekday evening in small town Louisiana.

"Carryout," Avery said. "I'll order."

"Fine."

"Give me five minutes, and then come up to the outside bar."

"Okay," I said. "I'll be Biff from sales. We'll hook up."

She shook her head, combing her fingers through her hair, and strode purposefully toward the stairs. "Not if I find a better offer."

So there. I waited the prescribed time, plus a few minutes longer for good measure, then made my way up the switchback stairs to *Maglieaux's* deck where Avery sat at the far corner of the outdoor bar. Smart; a commanding view of the deck, the doors from the restaurant, and the nearly deserted street beyond. I'd sit across from her with a view of the steps and the landing, plus the river and the far shore. I eased onto a bar stool, trying to decide if the shade called for sunglasses or not.

"Something to drink?" the man behind the bar asked, drifting our way.

"Any light draft," I answered. He nodded and moved towards the taps near the center of the bar.

"Wuss."

"Hi, I'm Biff. Live around here often?"

"You wish." Avery sipped from a tumbler of smoky dark liquid, neat. "And I'm trying to picture your stasis conference. I see a bunch of old man professor types in bad casual clothes sitting around a table."

"Not even close. Last one I sat on, we had a pair of twenty-something female psychology grad students who are TAG researchers, a retired sheriff's deputy who does all of our licensing, a woman my mother's age with a Ph.D. in anthropology, me, Tu'u, and two research analysts. Plus Red, of course."

"Why doesn't that inspire confidence in me?"

"Probably because you've had a career of old school police work," I offered. "We're problem solvers. Intellectual force, and multi-threaded logic rather than simplistic, linear thinking, and brute force." I scanned the far shore, admiring the post-WWII ironwork suspending the old bridge over the Cane. "Old school guns and cuffs and car chases are too clunky, inadequate in the digital world. That's why you guys hired us."

The bartender placed a tall, sweaty glass on a coaster in front of me and moved away. Avery downed a swig, then put her tumbler down with force. "Let me take a stab at this, whatever you call it."

"Meta-cognition, if you want the term."

"Whatever." She waved a hand. "Try this; in the big picture, all TAG really needs is Fuego on audio and video to blow this wide open."

"Plus bank records."

"That's a separate objective. But sending you and me back at Creed and Boucane is not necessary, except for one thing—bait."

"Bait?"

"Yes—Red is using us as bait, poking the bear, getting a response that he hopes filters down to Fuego. Forces his hand."

She had a point—I decided, scanning the darkening blue on the far side of the riverbank as dusk sent the daylight west, emptying the sky and deepening the blue. Red was in a rush, but could we afford to be, just two people against unknown numbers?

"Well," I said at last. "You're right."

"So, do we want to be bait?"

I sipped my draft beer, letting the cold burn slide down my throat with the reassuring comfort of an old post-workday ritual. "I think we do."

"Is that logic talking," Avery asked, "Or just the urgency of being hunted and wanting to see an end to that?"

"Probably both, but mostly the former; this only gets worse once warrants are issued. Then every law enforcement agency in the country takes up the hunt."

"Red said to 'work the Creed,'" Avery repeated, "But he didn't say how."

"Go on."

"Marcheaux will pass the Molly Hatchet contact back to Creed," she said. "Isn't it better to let them come to us, then we can choose how we respond?"

"I think," groping for words; I traced small circles in the melting frost on the side of my glass, "what you're suggesting makes only a marginal difference in the timing, which is acceptable, but a major difference in the overall dynamics."

"Good or bad?"

"Good—your theory gives us the ability to act rather than respond."

She nodded. "How's that for centrifugal thinking, Perfesser?"

"Smart—damn smart," I said, finishing my beer. "Red

manages this op strategically, but you and I have to have the final say on tactics."

"So," Avery continued. "Let's throw out some bait and see who comes to us. Give me your phone."

I handed it over. She dialed.

"Hey, Mags," Avery said in an uncommonly perky voice. "Is Bozo there? Yeah, I know it's his day off, just thought I'd check…look, I'm going to need a ride home from the airport later this week."

A pair of broad-winged egrets rose lazily from the shallows across the Cane and swooped off towards the old bridge.

"Well, I'll tell you what, could you just put a note for him on the schedule board? Yeah, I've been in Utah," she glanced at me, "helping my idiot cousin with some family issues."

She looked directly at me; "thanks," I mouthed.

"Be by soon to pick up my check. Have him call me; wouldja? Yeah, he has the number. Thanks."

She handed the phone back.

"Bozo?" I raised an eyebrow.

"Brozowski. Bar manager at *The Saint*."

"Hope there was nothing special you ever wanted to see again at your place."

"My place…" she said, polishing off the last of her Scotch, "…is a corporate apartment not far from your campus in the Garden District."

The egrets swooped by, headed upstream.

"The apartment you've been to with me is a DEA set up, Perfesser, which should be our first stop in the Quarter. Get us on audio and video there and I guarantee Fuego will make a move."

A woman in a white apron stepped out of the restaurant door and walked our way with two carry-out bags.

"Pay the lady, won't you dear?" Avery said sweetly, patting her handbag. "I don't have my wallet."

That's because a loaded 9mm semi-automatic

handgun completely fills your purse, I thought but didn't say. I paid cash, we gathered everything, and headed down the winding steps to the dock.

I cast off the line, and Avery motored us upstream to a half-moon shaped cove under a canopy of fragrant magnolias. She killed the motor, and I tied us alongside a tangled knot of roots, then hauled us aground on the sandy shore. We broke into the Styrofoam carryout containers.

"How perfect is this," Avery said at last, putting down her plastic fork. "The creamiest, richest grits in all of Louisiana, and blackened shrimp, on the Cane River."

I nodded. The *Maglieaux's* grits were perfection, the shrimp, too. Couldn't ask for a more picturesque setting, there on the glassy smooth Cane under the shade of a broad magnolia. But...

"The thing is, every time I'm on the water," I said quietly, thinking back to Big Lou's swamp boat, then the *Natchez*, "some disaster always follows."

Avery narrowed her eyes, closed her nearly empty carryout container, and pointed the blunt end of her fork at me. "There are times, Perfesser, when you need to stop over analyzing things and just live, enjoy."

She cocked her head, waiting for agreement. I nodded. She was right, of course. But I knew deep down that so was I.

Chapter Ten

Highway 55 split the Mississippi sky into a verdant "V" of tall pines, cedars, and oaks dressed in kudzu, and lush green undergrowth, topped by a furious blue stacked with thunderheads to the north.

"Who buys an old VW bug for an intel op?" Avery practically shouted above the slipstream from the rolled down windows and wedge-shaped side vents.

I liked the Bug—a 1971 Super Beetle. I'd had one in college, and nothing flew under the police radar like a Bug; if you were speeding in the vicinity of any other vehicle, cops seemed to take pity on you, and pass you up to ticket the more affluent ride.

When I got back to her trailer, she'd already docked the boat and was waiting, hands on her hips, shaking her head when she saw the beetle.

"You've got to be shitting me."

"Where's your sense of history, Miss O'Toole?" I'd asked. We sat outside until spotty rain; then a thunderous downpour drove us inside. That night, I decided to take her up on her offer of half the queen-sized bed rather than the sofa and shotgun. Besides, anyone braving the thunderstorm to sneak up on the trailer would have to dodge the closed-circuit TV cameras as well, and though Avery didn't realize it, Tu'u had engineered a tap into that feed as well.

We'd set out northbound after breakfast, through Louisiana and finally, Mississippi.

"Glad you're driving," Avery said, scanning the map. "I'm not a fan of rickety standard transmissions. And underpowered engines."

"Ah, but you're riding in a classic, not some government contract economy shit box," I answered, feeling a buzz in my pants. I tossed her my phone, which was barking like a dog.

"What the hell, Mosby?"

Spike's face popped up on my caller ID. "Text alert, read it, please."

"Says TAG capture Delta voicemail off of Alpha phone. Red suggests Alpha return contact."

I nodded. "That's Tu'u. TAG intercepts my calls and pre-warns me what's headed my way. I think he just grabbed a call to your DEA phone. The one driving to Utah."

"Honestly, Spike is my favorite part of TAG so far," Avery said, tapping the speaker button and then play on the voice mail. "Including you."

"Message follows," a mechanical voice recited, then after a moment of static, "Agent O'Toole, this is acting special agent in charge Raton…"

"Special agent in charge?" Avery growled. "Pompous ass."

"Anyway… Avery, hey, I've just inherited this big

mess since Fuego is out on medical…look, we can work this thing out, just you and me."

She laughed. "Yeah, like I'm stupid."

The road bent west and mist from the recent rain steamed off the raggedy pavement.

"Just come in, Avery…we can straighten this confusion out before headquarters starts talking warrants."

"As if they haven't already," Avery said quietly.

The Bug eased down an uphill as a stream of cars and pickups zoomed past us to the left. I claimed the calm of distant, bygone days driving my VW, when no one, except maybe a renegade tractor-trailer rig, was trying to kill me or my passenger.

"Call me back. I'll meet you in New Orleans or Zulu, your choice. Let's fix this, while we still can. Okay, bye." The line went dead.

"Zulu?" I said with a touch of curiosity.

"We always specify an alternate reconstitution point," Avery said, staring out the window. That's Baton Rouge, in this case."

I filed that factoid away.

"I'm surprised, actually," she said, still staring out the window. "That it took this long long for DEA to reach out."

"Glad they did," I said. "Because we really don't have long."

"I get the feeling," Avery said, "That Raton's on a short leash."

"You buying his 'inherited mess' thing?"

She shook her head. "No. He hasn't had an original thought in his empty head in five years. He's scripted. The only question is by whom."

"Fuego?"

"Maybe."

We sat without talking for a few miles.

"Either way," I said finally, "The only thing we need from either of them right now is a little more time."

"So, let's give him something to slow him down."

I thought about that. "You have his cell number?"

"Yes."

"If we're buying time, seems like you'd give him back the same vague, confused act."

"I'd like to tell him to go fuck himself," Avery said, digging her TAG phone out of her bag. "But let's buy some time." She started to dial.

"Wait."

She looked at me, an eyebrow raised.

"If you want to go directly to his voicemail, hit 'pound' then 'star three' before the number."

"How does that…work?"

I shrugged. "Ask Tu'u. All the calls go through his server. He designed that."

She dialed. "Todd, Avery here…thanks for reaching out…sorry I couldn't talk to you…call back when you can, we'll see what we can work out." She disconnected the call, then added, "Asshole."

I laughed. "The number on that phone is untraceable."

"That voicemail will have him scrambling for what to do next," Avery said as I eased us toward the highway off-ramp. Backroads to Oxford, from here.

It was a rolling, four-lane divided road with a surprising number of huge, modern-ish brick homes on wide setbacks and spacious acreage mixed with squatty farm homes that led through a genteel countryside that reminded me of rural Kentucky, only more lush, on the way into Oxford. The old downtown appeared abruptly, like blundering onto a movie set; suddenly, you're on the old square around the ancient courthouse.

"What is this place," Avery breathed, taking in the Victorian era architecture mixed with early twentieth-century small town downtown, snarled with parked cars and a surprising amount of traffic for a weekday noontime. A striated, bruised blue stack of cumulus blocked the afternoon sun to the west, but the town stood brightly lit in what was left of the midday light not shrouded in thunderheads. The town looked bright, the square washed by morning storms and on the verge of more thunder and rain.

"Set your watch back a hundred years," I told her, veering off on a side street, then down an alley off the square. Best get parked and inside before the next cloudburst.

I pulled in near the back door of a narrow, three-story brick building that fronted the square to the south of the courthouse. The front door was for tourists, book collectors, and wannabe writers. The back door was for, well, real writers and business. I locked the Bug and led Avery up some steep, crumbly brick stairs to a loading dock, then to a blackened steel sliding door. I texted "back door" to an old, familiar number.

After a moment came the clanging of a chain sliding across hasps on the far side of the door, then it creaked and groaned on rusty rollers, and slid open a couple feet. I stepped in and waited for Avery to follow.

Inside, it took a minute for my eyes to adjust, but there was no mistaking who'd opened the door; tall, balding, and gray, white oxford button-down, dress slacks, slouching posture—Christopher Sly. He dragged the steel door shut, chained and locked it, and scowled.

"Avery, meet Sly. Sly, Avery." He nodded, looked her up and down, and shook his head, then led the way up a steep flight of steps.

"You know, we have a front door, Ghost," Sly said as he unlocked another door at the top of the staircase.

"This is business, Sly." We walked down a long hallway paneled in deep mahogany, then into a high-ceilinged room with one wall lined with bookshelves.

"It always is." He sighed. "Ain't Bee is in a mood, I'll warn you right now."

"No, I'm not." a booming female voice interrupted. A tall woman with a stacked beehive hairdo swept into the room. She was big-boned but graceful, commanding the room with a dignified presence. Full metal makeup, a classically southern matron. I'd guess Ain't Bee's age to be somewhere between fifty and sixty, but with southern ladies, it can be hard to tell.

"Christopher Sly," she said, "Don't be rude to our guests. We're happy they're here."

'Here' exactly 'where,' the look on Avery's face said. Ain't Bee knew.

"This upstairs loft is a 'salon,'" Bee purred, "a writer's salon, to be exact. The sign out front on the building says 'The Bindery,' as in old-fashioned, handcrafted book binding. But our passion here is writing. Dr. Sly hates being interrupted when he's writing, but in this case…" she glanced at Sly, "…it's your story he's writing."

"Downstairs," I pointed at the staircase beyond the burnished dark balustrade, "Mint juleps and half the liberal arts faculty and grad students at Ole Miss writing, talking, and envisioning themselves as Faulkner."

"Up here," Bee continued the thought, "A very specific genre; backstory. Now, what assets do we have so we can create a plotline?"

Sly scowled. "Not much. Credentials just coming in, but at least enough to get started."

"Credentials?" Avery asked.

Bee nodded. "Yes. Red was very specific about your rewrite. Investment firm, a retirement fund, which I believe he is embedding right now. So Christopher, start writing. I'll get the digital copy as soon as we have the data from TAG."

I had to laugh; this was going to cost Red a small fortune. But that fact alone underscored the urgency of this scrub and rewrite. Plus, the financial credentials gave me an inkling of the developing TAG strategy.

"Does he get a rewrite?" Avery asked, nodding at me.

Bee shook her head slowly. "Well, Dr. Mosby has several backstories to choose from. But a digital scrub, yes."

Avery's eyes narrowed, as if wondering which

backstory she'd been told, although what she'd been told was true. Mostly.

I nodded toward Sly. "He's in a bad mood because this kind of writing takes him away from the literary fiction he usually writes."

"Always writes," said Sly. "Even such genre fiction as this," he waved his hand at the stack of notes from TAG for Avery's "new" identity, "will be literary, so help me."

"No one reads literary fiction any more, darlin'," Bee said softly. "But good writers still write anyway. That's why we're here."

"To read the story is to live it," Sly said, typing away furiously on a compact notebook. "If it's a decent story."

"Meanwhile," Bee explained for Avery's sake, "We create authentic, hand-crafted replicas of classic books, most of which are out of copyright, or old law books. Our customers buy them mostly for decoration. If you're ever sitting in a lawyer's office, admiring the impressive legal tomes bound and shelved around the room, chances are good we printed them. They just look antique."

"And nobody's ever read them," I added.

"Of course not," Ain't Bee said with a pleasant smile. "Books are mostly for show nowadays."

"We are doomed as a civilization," Sly grumbled, typing. He paused to crosscheck some hand-scrawled notes, then resumed typing.

The clock ticked slowly, the hush broken only by Sly's fingers tapping keys, reminding me of nothing so much as sitting in my grandparents' breezeway, time dragging, the furniture ponderous and old, from another time, a distant life. The lugubrious clock hands sucked the life right out of you, just like this parlor with heavy drapes, oaken, book-lined walls, and Ain't Bee staring sweetly as if she hadn't seen her precious child in way too long. That's the drag that Tu'u and I dreaded.

"So he writes the story," Avery said, "That I'm supposed to be? The character I'm going to play?"

"No!" Sly snapped, annoyed. "Read the character setup, then *live* your story. This is an intense, effective way for you to not play act, but to live and own the very detailed backstory you'll need to pull off whatever undercover role you will inhabit."

"It's not your usual federal—"

"I know, I know," Avery cut me off with a raised hand. "Not your usual law enforcement methodology. Which you didn't seem to mind when I used it on the Creed thug trying to rearrange your face in Krotz Springs."

"I manage to get by on my own pretty well," I answered.

Sly's head popped up. "You'll have to tell me that Creed 'face rearranging' story—I may write that into one of my novels."

Ain't Bee handed me a mini tablet of notes from Red specifying the identity and credentials Red—or as likely, Tu'u—was painstakingly implanting into a series of banking databases. Avery huddled with Sly, answering his questions, giving him feedback. He nodded and typed.

"When we finish here, looks like we'll have full-spectrum financial institution credentials," I said, looking at the TAG notes.

Ain't Bee nodded, perched on the end of a large, round divan near the staircase. *If we ever get out of here,* I thought but didn't say, as the ornate hands on the big armoire dragged ever so slowly across the flat white clock face. The Roman numeral "four" was depicted wrong, I noted. Yet another throwback to the late Victorian parlor standard; Big Ben used four "I's rather than "IV" to represent the four on the clock face.

"Looks like Red has her set up as the trustee of a statewide retirement fund," Bee said. "With you as her administrative assistant."

"My assistant. As it should be," Avery added.

Fine. Much more operational leeway for me with her as the ostensible focus of whatever configuration we'd be using.

After the spindly brass hands dragged themselves through nearly an entire trip around the clock face, Sly snapped his notebook shut.

"That's it," he said, standing. Bee stood, smoothing the front of her dress with large, jeweled hands.

"Do I get a hard copy?" Avery asked.

"Only if I use any of it in my next book," Sly tossed over his shoulder, headed for the stairs.

"It'll be available on your phone as an audio book within the hour," I explained. "We don't want any paper trail floating around."

"But you will need *some* paper," Ain't Bee said, sweeping her hand toward a heavy oak door between the two main bookcases. She tapped a cypher into a small keypad next to the door, and it unlocked. We stepped into a brightly lit room of copy machines and photo printers.

"Over here, please," Ain't Bee ordered, standing by a digital camera mounted on a small tripod atop a hard drive server cabinet.

I stepped in front of the camera and froze for just a moment. I nodded to Avery. "Next."

"How does this, this equipment fit into a collectible books scenario?" Avery asked.

"We're mostly about digitalizing law books," Ain't Bee stated softly. "We rent and sell digital texts. It's the way of the future, and there's a good profit margin in law books, especially for new or small law firms, not to mention college books."

"Exactly the stuff Sly hates," I added. "Digital is the giant asteroid sending paper books into the extinction of the dinosaurs."

The hum of machinery filled a long silence, and then Ain't Bee gathered up an armload of documents, stacked them neatly, and placed them in a plastic folder.

"When I write the great American novel," Sly growled, "you are not included in those who can say they know me."

"So your primary income is from digital books and replicas?" Avery asked, running her hand over a richly bound volume of Ruskin's *Modern Painters*.

"Of course." Bee continued, "We offer some custom printing and digital services for select clients." She handed me the folder with several photo IDs, passports, and certificate-quality credentials.

Avery's jaw dropped as she examined the passports.

Ain't Bee smiled so hard that her eyes nearly closed. "Honey, we can print and bind you an authentic mid-nineteenth century volume of Swinburne's *Laus Veneris* with perfect woodcut etchings tipped in. So a little old passport is nothing."

"It's an art form," I added.

It's a forgery, Avery's look said.

"You can use my office," Ain't Bee pointed to a glass walled room, "if you want to confer with TAG before you fly out of here."

Inside, I propped my TAG phone on Ain't Bee's inbox and video-called Red. In a moment, the screen came to life. Red looked even more tired than he had in Tu'u's truck, which I took as a good sign; they'd been working this case hard. And they had to, of course, if they ever wanted another government contract, never mind avoiding a multi-count organized crime indictment.

"Ghost, Miss O'Toole," Red said without any preliminaries, "Tonight you start backtracking the DEA dollars, starting with The Quarter."

Avery glanced at her watch. Yes, dear, I thought to myself, New Orleans is a five-hour drive away. Did you catch Ain't Bee saying *fly out of here*?

"We're coming up on a federal holiday, which will be perfect for our purposes," Red continued.

"What are we talking about?" Avery asked.

"When we locate the transfer institution," Red explained, "you'll get there when all of the federal offices are closed, so your credentials will be validated on line."

"So, you've uploaded us to the federal banking databases?"

"No," Red stated flatly. "They'd get purged within twenty-four hours. Except on a holiday. The databases won't update until after you're gone."

"Tu'u will do a digital overlay of our credentials on a set of actual credentials right before we infil," I explained, having done this before. "That'll show up as a corrupt file on the federal server *after* the weekend. They'll fix it, and go on. But we'll be legit until they do."

"Now, the money is tied to your boss, according to our best run of the relational models."

"Fuego?"

"Yes."

"So you found him?"

"No," Red answered. "Your partner did. And we found your partner."

Chapter Eleven

We hurtled down the saddleback asphalt runway, the big radial thrumming like a locomotive, till I eased the stick back gently and the earth fell away. Through the big four-bladed prop, trees,\ and rolling hills gave way to clear blue sky as we climbed, and I eased us into a gentle bank toward the south.

By the time we passed over rolling, elegant leafy-green canopy of Ole Miss, then the town square and The Bindery's brooding façade on the Oxford Square, we were at nearly three thousand feet, an abnormally high altitude for the Air Tractor, the sturdy crop duster with an ungainly look but which was nonetheless a beautiful, tight handling air machine. I could see over Avery's head and headset, seated as she was in the front while I flew the plane from the rear cockpit.

She reacted as I expected when we pulled up to the corrugated steel hangar, doors open and the school bus yellow, boxy low-wing airplane staring back at us.

"This, this…*thing*? Who's flying us?" She stood with both fists on her hips, her jaw set. "What kind of bullshit is this?"

"This *thing* is a fast ride to New Orleans. Gimme a hand." I pulled on the tow bar. Slowly, the Air Tractor rolled forward. The trip would take less than two hours flying time, versus at least five hours on the road. "More TAG resources you should be grateful for."

"No way," Avery said, pulling with me on the tow bar. "You know how to fly this thing? You're a, a…"

"Backstory," I said, easing the rig to a stop as the tail cleared the hangar. Sixty feet of thick, high lift wing and a big ass radial engine. At times like these, I really loved my job. "You're about to live some of my backstory."

We'd been mostly silent as we'd driven the seven miles to the airfield, both of us trying to make sense of Red's bombshell revelation. Fuego was in rehab and somehow, Jesse, Avery's partner, was in the same facility.

"So your 'nerd herd' believes Fuego's in hiding?" Avery said as we left the Oxford Square. The stasis group at TAG; I had to admit, "nerd herd" fit.

"Adding up all of the weighted probabilities, that's the most likely scenario the relational model predicts."

She waved a hand. "I don't know about your model mumbo-jumbo, but I knew Jesse didn't just vanish. He got a lead on Fuego and went after it. I don't think Red believed me when I said that."

"He doesn't take anything at face value," I said, easing us off the main road and onto a private drive. Plus, I, like Red, wasn't convinced; Fuego maybe was hiding—or being hidden. How could we know for sure?

"But why would Jesse suddenly vanish and magically turn up on Fuego's heels?" I asked.

"Lourdes?" Avery said quietly.

"Who?"

"Lourdes Lafimen. At DEA Headquarters. Remember?"

"Jesse knows her?"

Avery shook her head. "I may have mentioned her, but he's never met her, I don't think. But she'd know of him."

"Why didn't you tell that to Red?"

"Because I don't trust him," Avery answered matter-of-factly.

I couldn't fault her for that and of course, the feeling was mutual; I could tell that Red didn't trust her either.

"What makes you so sure that Fuego is hiding, rather than being hidden? By Raton? Or anyone else in the multi-million-dollar food chain."

"I don't give Raton that much credit," Avery said. "He's an empty suit, empty head."

Motivation. I knew, the TAG group would be searching for that piece of the puzzle, and I knew where they'd look. If they didn't already, they'd soon have all of Fuego's and Raton's credit and banking records.

"Well," I said, concentrating on the narrow road under the tree-lined drive, "Boucane is not somebody you just conjure out of thin air." That was, I decided, not entirely true; the man of smoke just sort of appeared, normally at *Old Masperos*, but you never knew when or exactly where he'd appear.

"Creed," Avery said with a sigh, as if resigned or disappointed, I couldn't tell which. "We get into that hornet's nest; word will spread."

That was true enough. The outlaw grassroots, Creed, would conjure the man of burnished, wispy smoke. Word would move up the food chain; then Smokey would decide when, where, and most importantly, what, if anything, he'd reveal about money changing hands under the table.

"Well, how about this," I offered. "I can get us to Barataria. That's the outskirts of Lafitte. Can you get us into the swamp hangout where we'll find Creed?"

"*Sale Chien*," Avery said flatly. "The Dog, Creed calls it. It's near Lafitte."

"You can get us there?" I asked, dreading the thought of a few dozen drunk Toilet Guys.

"I can do better than that." Avery typed away on her phone. "I'll get us an under-the-radar ride." She paused. "Not some half-assed beetle car either."

I took a deep breath, then let it out slowly. "Okay," I said carefully, "Now, I'm going to just ask this, and you need to not poke my eyes out for asking."

"No promises."

"Is there any point in this where you think your sister can reach out to her old colleagues in the DA's office in Baton Rouge?"

"Way ahead of you, Perfesser. Spoke with Audrey last night. She said every case in the DA's office is on the back burner while they search for their trooper's killer. So yes, whenever you and I uncover solid links between the money and Fuego and Raton, she'll reach out."

Big asset, contingent on a big if; *if* we could find the money trail. Of course, she hadn't told Red about talking with her sister either. I let the idea drop.

To save fuel, I decided we'd climb on course. The big engine leaned out and saved gas at a higher cruise altitude, so I eased us up to 7,500 feet—cooler, quieter, and the best fuel economy without adding the physical stress of high altitude on the two of us.

"Okay, so you know how to take off, Perfesser," Avery's voice came through my headset, sounding high-pitched and mechanical. "Have you read the instructions on landing this thing?"

"I thought I have a couple hours to read the quick start manual."

"Seriously, Mosby," she asked. "What else don't I know about you?"

I nudged the stick to the right, rolled the Tractor up on one fat wing, eased the stick back, pressed the rudder and we inscribed a perfect, gentle barrel roll in the dusk-deepened sky. I said nothing. That would do for now.

She plugged in the audio book that Sly had created, listening to the story as Ain't Bee had recommended, over and over, until it was second nature. At least that was the plan.

I paged forward on the GPS navigation display, counting miles and waypoints and dividing them into the pounds of fuel we had remaining on board. At the high cruise and leaned-out fuel mixture, we would be fat on endurance when we reached the delta. I paged back to the navigation cross-track angle error display and zeroed out the fraction of degrees showing up as we headed south.

There was no doubt in my mind that Avery was trustworthy and on the right side of this war, so I had to believe her partner was too; she was shrewd and a very good strategic thinker. She wouldn't be blinded by the partner bond.

TAG giving us financial credentials was an all-in bet on one number, something Red wouldn't normally do. But I had to think the urgency of imminent warrants distilled the "nerd herd" deliberations to one best bet option. In a way, that was a positive; this would not be a long and tortuous road ahead of us. Things would move fast, whether they were good things or bad. I broke into Avery's audio through the intercom.

"I'm going to drop us down low for the last forty miles," I said.

"Why?" We're practically in the treetops now."

Not exactly—7,500 feet was the highest that Tractor had seen in a year of crop-dusting and firefighting, I was sure of that. But nowhere near the airline cruising altitude, Avery was accustomed to.

"Call it ancestor worship, Aivs. I like to ingress below radar."

"I need to unravel this backstory mystery of yours, Perfesser," Avery said with a sigh as I pulled back on the throttle and let the nose fall. The altimeter unwound steadily.

The bayou dusk crept from a darkened layer above into the horizon to the east, graying the dusty sky, while the sun burned furious red and low to the west. As always, a morality play, where daylight makes a brave stand but weakens, fades, then cold, quiet darkness always wins—until dawn, anyway. For now, though, it looked like we'd have just enough daylight left for the landing. I aimed for the final approach fix for the small utility field.

"Are you getting a decent cellular signal?" I asked. Should be, at the lower altitude and our relatively low ground speed.

"Yeah, I am. Want to conference call?"

I switched the GPS to the runway threshold coordinates, our last waypoint. I typed them into my phone and texted them to Avery. "There. You have the destination coordinates if your pickup person needs them."

"I'll send them," Avery said. "But I never said 'person,' did I?"

That sounded ominous, but I left it alone, concentrating on the final approach course and a constant rate RNAV descent, slowing the trusty bird. I always hated the end of a flight, especially in twilight. The feel was so uplifting, otherworldly, legless, and footless, but with broad metal wings and a smooth freedom to cut an arc in the sky. That evening the instinct was strong; trading the freedom of flight for the uncertainty of dangerous liaisons and hateful, volatile, and largely lawless people, well, I really wanted nothing more than to stay in the darkening sky forever. Ahead, the airfield beacon winked white and green, seeming more like a lighthouse warning of a treacherous shore. I aimed us right for it.

Chapter Twelve

A solitary yellow light glowed from the window on the hangar near the office door as I taxied the Air Tractor to the line of other aircraft parked in a neat row in front. The jaundiced light meant Tork was in the hangar office, minding his own business. Callieu Aviation Services was famous for that; they just minded their own business, never questioning the peculiarity of say, a turbo-prop re-engined DC-3 wandering up from South America, the light twin with no markings, or the big yellow Air Tractor I swung into a parking spot between the two.

Tall, stooped, sixty-something, Torkle McCorkle was known as the airfield "host" rather than the night watchman designation most likely in his job description, because he didn't watch anything, save an ancient black and white TV on top of the desk. "I just stay inside this here office," Tork told me once, "And I ain't never seen any type of crime." Callieu Aviation gassed up planes, did certified maintenance, minor airworthiness directives, but most importantly, they asked few questions.

"She in for her annual?" Tork asked me, holding a clipboard at the ready. The smell of burnt coffee wafted from an urn left too long on its hot plate near the counter.

"Yeah," I answered. "How long you figure?"

Tork flipped through a page or two. A *Gunsmoke* rerun droned from the tiny TV. "Just one ahead of you. With no major squawks, a week, maybe less. You gonna fly her back up to…" he paused, glancing at Avery, standing at the door with her travel bag slung over one shoulder. *She knows where we came from*, I wanted to say but didn't. Tork's discretion was one main attraction of Callieu, as far as I was concerned. That, and the fact that they always had Cream Soda, ice cold, in the relic of a vending machine by the shop door. "Back to wherever ya'll come from," Tork finally finished.

"I wish. Maybe, if we're around." I wanted to fly the big bird back north now, skip the upcoming dance of death in the swamp and later, The Quarter. Avery dropped her bag on a vinyl chair and walked toward the back door. "Restrooms?"

Tork tossed her a key wired to a red canvas tag that read "Remove Before Flight."

"Just inside the hangar, left side," he said, pointing.

There was only one restroom, and besides an ice-cold Cream Soda to wash down five hundred miles of trail dust, the bathroom was my highest priority. So once the vending machine ate my bills, refused to give change, and sent my soda clattering to the hopper, I twisted off the cap and stepped outside, then walked around to the side of the hangar under the pale moonlight. There I unzipped and relaxed into the blessed paradox of cold sweetness flowing in even as hot relief poured out.

Then I heard it. Faint at first, but growing,

unmistakable, gathering strength, and eventually, the deep roar of motorcycles, many motorcycles. Headlamps from a half dozen, then a half dozen more heavy bikes spilled out of the scrubby, moss-draped tree line and roared up toward the hangar. I hoped whoever they were, they hadn't seen me finish, put everything away, then zip up. The bikes surrounded me in a semi-circle. A gloved hand raised, then the motors rumbled and died.

Bug sounds reclaimed the night once the mechanical thunder subsided, and mixed with the ticking and cooling of a dozen motorcycle engines. I couldn't tell who or what was under the helmets, although the one who'd raised a gloved hand had a pink Mohawk glued across the top, front to back. I wanted to steal a look at the back of the vests and jackets, looking for a familiar biker gang name, but face-to-face, that was impossible.

"You should try the Cream Soda," I offered, then took a deep chug from the bottle. "Ice cold."

The gloved hands pulled off the helmet with the pink Mohawk. A woman with squinty eyes and a pointy nose shook out short, bleached-white ringlets of hair. She looked over her shoulder and laughed. "Cream Soda, he says."

Other helmets were pulled off—all women. They weren't laughing.

She turned back to me and pointed. "And whose bitch might you be?"

"He's my bitch," Avery said confidently as she rounded the corner of the hangar.

The ringlet-haired leader rested her helmet on the fuel tank of her Harley Roadster and leaned on it with both gloved hands. "He's like a donkey out here, pissing on the wall," she said at last. She swung a leg over the bike and crunched the gravel towards Avery in heavy biker boots, leathers groaning.

"Long flight," I offered.

Avery put both fists on her hips, stepping between me and the biker woman. "Well, you can put lipstick on a pig and call it Monique," she said. "But it's still just a pig.

I wasn't sure if I liked being seen as a pig or a donkey, or Monique. But neither of them seemed to even notice me, and they stepped toward each other. They hugged, slapping each other's back, then stood apart.

"So, you busted Ray-Ray's nose?"

Ray-Ray? Ah—Toilet Guy.

Avery shrugged. "It's not like his face wasn't already butt ugly."

I cleared my throat.

"Oh yeah," Avery said, "Let me introduce you guys. This is Mosby. Mosby, Gibby, and C3."

Crescent City Curves, the three cees, or C3 as they called themselves. All female bike club. I sighed; could have been so much worse. But was this our "ride?"

Gibby looked me up and down. "He's a geeky one, this bitch."

Avery shrugged. "Yeah well, a little variety, ya know? And Ray-Ray was being an asshole."

"Ray-Ray *is* an asshole." She looked over her shoulder. "Right, Cassie?"

One of the many women who'd shed their helmets nodded. Cassie was short, slight, and olive-complexioned—clearly Cajun. They all looked so serious—what the hell?

"No love lost between Creed and the Cs," Avery said over her shoulder as if reading my mind. And seemingly none lost between Cassie and Toilet Guy, I wanted to say but didn't.

"Grab your stuff," Avery said. "We need to get going."

"You're kidding, right?"

"Do I look like I'm kidding?"

Gibby laughed. "You'll fly in that ugly yellow lunch box, but you won't ride on the back of a bike?"

It wasn't that, although I believe motorcycles and organ donorship had more than a coincidental relationship. But worse, I couldn't imagine how such a large group would be anything but a liability, especially going into an incendiary situation like a swamp bar with an unknown demographic mix of prison gang alumni, drug dealers, and assorted lowlifes.

"C'mon, Moses." Cassie gestured with one hand. I was twice her size, but I was to ride on the back of her bike? Avery swung a leg over Gibby's Roadster. What could I do?

"Mosby," I said. "It's Mosby." Cassie jumped up and landed hard on the starter. Her Harley roared to life.

"Moses sounds better," Gibby yelled above the din. "More biblical, less nerdy."

"You are so right," Avery said, smiling that dangerous smile at me. I longed for simpler times, like when I was embedded in Mexico City for their first elections after Vincente Fox in the era of the Sinaloa cartel, or Bosnia overthrowing Milošević. Safer, more predictable, more defensible. I slung my travel bag over my shoulder—the 9mm smacked my ribs with a thud—then I headed for Cassie's rumbling bike.

She stared straight ahead and jerked a thumb toward the back of her rumbling bike. I glanced back wistfully at the big-winged yellow Air Tractor, making myself a promise that I'd fly her back north, at least some day. If we lived. Cassie tapped the clutch, and we edged forward like a roller coaster ride released from the loading deck, waiting behind the front car to engage the track chain and climb the big hill.

Avery shot a look over her shoulder that was two parts enjoyment of my obvious unease, one part the loyalty of one who'd slept with me like it meant something the night before. I put my hands behind my head and acted as if I didn't care, about the ride or the night before. Of course, I really did care about both. A lot.

Cassie flew the bike as much as rode it, leaning into curves like the Air Tractor banking to slice through a turn. The bikes cruised two abreast like the formation flying jets in tactical echelon I recalled from what seemed like another lifetime. The low-hanging, gnarled tree limbs grew horizontally abeam the road, laden with hanging moss like the silk-draped arms of a ball gown. Patches of moonlight, bone white, spilled through gaps in the canopy as the bike drew the road forward as if we were motionless, save a lean to either side on curves, the asphalt playing out before us like an endless ashen conveyor belt rolling below.

"We're going to help each other out, Moses," Cassie yelled over her shoulder. "You and me."

"Right," I yelled back, straining against the rush of the wind and the deep-throated rumble of the Harley. I figured I'd just agree but wondered what exactly "help" meant and how that included her. There was no way to discuss anything at sixty miles an hour, so I leaned back and tried to just enjoy Cassie's unusually smooth way of easing the bike through its paces.

Gibby raised a hand, ahead and to our left, and the column of bikes slowed as one, then turned off the main road onto a narrower, crumbly road. You could smell the swamp for miles when the wind's right but from this turn-off, the air of Lafitte announced itself more strongly with every mile. The pavement paralleled a tree line which, given the moon's position, must have been to the south. A broad, empty field fronted what had to be the edge of the swamp and by the far shore, a long, tin-roofed shed-like building squatted under neon lights proclaiming "Sale Chien." The "Dirty Dog." I had a really bad feeling about that.

"So what kind of help do you need?" I asked as the bike slowed and the slipstream weakened a few decibels, allowing conversation.

"I'll help you first, Moses," she answered. "Then I'll tell you what I need."

I wasn't sure what that meant. Why did I need help? Or, why *would* I need help, I wondered, as we drew closer *Sale Chien.* A collection of beater pickups, ramshackle cars, and a scattering of motorcycles cluttered the parking lot. I sighed, making the connection; The Dog, Creed, and the inevitable explosion when we lit the fuse.

"If I need you I'll find you," I said as we slowed, C3 pouring into the lot with revs and roars, circling around Gibby's Harley. I dismounted awkwardly, feeling unlimber after the ride.

"No, Beb," Cassie said. "It'll be the other way around. I'll find you."

A light, humid breeze rustled the marsh grasses and birds called to one another in the moonlight. Avery hopped off Gibby's bike and walked my way. She was all business.

"A few Cees are inside, a few more will go in after us," she said. "The rest will hang out here."

"Fine." Faint strains of an electric bass mixed with zydeco notes drifted from the distant doorway.

"What we need is either your buddy the boatman, or a few others I know who aren't overly happy about El Hefe and the other two idiots running Creed."

I filed the name away, wondering why TAG seemed not to have provided them to me during the entire operation. What else didn't they—or I—know? We walked shoulder to shoulder toward the shack.

"There's a front door, two side doors, both on the east side." Avery continued, pointing. "And a large open deck up against the dock on the south side."

I nodded. Ingress, egress, and contingencies.

Once again reading my mind, Avery continued, "The best bailout is the side door towards the parking lot. That's where the dumpster, compactor, and grease pit are. Just follow your nose, hop the stockade fence, and you're back in the lot."

"Got it. And the idea is, see and be seen, then get the hell out of here. An hour, max?"

"Well, that's why you're the perfesser, Perfesser." Avery smirked. "You're just so dang smart."

That remark was a bad sign; I knew Avery was at her most sarcastic when she was most worried. I let it go.

I let her get about ten yards ahead of me, not wanting

to impress anyone's memory if asked later if they'd seen a pair that looked like us. Better to act like we weren't together, as we did in Natchitoches and I looked around for Cassie to perhaps walk in with. She was nowhere to be seen.

"*Molly*," a huge man at the door with a mullet and a Fu Manchu growled, pointing a fat finger at Avery. "Don't you be starting no shit in here tonight."

Avery just kept walking but raised a hand as if testifying, or telling him to "talk to the hand," no one could tell which, but I was pretty sure I knew. I filed away the fact that the bouncer seemed to know her, and better yet, that Molly Hatchet had "started some shit" there before. I'd have to ask about that later.

A varnished-timber bar ran east to west through the center of the pavilion, with pool tables on the west side where most people had congregated. The corrugated roof was nailed to large, rough-hewn beams that were strung with barbed wire, although a guy with a crewcut in the far corner had managed to climb into the rafters anyway, ripping pieces off a beer can with his teeth. The mullet guy from the front door strode his way purposefully.

Under the cavernous roof, broad four-bladed fans rotated slowly, stirring the air, connected by an elaborate series of belts and pulleys. I took a seat near the center of the bar so as to be close to the fat, main bar tap, housed in a rounded stainless steel cylinder that would allow me sort of a half-assed rearview mirror if anyone should approach me from behind. I had a decent panorama of the dock side, and I kept an eye out for Avery.

A bartender with a scraggly beard drifted my way and stood scowling, as if I didn't belong there. Of course, I did not.

"A *Saison D'Ecrevisses* draft," I said, and slapped a twenty on the bar. "And let me know when that's empty."

He eyed me warily, then grabbed a mug and drew a draft out of the tap in the center of the shiny aluminum pipe before me, then placed it on the bar in front of me and moved away.

This is what I hate about such fieldwork; I decided as I took a deep draft of the cold *Saison*. The music, the damp darkness, the zydeco, the beer; I could really enjoy such a night in such a place, but there was the catch; all of those factors reminded me that I wasn't just blowing off steam from a long day. I was embedded, trying to look like I was not.

I scanned the room as Avery took a seat across the bar. Two thuggish men, both with the familiar, bad-news neck tattoo, sat next to her, the smaller man closest. She spoke to the big guy beyond him, a man with a shaved head and a teardrop tattooed near his left eye. Creed, no doubt, likely an Angola alum. The smaller guy stared at me, almost glaring, so I deliberately avoided direct eye contact. Avery drifted off toward the pool tables.

One beer, then a second, then I cursed myself for not prearranging a signal that I could pass to Avery or vice versa to subtly signify that it was time to leave. She was nowhere to be seen anyway, another problem I could do nothing about as I slipped off the bar stool and headed for the men's room.

As I pushed the heavy wooden door open, three scruffy men tumbled out. Offshore oil rig workers, I'd guess. Inside, the short guy who'd been sitting next to Avery sized me up. I didn't make eye contact, not wanting to set him off, at least not before I'd had time to tap off a couple of beers and a cream soda.

"The *fuck* you looking at?" he asked. High-pitched voice; the larger guy with the tear tattoo stood nearby. Here we go, I sighed.

"Me?" I asked innocently, unzipping my pants. "I'm looking at probably just a number one right now, but maybe a deuce later."

"Let's go, Moses." Cassie appeared from a stall. In the men's room.

Without looking, the teardrop tat guy swatted a rough

backhand that knocked Cassie back into the stall. While his arm was outstretched, I put my whole torso into a roundhouse blow with the butt of my open palm hard into his solar plexus. Like clockwork, he seized up as if he'd been tasered, and as he hunched slightly forward, playing out in slow motion in my mind, I waited for just the right angle, then used the elbow of the same hand to chop down in the sweet spot at the tip of his mandible below his right ear. I felt the muffled crackle; jaw dislocated, if not broken.

The short guy jumped me from behind, one arm around my neck. I let him have his way, turning slightly then driving backward and falling against the stall door, now held open by Cassie, and let my one hundred and ninety pounds fall, driving the door stanchion into little guy's back. He folded with a grunt; then Cassie punted his head with a motorcycle boot. The thug with the teardrop was on all fours, struggling to get up.

"Probably don't want to see what he has stashed in his boot, do we?" I asked Cassie.

She shook her head, brown eyes wide, grabbed my collar, and pulled me toward the door. "No, Beb," she said, and then the door banged open. Avery stood with her hands on her hips.

"Well," she said to Cassie, "My thanks for rescuing his sorry ass."

Before Cassie could speak, I said, "She has a mean roundhouse."

Cassie said nothing, studying me even as she held me by the collar, while the big man struggled to his feet. Avery took two quick steps forward and swept a leg against his ankle, dropping him to the floor again.

"Guess we're not getting a Christmas card from these two this year," I said, stepping over the short guy.

Avery grabbed the door handle and paused. "Your pants are unzipped."

Oh yeah, never did finish that business. But no time; the door burst open and more roughnecks, and Creed tumbled in.

I grabbed Cassie's small hand, and we slid by behind Avery, headed for the side door.

"Guess we've done the 'see and be seen' thing," I said, as the bouncer with the mullet and two others rushed our way, slowed by the ever-growing crowd streaming into The Dog. Between them and us, Gibby and a few Cees milled about, creating a traffic jam that impeded the growing tide of angry men heading our way.

"We can probably call that part good," Avery said. "Side door."

"No time," Cassie said, dragging me toward the dock. Avery looked at the onrushing mob cutting us off from the side door. She pivoted toward the dockside deck. We stopped at the edge.

"Jump!" Cassie shouted, pointing at the water.

"Jump?" I echoed. "Are you shitting me?"

"You got a better idea?" Avery asked, doffing her boots.

"Gators," I said. "And snakes. This is a friggin' swamp, and—"

Cassie threw a forearm at me with her full body weight, and we tumbled off the dock, Avery jumped right behind us. There was a split second, a slow-mo replay reel of the three of us in the air at once, the deck receding at an odd angle, Tiki torches burning bright with a mane of oily smoke, the silent moon peeking through cloud breaks, angry voices yelling at us, then everything went cold, dark, and wet.

Chapter Thirteen

I frog-kicked lazily underwater, trying to put some distance between me and the mob gathering on the dock, or at least where I'd last seen it. I surfaced eventually, located the dock from the light and the noise, and then cruised on my back away from the mob. A dark object—a beer bottle, probably—plopped into the water a few yards short. More followed.

Avery swam a few yards ahead of me, and I could barely make out Cassie's dark head bobbing beyond Avery, swimming strongly deeper into the moonlit swamp. I tried not to think about the gators, snakes, and even large rats I'd seen lurking in the muddy water from the safety of Big Lou's tour boat. Nighttime was the gators' feeding time, and there were likely more than a few lying in wait for food scraps and garbage dumped from the Dirty Dog.

Avery dropped back and swam beside me. "Try to stay with the group, Moses."

"Where exactly…" I asked, rolling onto my stomach and switched to a quiet breaststroke so as not to attract any stray gators, "…is the group headed, Miss Hatchet?"

"There," Cassie shouted, pointing with a dripping hand. Ahead, a bulky, dark object floated our way. As Avery and I neared the bulbous, rubbery float, a hand reached over the side and grabbed Cassie's outstretched hand, and then hauled her aboard, dripping along the side. The silhouette of a Zodiac boat took shape in the moonlight, oars reefed and motor hanging. A rope ladder flew over the side, which Avery grabbed with both hands. Cassie helped her aboard; I climbed the ladder. I tumbled over the side, saying a silent prayer of thanks that no gator or other reptile had tried to take a bite. A flashlight shined in my face, and then a familiar growl announced, "This is goin' cost you, Mosby."

The outboard motor sputtered to life, and we pivoted away from the Dog and deeper into the swamp. Goddam, I said to myself. How in the hell am I—are we—on a Zodiac boat with Big Lou, of all people, of all places?

Overhead, a grayish shadow swooped by, wings whistling lightly just over our heads, and disappeared into the gloom ahead.

"What the hell was that?" I asked.

"Probably an egret," Avery said. "Or a heron."

"That's my pelican," Cassie said. "He knows me."

She plopped down beside me wrapped in a blanket, her hair a dripping snarl of ringlets. "So, we just helped you, Bebette," she said, shivering. "Now you help us."

"Who is 'us'?" Avery asked before I could.

Cassie nodded to the man at the stern, steering the boat with the small outboard. "My uncle. My uncle, my father, and me."

Big Lou tossed me a coarse towel that smelled like motor oil. I dried my face and hair as best I could, then peeled off my sodden shirt.

"What kind of help are we talking about, Lou?" I asked noncommittally.

"The kind that keeps me from tossing you overboard," Lou said, although, with his Cajun accent, it sounded more like "ova bahd."

I looked back and forth between Cassie and Lou. Uncle? Or was he Cassie's father? Avery's eyes narrowed as she looked at the pair, then me, but held her silence.

"I figured we were on the same side," Lou continued, "when you whipped Ray-Ray's ass."

I raised a hand. "Well, I—"

"Not you," Lou interrupted, nodding at Avery, "Her."

I sighed. Sure, she did kick him in the nuts. And bounce his face off the parking lot a few times at Tommy's Gas & Meat.

"How does that make us on the same side?" Avery asked, meeting his eye with a resolute look.

"We know you a narc." Lou let that dangle like Spanish moss in the breeze. "So you know where the money come from."

The missing $3.8 million, I thought but didn't say. The Dog receded in the distance, and we motored further into the swamp.

"So do I. Thing is," Lou continued, "It'd save your ass if you outed the Fed asshole who kept most of it."

"And what do you get out of it?" Avery asked, toweling her hair, then shaking it out. Cassie sat quietly, her eyes darting back and forth between the two.

Lou eased off the throttle as we rounded a bend into a large alcove lined with cedars. A dark hulk loomed near a broken down dock. "I walk," he said. "And, what money is gone, is gone."

I did a quick rewind to Lou's comment on the swamp tour last week. *You tell Meng my price just went up*, he'd said as he'd passed me the phone. He—and then it must follow—Meng were in the payoff chain. She figured he'd be killed in the crossfire, but he knew the full story and stayed clear.

Again the whitish, grayish shadow swooped over my head just inches above, and I ducked out of reflex. A huge, fat bird flapped, spread wings larger than any I'd ever seen, then pulled them into his side, eying us from the bow rail.

"What the hell is that?" I asked, pointing.

"Barnabas," Cassie said. "A brown pelican. I told you—he likes me."

"Came with the boat," Lou added. "You don't speak bad about a seabird on a boat. So shut up."

"Turning back to the business at hand," I said, watching the fat bird carefully, even as it seemed to do the same to me.

"You basically set Creed up for the Tombs massacre," Avery said.

"No, your Fed scumbag asshole did, and tagged you for it," Lou said.

Now it made sense; Fuego or Raton, one or the other, had the money, set up the guns deal, and blamed Avery. Come to think of it, must have been both of them, each corroborating the other's story.

"Which brings us back to why we're here," I said. But that was becoming clear; Big Lou was willing to put us on the money trail, as long as he stayed out of the investigation. But there was an ugly reality that I was beginning to realize; I was supposed to be the Tombs scapegoat, not Avery. She would have been dead if we hadn't both heeded Boucane's warning, and I'd be rotting in a federal super-max prison without bail right now if not for Boucane and Avery.

Which brought me to Boucane. Why *wouldn't* he want to let the Tombs play out without warning me? I looked at Avery. What could be the motivation for Boucane saving her ass, and mine? That act had not only saved us both, but had ruined the strategy Fuego and Raton needed to have a dead, dirty DEA agent, a dead intel contractor, and their own hands clean.

"What doesn't add up," Avery said, "is why you're telling us this?

The Zodiac slowed, Big Lou killed the motor, and we glided up to the broad, low-slung stern of what looked like a trawler. I squinted to make out the name.

"You put your Fed buddy away for what he did here," Lou said, "and we both walk. Or, you take your chances with both Creed and the DEA wanting you dead."

"Grub Tub?" That was the name painted on the stern. She wasn't a new boat, but she'd been extensively refurbished; that became clear as we climbed aboard. I began to see where the money went.

"We're going to make a living on this boat," Cassie said. "Away from here. Upriver."

Avery sighed. "You have a contact with a name, I assume, at the DEA?"

"Fire," said Lou with a shrug. "I'd know him if I saw him, but that's what he went by. Fire."

Fuego…*Fire*? I glanced at Avery. Her eyes widened.

"I will kill that sonofabitch," Avery said in a cold, calm tone.

"The *Grub Tub* is like a food truck," Cassie continued, as if discussing murder was just chit-chat. "Only on the water. We dock at public wharves, docks, tourist spots. We sell mudbugs, Etouffee, gumbo."

"What is it," I asked Cassie, "With you and Ray-Ray?"

"Ray cut a plea deal," Lou said, "Testified against my brother, who went down for twenty-five years."

"My father," Cassie added. "But he'll be out soon. We'll make a straight living, away from here, away from Creed."

"I want out," Lou said. "That's what's in it for me, for us."

"So this," I swept my hand around. "Is where your money went."

Lou hooked an electric winch to the Zodiac boat. He nodded. "Paid cash. Plus my tour boat. Ain't a dime left, except what I put aside for fuel."

"Then you have the money transfer details from Fuego?" Avery asked.

"Some," Lou said. "Boucane has the main part, the account numbers, and payors."

Avery stood, wrapped in a blanket. "Well then, give us that, and then we'll get what we need from Boucane."

"No," said big Lou. "You get from Smoky first. If you can. Otherwise, no deal."

That made sense; Lou wouldn't commit anything till the full paper trail was possible, which hinged on Boucane.

"Gibby's got all your stuff," Cassie said. "And mine. We can meet her somewhere, get you two downtown."

Avery gave me a look that said *I guess we don't have much choice*.

"I give you two days," Lou said. "Then we're headed upriver, and we never saw you, either one."

"Two days?" Avery snapped, "That's—"

"More than enough," I interrupted. Either Boucane would show tomorrow at *Masperos* or he wouldn't show ever.

Avery tilted her head, considering the proposition. "And throw in a ride up to Baton Rouge on this thing."

"She's a food boat, not a thing," Cassie corrected.

"And we'll have a deal," Avery concluded.

Lou edged us away from the dark, deserted dock and out of the alcove. He nodded.

"Get Boucane's blessing; then we sail for Baton Rouge."

"And one more thing," Lou added. He nodded at Cassie. "She goes with you."

"She's just a kid," I protested. "You don't want her in *Masperos*."

"I'm twenty-five," Cassie said. "Or will be soon."

Avery shrugged. "She might have to save your ass again, Moses."

"She's my eyes and ears," Lou said, turning the wheel

slightly to avoid some roots poking up from the black water. "She goes."

The four of us sat in silence as Lou eased us quietly out into the moonlit swamp, headed god-knows-where.

Chapter Fourteen

"I thought Molly Hatchet a civil war ghost," I said. "Brought soldiers home, then beheaded them with a hatchet?" Just trying to make small talk, to stay awake, really, in a dingy all-night laundromat in the seediest part of Faubourg Marigny, a few body-slams from our haunted mansion digs for the night.

"Right," Avery said, talking over the squeaky dryer spin cycle. "I've got a big picture of a bunch of Creed mouth-breathers sitting around, discussing antebellum history."

Our clothes from the impromptu evening swim in the Lafitte Swamp flailed about behind the round glass window of the dryer. It was late, and I was tired.

"So, where did they get that nickname for you?"

She rolled her eyes. "The Molly Hatchet LP."

"'Flirtin' With Disaster' is on my cloud, coincidentally."

"Of course it is. Dork." She propped her feet on a laundry cart and shifted her 9mm to her lap. "And I may or may not have shown a willingness to use a blade on one of them."

"These are the things that make you regret your life choices," I said with a resigned sigh. The dryer had at least thirty more minutes to go.

"Well, one big Creed idiot regretted his choices that night."

"That's not what I meant," I said, shifting uncomfortably in a plastic chair. It was hot and humid in the dingy, poorly lit laundromat. "I mean sitting here now in my boxer shorts waiting for my clothes to dry after jumping into the swamp to escape a mob of angry drug lords."

"They're not drug lords." Avery blew a lock of air-dried hair off her forehead. "Just a bunch of lowlife dopers. And we're a step closer to the smoking gun we need to nail Fuego."

True enough; we had Lou's end covered, and he'd see to it that Boucane showed up at *Masperos*. If we could get banking records documenting the DEA money changing hands, or at least the location of the banking records, from Boucane, we might just be able to indict Fuego before he set the entire federal law enforcement dog pound loose on our trail.

"When our stuff's dry," I said at last, "We need to contact Red and see what they have, then fill them in on Big Lou."

"At five in the morning? Or it will be by the time this damn dryer finishes."

I nodded. "Yeah, I like waking him up, reminding him that we never did sleep. He forgets what field work is like."

Gibby had met us at the deserted dock in a pickup truck with all of our stuff piled in the bed. I had her drop us off here, not wanting any of the Cees to know of the safe house where we'd spend our time in the Quarter, keeping a low profile. We left Cassie on the *Grub Tub* with a promise to meet before we went to *Masperos* together, an idea I still didn't favor, but there seemed to be no other choice.

"Fine," Avery said. "Where's this so-called haunted house?"

"Dauphine Street, not far from here. Top floor of the LaCogne building. Lots of legendary ghost bullshit, but the perfect place to hide in plain sight."

"Explain, Perfesser."

I shrugged. "The building was built with slave labor in 1811, paid for with money the LaCogne family made off the sugar mill. Former slave butchered them both in their beds in the penthouse, blah-blah-blah, Madame LaCogne's ghost appears in the window some nights, end of story."

The dryer buzzed. Avery reached over her head, wearing just a *Grub Tub* loaner towel, opened the door, felt the clothes then slammed it shut. "Almost," she said, as spinning resumed.

"Tourists from about a dozen ghost tours trudge by on the street below every night, point and gawk, consider it proof when they see a shadowy figure behind the drapes late in the evening. Which is in reality, whomever TAG is sheltering for the night."

"Alcohol," Avery said. "And ghost tours; they go hand in hand."

"Good cover for us. Hiding in plain sight. And maybe they'll spy Molly Hatchet in the window some night." She gave me a withering look.

My phone started barking, so I dug it out of my bag. Spike's face smiled up at me.

"Hey, brah," Tu'u appeared on the small screen, Spike in his lap. "We've got a smartphone ready to be passed this morning to Avery's partner in rehab."

Avery sat up straight. "Jesse? How?"

"Just a dead drop. What Red suggested is you text the phone a short video letting him know you're on the other end of the line."

"Then he'll contact me," Avery said. "Excellent—he's in there working Fuego."

I still wasn't sure of that. How could she know her partner wasn't working with Fuego? But, Red obviously decided the phone was worth a shot. Opening another line of communication, even if her partner was colluding with Fuego, was still a positive asset.

"Is this a bad time?" Tu'u asked politely, probably noticing Avery's towel and me in my boxers.

"No, this isn't what you think," I said, wishing it was. "It's a long story. We're going to regroup in the haunted mansion and call Red shortly."

"So maybe do the video, and then call Red, with your clothes on?" Tu'u suggested. "Mo bettuh."

Avery yanked open the dryer and started dragging some dry pieces of clothing out. "Now I see what you mean about regretting life choices."

"We'll do both within the hour. Conference you in with Red?" I suggested.

Tu'u nodded. "I'll text you the number for the phone that's going into the rehab facility."

Once the dryer finally wheezed itself into silence we dressed, then trudged the block and a half to Dauphine Street. I unlocked a padlock on a cage around two trash carts and a recycle bin, then refastened the rusty chain with the heavy lock once we were both inside. I led Avery into a ramshackle tin-roofed shed that concealed a right turn from the street into a mildewed back alley of jumbled cobblestones and weeping brick walls.

"You sure this place *isn't* haunted?" she asked quietly, both of us walking carefully on the rumpled, slippery bricks.

"So here's the woman who isn't afraid to swim with gators, worried about ghosts."

"Not ghosts so much as slime and stink."

"Now that Molly Hatchet is in residence, I guess it is

haunted," I said, feeling along the wall for a pipe stem embedded in the brickwork. *There.* Above the pipe stem, a cipher box.

"Can you hold your phone up and shine the flashlight on this keypad?" I asked.

Once I could see the keypad, I hit enter, and a dozen lit keys scrambled. I entered the correct code; then a steel door buzzed next to the pad. I pulled it open, and we stepped into a small, dank room with cement walls, lit by a lone, bare incandescent bulb. I sealed the door closed and went to the door on the opposite wall and placed my palm on the handprint reader next to another door.

"Overkill much?" Avery asked in a tired voice. The door unlatched.

"Can a safe house really be too safe?" I asked, pushing the door open, then closing it behind us. I led the way to a corrugated metal staircase. "Fifth floor," I said, pointing upward. Avery rolled her eyes.

"I know," I said, exhausted. "Me too."

Once inside the cool, blessed air conditioning, we dropped our gear on the burnished wooden floor. I went to the fridge and pulled out two Voodoo beers, twisted off the tops, and handed one to her. We clinked bottles, then took deep draughts.

"We'd better do that cellphone video before I fall asleep standing up," Avery said.

"And call TAG," I added, "Fill Red in and get the latest they have. We can sleep all day after that, hit Masperos after dark."

The apartment spanned the southern corner facing Dauphine Street. Floor to ceiling French doors, masked with sheer curtains, opened to a narrow balcony above the street. Two separate bedrooms opened off a hallway to the west, and a full kitchen tucked in between a small library filled floor to ceiling with antique books.

"This place," Avery said, brushing a hand over the spine of several antique, Pre-Raphaelite volumes. "It looks like you."

"It's my place," I said. "In keeping with our policy of mutual honesty," I gave her a pointed look, "I'm telling you."

"Holy shit," she said, viewing the rotating display of security cameras showing various views of the exterior and the entryways. "Weird, but it feels like I've been here before. The feel, the hallway."

I shrugged. "Feels like home to me."

She stared at the brick archway into the study. "I just feel this place in my bones."

"It serves as a safe house when needed," I added. "Happens now and then. But mostly, this is home when I'm not working."

"So, you're the ghost in the window?"

"No," I said, grabbing her around the waist with one hand, the other on the nape of her neck in her thick, dark hair. "You are. It's about time."

"Business, Ghost," she said, slipping away. "The video, the TAG conference …"

"Fuck business," I said. I drew the drapes, took her hand, and headed for the west wing.

Chapter Fifteen

"Jesse," Avery said, looking into the cell phone on a small tripod on the desk before her. "Call me. Tell me what you're doing. I'm okay, and I need to know you are too. This is a secure line, just call or text me back."

She touched the stop button, then sent the video.

"Alright," I said. "Ready for TAG?" It was mid-afternoon, after we'd had a much needed six hours of sleep. Deep ops can be insidious; you run on adrenaline and don't realize how exhausted you are. Then, judgment, execution, and ultimately, survival begins to unravel. So, I chose this break, in my place, with Avery.

She nodded, taking a seat on a Corinthian leather sofa next to me. I tapped a few codes into my tablet, and then the screen adjacent to the north wall lit with a tapestry of scrambled pixels, which snapped into focus. Tu'u appeared with Spike seated on a chair next to him in the plumbing truck.

"Okay, patching in TAG," Tu'u said, pointing a remote.

The image on the screen split. A lone man with thick glasses, shaved head, and a soul patch faced us, wearing a headset.

"Afternoon, Ghost."

"Maestro." I nodded. He coordinated comms at TAG, especially for some real-time ops, a vital link between many players and moving parts when action becomes chaotic. "The Maestro," as we called him, conducted the TAG assets like a symphony. I'd explain that to Avery later.

"I'll get Red," he said, stepping off screen.

I shot Avery a wary look meant to reiterate what I told her the first time I'd warned her about talking to Red, but she faced the screen, intent. In a moment, Red settled into The Maestro's chair and without any preliminaries, started talking.

"Raton's credit is shot," he said, poking a finger at the bridge of his nose, pushing his glasses up further on his nose.

"He, like Fuego, has gambling debts, we believe," Red continued, "Because they both keep channeling bulk deductions from various accounts in amounts way beyond what he'd make as a DEA agent."

I put my left arm behind my head and stretched.

"Saw that," Avery murmured. She was more observant than I'd figured; Red's gesture was inquiring if I was under duress. Mine said no.

"So we went deep into gray sources, some black," Red continued.

I'd have to explain that to Avery later; gray sources were those behind firewalls, but which, if you could get around them, were accessible and therefore, fair game. Black sources, well, we shouldn't even be there, but once we were, the data was ours.

"Recently, an offshore account popped up on his financial array. We're trying to match that with Fuego's financial footprint," Red continued. "We're running the relational model connected to the FDIC and IRS databases, but we lack an ID to connect Fuego's multiple accounts. He receives funds from several dummy sources, but we need a commonality to deep drill on his source data."

"Try the name 'Fire,'" Avery suggested.

I nodded.

"Possum gave that up yesterday," Avery added.

"Big Lou," I said. "DEA calls him Possum."

Red nodded to someone off-screen. I smiled; several researchers were about to run "Fire" in cross-reference with Fuego.

"Well 'The Possum,'" Red said, using Avery's term, "Just caught two large deposits from Banco Delgado, the fourth largest bank in the Caribbean last week, and none of it's in his account now. We need to know if he bought into the arms deal."

"I doubt it," I sighed. "He bought a *Grub Tub*." Delgado would mean a trip to Haiti or the Dominican, if that was where Boucane's money trail led. Please God, no.

"Appears to be a refurbished shrimp boat," Avery explained. "Medium-sized trawler."

"Get on the boat's title and the lien," Red said to someone off screen. "Now, Miss O'Toole, your partner in rehab with Fuego."

Avery said nothing, her head cocked and jaw set. A tough one, she was, and loyal. I admired that, but only to the point where her partner could actually hurt her; she had been set up by her supervisor; who's to say her partner hadn't been part of that?

"We're talking more gambling debt, but—"

"You mean Fuego," Avery snapped.

"No," Red continued calmly, "Your partner owes over $100,000 to Rager Poker and Black Dog Game World."

That vein near Avery's temple began to throb. She said

nothing.

"We found a line of credit recently opened under the name Colby Romero, but all of the other info matches with your partner."

Avery closed her eyes and let out a long breath. "That's his son's name. Colby."

"What I was trying to say," Red continued in a quiet voice, "Is that we don't have any big deposits into his accounts like the other two. Just the debt."

So, we weren't really sure whose side he was on, but Red was throwing Avery a bone. I was thinking along the same lines as Red; we couldn't know which side of the law Jesse Romero had landed on—and neither did she. My guess was that the TAG relational model found the question too evenly divided to conclude either alternative. Avery believed in what she believed because he was her partner. I reserved judgment.

"Jesse will wear a wire," Avery said. "That'll prove it."

Red smiled for the first time in ages that I'd seen. "We don't do that kind of thing. I'll let Mosby explain to you."

She looked at me, her brow furrowed.

"Later," I whispered.

"The piece of the puzzle we need now is whatever banking trail you can pick up from your *Masperos* contact," Red continued. "Anything, however slight. Mosby can explain that, too."

I nodded.

"Once we can be sure which of the three—Fuego, Raton, or Romero—are able to act in this negotiation, we'll be able to act ourselves."

That was uncommonly diplomatic of Red. Normally, he'd have said, "Once we determine which of the three are dirty, we can target our efforts to out them." The deference to Avery was clear, and knowing Red, that meant her help was going to be crucial. That was both good and bad; I knew she'd do whatever was necessary to nail the rogue DEA people, but that also kept her in the line of fire.

"What does TAG have on Boucane?" Avery asked.

"Nothing," Red answered flatly.

"Nothing?"

Red shrugged. "Nothing for the last fifty years—no public data."

"What is he, a *ghost*?" Avery asked with exaggerated surprise.

"Probably not," Tu'u answered. "Probably a really deft cyber sweep by someone, some organization, that doesn't want him known."

"His digital and paper footprints dead ends in the last century," Red added.

Avery glanced at me; I shrugged.

"We collect intel data," I said, "Add it to our total source database."

"With an asterisk beside it," Red continued, "Because we don't have ethnography on Boucane."

"But so far," I continued, "Everything Boucane has forewarned has come to pass."

Avery shook her head. "This 'source,' if you want to call it that, would be totally ignored in federal law enforcement."

"Exactly why we pay attention," Red said, folding his hands before him. "So get what you can from out of *Masperos*, and then get out of town."

I nodded. That's exactly why I'd made a ride to Baton Rouge as part of the deal with Big Lou. He was a master at disappearing before any ambush.

"Anything else for me?" Red asked.

Avery glanced at me then shook her head. I contemplated telling Red that Cassie was going in with us to meet Boucane at *Masperos*, but decided to hold back—that hadn't actually happened yet anyway.

"Okay," Red said, glancing at an iPad. "That's all from here. Tu'u's tracking; contact when you've egressed safely."

Avery's eyes narrowed at the "tracking comment."

There was a lot I'd need to explain to her later. The TAG screen went blank.

"Okay, brah," Tu'u said. "And Avery. You two be careful."

"We will," I said. "You too." The other screen went dark.

"He pisses me off," Avery said.

"Tu'u?" I asked.

"No, Red."

"Because of Jesse?"

She nodded.

"Look," I said, "He's your partner, but an unknown quantity to Red; a variable in the moving parts he's trying to define so that he can accurately predict an outcome that saves all of our asses."

"Still don't trust Red."

"And you don't have to," I said. "Look, let him be the devil's advocate. That needs to be done to see all sides of this situation. Let him do that, which frees you up to focus on what we're doing."

"What's with the 'tracking' thing?"

I took her hand and lightly ran it over my right forearm. She had to feel the aspirin-sized bump under the skin. Her eyes widened.

"You're chipped like a dog?"

"I prefer to think of it more like a toll tag. And some places I've been sent, I really needed someone to be able to find me."

She shook her head as if she was trying to clear it.

"And why is 'wearing a wire' so funny?"

"It's not funny," I explained, "Just archaic. In effect, he's wearing one now, or whenever he's holding the phone TAG passed him."

I wanted her to be aware, at least indirectly, that her partner's new phone, like Fuego's, had had audio and video capture features that were hot, or "on" and recording, sending data to Tu'u, most of the time. She seemed unfazed.

"How does that stand up in court as evidence?" Avery asked, arms crossed.

I shrugged. "Probably doesn't. Nor does it need to; don't you think that once the audio and video appears on YouTube, Snapchat, and a few other social media platforms, that every law enforcement agency with jurisdiction will be getting subpoenas and warrants?"

"And the bit about 'anything, however slight?'"

"That's zero-based intel," I explained. "You all have a hypothesis, a theory, and eventually, a suspect you go after. We look at the entire situation, sweep the room, then examine every shred of information—including Boucane—to assemble a defined image, a picture with as many pixels as possible."

"How is that better?"

"Because that method—examining every information shred—leads to real answers, not just confirmation of your best guess."

Neither of us spoke for a while, making it clear that she wasn't convinced. And just as Red could be, maybe should be skeptical of Avery's partner, for the same reason it would actually be a good thing to have her try to shoot holes in our methodology. That's just more quality assurance at no additional cost.

Time to change the subject.

"Where should we meet Cassie?"

Avery pursed her lips. "Certainly not the *Ole Saint*." Avery's cover job for her DEA undercover work—that would be covered by DEA and by now, FBI and ATF agents. "Let's do *Chouette* on Rocheblave Street."

"Are you kidding me? That's a major crime area. BYO knife and gun."

Avery smiled sweetly. "I'll bring both."

Chapter Sixteen

A mechanical monkey pedaled a bicycle across a saggy tightrope slung just under the ceiling, wall to wall, back and forth about every thirty seconds, right over the bar.

"A Bourgogne," I told the bartender at *Chouette*. "But put it in a tumbler, so I don't look like such a pussy." The bar reeked musty and stale from too many spilled drinks, the French Quarter summer humidity, and the swirling mix of ancient crumbling plaster infused with tobacco smoke, booze, and rumbly, deep-throated laughter from sailors, hookers, and all manner of lowlifes who frequented a place seldom paid any attention by NOLA PD. "The Owl," the name proclaimed in French, suggesting a wry chiasmus; stately and wise, maybe, but a voracious raptor nonetheless. *Chouette* was a favorite watering hole among Mississippi freighter crews, and God only knew why.

"Just don't drink pussy drinks, Perfesser," Avery said in an aside to Cassie who sat on a heavy oak barstool between us. "Then you won't need to worry about the glass."

Cassie perched on the front edge of the battered wooden seat, wary as a cat, eyes darting left and right, and I couldn't tell if she was fending off predators or looking for prey. Big Lou was a fool for sending her with us—she didn't have Avery's way of melding into any circumstance, or mine of vanishing. Large, brawling types roared and yelled at their bar pals, one eye on Cassie, the other on Avery, letting me be invisible. As for me, I felt like having a decent, non-fruity, crisp French Chardonnay. I needed a refreshing drink, not a piss-bucket draft beer, at least not today, or a gas station quality wine either. The monkey wheeled by overhead, grinning.

"I don't know what the hell a 'bear-gone' is," the ruddy, roast beef-faced man on the far side of the bar snorted. "But we have white or red wine. Them's yer choices."

"Then just a piss-worthy draft beer," I said, resigned. Clearly, this night would be a disappointment. "Anything light, and a large whatever."

The man had one wonky eye, and I couldn't tell which it was, so I stared at the bridge of his nose. He froze for a minute, as if to emphasize that he really would rather stab me than serve me—it was that kind of place—then moved towards the taps.

"Was it really good manners to call his beer 'piss-worthy?'" Avery asked pleasantly.

"Hard to find a decent Chardonnay these days," I answered. Really, it was; everything in the US seemed either too oaky or way fruity.

"Mosby's a high-strung poodle," Avery said to Cassie, turning a tumbler of whiskey back and forth against the lone bulb in an Elvis lamp on the bar. The monkey whizzed by again, unconcerned.

"Moses," Cassie said, nursing a bottled *Voodoo Dreams Dark*. "Just needs someone to look after him."

Yeah, maybe I did. But I also needed to move this soiree along; we'd hooked up with Cassie; now, we needed only sundown and darkness to conjure the man of smoke at *Masperos*.

"Tell me," Avery said so quietly that Cassie leaned in closer to hear, "How *Masperos* plays out. I've always avoided the bad karma that place is famous for."

The barkeep drifted our way, eying me, and I only wished I knew which bloodshot orb was his good eye, like a newscaster needing to know which camera to look into. Again, I fixed my gaze on his nose.

"We got white," he growled. "Toldja." He plunked down a water glass of jaundiced, piss-looking wine, no coaster, glared, then left.

"We need entre to the back bar at *Masperos*," I started to explain, then sipped the wine. Vile. "But there's a gatekeeper first." I explained that first Amédée would glide by behind the bar like a long-billed, lazy-winged seabird, a Gannet seeking prey with dangerous grace.

At the mention of Amédée, Cassie crossed herself, her eyes wide. "Uncle Lou says you messing with Vodun."

"Voodoo?" Avery asked. "Seriously?"

I ignored the subject. "Amédée will pour drinks and study you—act like you don't notice; never make eye contact."

Avery's eyes narrowed. The monkey hit the wall, hard, then fell off the wire.

I met her eyes. "Then, watch the big mirror behind the back bar."

"Mère de Dieu." Cassie crossed herself again. The barkeep examined the monkey, banged his head on the bar a couple of times, then put him back on the slackwire.

"Boucane doesn't like eye-to-eye stuff," I said. "At least not face-to-face, if that makes any sense."

"Not really," Avery said. "But continue, Moses."

"So just watch the mirror, talk to him in the mirror."

"And we press for any type of money trail for the Tombs he'll give us," Avery said, although the inflection made it sound as much like a question as an answer. I nodded.

"I kind of listen more than talk," I said, "When it comes to Boucane."

"Uncle Lou says Boucane's a demon, not real," Cassie said quietly. The bartender cursed the monkey, frozen, it seemed, on the high wire.

I sighed, sipping the drink, which was losing its harsh bite and becoming tolerable. "Nice of your uncle to send you with us to meet the devil."

Dusk stained the outside walls a mahogany they didn't have earlier and sketched the intricate wrought iron balcony latticework in ashy Conte crayon. The temperature dropped, but the air held a full bayou breath of steamy Mississippi funk as the sun burned red, then expired, giving way silently to deep blue, then black. Thunderheads stacked themselves against the Mississippi and wisps of rain in swirling mists came in light sheets, cool almost. We walked in silence, mindful of crumbly Quarter cobblestone, fractured curbs, and crowded sidewalks. Somewhere, a church bell tolled the hour like a dirge.

Music drifted out of open doorways, and we approached from the river side, avoiding the *Ole Saint* as well as the old police headquarters of brooding granite behind ponderous wrought iron fences, the outside littered with police scooters parked every which way. Evening roll call going on inside, I imagined, a good time to slip by, a good thing to miss. Depending on what strings Fuego was pulling, what cards he had in his hand, there'd either be Avery's and my face plastered on "BOLO" handbills, *be on the lookout*, or maybe nothing at all. We had no choice but to count on the latter and just move quietly, unobtrusively down the steamy block, past the slave market—the words chiseled into the old cornice work were still there, if you knew where to look—then cross the street catty-corner to *Old Masperos*. Thunder rumbled in the distance, promising a cloudburst, likely within the hour.

Stepping inside was like entering another world; a musty, almost spice-like, a clove smell floated over more pungent traces of seafood, shellfish probably, that wafted in from the dining room. Gas lamps flickered from blackened wrought iron sconces on the rough brick walls, casting subtle, fleeting shadows on the faded red brick. I savored the coolness but dreaded the feel of smoke; Smokey, Boucane, studying me studying him in the big mirror beyond the smaller, inner bar.

We eased onto seats at the main bar, me in the middle this time, Avery on my left, Cassie near my right elbow, looking ready to clutch it at any minute. Avery, on the other hand, seemed relaxed, almost bored. A cool dampness claimed the air and a smell that was hard to describe; maybe, the scent of rain on hot pavement, flowing in from an open door mixed with a Caribbean spice, and incense of some type, plus the smell of whiskey and rum both poured and spilled on the heavy slate bar.

A glass appeared in front of me out of nowhere, and then Amédée glided up in profile, never eyeball to eyeball, of course. He poured me a Bourgogne, bless him, then a dusky whiskey for Avery though she hadn't said a word, and finally, he slid a cold-sweating *Voodoo Dreams Dark* before Cassie. She grabbed my arm but resisted the urge to cross herself.

I took a deep swallow, letting the Bourgogne burn its way down. Through the open sash on the French windows, a gust of cool air swirled in, the first breath of the coming storm rumbling closer. Avery knocked her whiskey back in two gulps.

"I just got another text from Raton," she whispered. Cassie squinted and cocked her head as if she'd heard, but didn't understand.

"One thing at a time," I answered, cursing to myself.

Why now? I took another deep swallow. "Not here, not now."

Avery nodded, and Amédée appeared and refilled her tumbler. Cassie looked like she was going to ask a question, but I caught her eye, shook my head, and she turned back to her beer and the rivulets of condensation tracing the curve from the neck of the dark bottle downward.

Rain began a light hiss, then a steady hammering, staining the scotia molding blood red over the dried, cracked timber board of the sill.

"Why all the ritual, the horror movie theater?" Avery asked. "Let's just go to the back bar, or whatever it is."

"Doesn't work that way. Be patient."

A flash of light scorched the walls blue-white, then a crack of thunder tumbled in the open windows, echoing through the downtown canyon of high-rises surrounding The Quarter like the walls of an old castle. The rain intensified, pouring as if weighted down, urgent. The temperature dropped.

Amédée refilled our glasses while Cassie fretted over the same beer. Finally, after I'd finished my second drink, thinking about a third, he floated by again, never looking at any of us, and held out his hand to show us the door. The small, back doorway framed by rough timbers beside the bar; I knew it only too well. Thunder crashed, then reverberated off the walls, and echoed down the street.

I led the way, stooping through the low doorway that must have been built over a century ago when men and women were more Cassie's diminutive size than mine. The lower bar was quieter, although muffled rumbles still shook the walls and lightning flickered through wrought iron framed clear story windows. I took a seat at the bar, a smooth, dark slate atop ornately carved and dark-stained mahogany. Avery sat to my left, Cassie, wide-eyed, to my right. Again, the drinks appeared, but once Amédée vanished, we were alone. Over the bar, the familiar mirror etched with the cathedral in silhouette and bordered on the bottom by a city skyline of bottles in various sizes and shapes.

A flash of light almost simultaneous with a thunderclap doused the lights and Cassie jumped, leaning against my shoulder. The lights flashed to life, barely, then died again, leaving the bar lit only by the flickering, golden gas lamp flame of the wall sconces. A cool rush of air coursed through the bar, and Cassie crossed herself for at least the tenth time.

"There," Avery murmured. "In the mirror."

Cassie leaned forward to see around me, looking at Avery, then the mirror.

I saw it too, the shape in the glass once my eyes adjusted to the dimmer light, Boucane, the man of smoke. "Let the games begin," I murmured to Avery.

"Where, bon Rien?" Cassie asked. "I don't see anything."

"So," Boucane said quietly, fixing my gaze with his in the mirror. "You took my advice, or you wouldn't be alive tonight."

I nodded. Cassie looked at me, then Avery, then the mirror again.

"Good advice," I answered. "And now I need some more."

The barest hint of a smile played on his lips, then he shook his head. "You're all out of favors, mon."

"Who are you talking to?" Cassie asked, squinting at the mirror. I put my hand on hers lightly, as if to say, chill.

"But I have some advice for her." He nodded to my left. Avery.

"I'm all ears," Avery said, as if only mildly interested.

"You're just like your sister," Boucane said, the hint of a smile nowhere to be seen. "Strong-willed, overconfident."

Avery seemed rattled by those words, and the vein near her temple throbbed; plus, her eyes narrowed ever so slightly. I hoped he hadn't noticed that, and yet I was afraid he had. I willed my own face into stone, but inside, a dagger of concern; how the hell did he know about her *or* her sister?

"Look for fire in the Carib," he said. "Look to Banco Delgado, the Radaloa people. They have what you're looking for, if you can make them give it up."

"I will," Avery said. "Now, how—"

Another flash, a clap of thunder and when my eyes adjusted to the dim light again, Boucane had his glass raised, signaling that our conference was done. I raised mine; Avery did the same, but I could see her anger rising. Perhaps this was a good time to end this anyway. Cassie stared at us, then the mirror. She raised her *Dark Voodoo Dreams* bottle but stared at me and Avery.

When the electric lights flickered back on, and Boucane was gone.

"What the hell." Avery turned to me. "My sister?"

I held up my hands. Cassie leaned around me.

"You saw him?" Cassie asked, "Or it, whatever it was?"

Avery nodded. "Are you saying you didn't?"

"No! I didn't see or hear anything!"

Avery and I exchanged glances. Why Cassie hadn't seen Boucane, I had no idea. But, the more important concern was deciphering his advice. That, and dealing with Raton's latest, then having Big Lou sail us upriver and the hell out of the Crescent City.

We waited outside in the rain by the riverside service door for Cassie's Uber. She seemed unconvinced, but in a way, relieved she hadn't seen Boucane, as if that was some sort of deliverance from the devilment that Lou had warned her about and in which Avery and I were hopelessly entangled.

"He said 'Banco Delgado,'" I repeated for Cassie, "Tell your uncle that. Has he ever mentioned that name to you before?"

"No," Cassie said, studying the rainwater rushing by beyond the crumbling curb. "But I've seen emails with that name, and electronic transfers."

Avery and I exchanged glances.

How about the name 'Radaloa?'" Avery asked quietly.

Cassie nodded. "Some type of investment thing. A broker, maybe?"

I sighed. Looked like we'd be headed to Haiti soon. Cassie glanced at her phone, then held it up smiling.

"See?" she said, her mood brightening. "My Uber."

The text read, "Jesus arriving now in a Toyota Camry."

I laughed out loud as the car rounded the corner and stopped before us.

"Dockside," Cassie reminded us as she opened the car door and ducked inside. "At eight."

The car drove off, and Avery and I walked arm-in-arm into the darkness, taking the roundabout way back to the Haunted Mansion in the diminishing rain.

"So, Cassie dodged the devil and has been delivered to salvation by Jesus," I said as we crossed a darkened alley.

Avery laughed. "But you and I, perfesser are clearly doomed."

That, I decided, was probably true. The lights of the Haunted Mansion beckoned.

Chapter Seventeen

"What do you make of this?" I asked Tu'u who sat with Spike in a beanbag chair, front and center in the large TV monitor, the side wall of my study.

"It's the same electronic signature with no spoofing," Tu'u said, "I break it down, and I get the original MSGID, library-name, and file as the first one. So it's most likely Raton."

"And the message?" Avery asked.

"We need to toss that to the TAG stasis group," Tu'u said. "But even if he isn't trying to manipulate you, this is a major vector change. Can you read it again, Ghost?"

A TAG technique was to read a message aloud to see if, through the semiotics of inflection, we could deduce the implications of possible vocal context.

"Sure," I picked up the phone from the granite-topped

coffee table and scrolled to the latest message from Raton. "It reads, 'Avery; this has gone way too far. I need to kill this before it gets any worse. Fuego swore no friendlies would get hurt, but they have and they will. I can't be a part of this. Call me.' That's it."

"So," Tu'u said after a moment. "You read it as if it's sincere, as if Raton is having an attack of conscience."

I nodded. "Guess I do."

Tu'u shifted the poodle to his other knee. "But Avery doesn't."

She shook her head. When she'd read the text, her voice conveyed a definite subtext of skepticism.

"So we bring Red in. We need to fill TAG in on *Masperos* anyway."

Tu'u nodded, punched his tablet with a pudgy finger and The Maestro appeared on a split screen.

"No rest for the wicked," The Maestro said in greeting.

"Then maybe you shouldn't stay up so late," I snapped back at him. That drew a wry smile from Avery.

"Touché," the Maestro said tonelessly. "I'll patch in Red. Hold one."

"I just read the Raton text," Red said abruptly as his image blossomed in the split screen. "We'll run it through stasis relational analysis, but for now we have to assume at the very least he needs a relatively prompt response from you, Miss O'Toole."

"I was thinking tomorrow morning would be soon enough?" Avery said.

Red nodded. "Should be adequate. Ghost?"

I shrugged. "Yeah, I think so."

What difference could the matter of a few hours make? And I knew what Red was thinking; if Raton was sincere and the text was a crisis plea, a little wait time would add leverage to Avery's response. If he was simply being manipulative, just trying to draw her out or wear her down, making him wait was also the best option. And the phone was untraceable, using a complex internet connection through Vancouver, British Columbia rather than cell phone towers.

"I should mention," Red continued, "That Fuego's phone is back on line. We think he must have had to find a new charger or some other technical problem."

I sat up straight. "Are you pulling in audio and video?"

Tu'u shook his head. "Not yet. We're monitoring the audio from a hot mike, but we don't want to use Snapchat or Meerkat until we have something significant. The modified apps are not stable over the long run without updates, which is a problem."

"Now," Red continued. "*Masperos*. Did you make contact with your CI?"

"We did," I answered, thinking back to Boucane in the mirror. I wanted to ask why Avery and I had seen him, but Cassie had not. Avery and I also had questions about Boucane mentioning her sister—how could he know? But, no need to complicate an already volatile, fast-unfolding situation. "He steered us toward Banco Delgado and an entity, presumably financial, called Radaloa."

Red made a few notes on an iPad mini, nodding. "We'll deep drill on that, have intel for you by tomorrow morning."

I sighed. A trip to Haiti would be the next shoe to drop.

"Miss O'Toole," Red resumed. "Given that we're probably going to need to execute the financial cover story, are you fully conversant in the Ain't Bee rewrite?"

"I cut my teeth coding on a ZX Spectrum," Avery purred. "And we are fully prepared to conduct 'deep dive' financial and strategic diligence for our investors, if Banco Delgado is up to the challenge."

A broad smile spread across Tu'u's face and for a second, I saw the inkling of one on Red's typically taciturn face. At least it seemed he'd gotten TAG's money's worth out of Ain't Bee's.

I shook my head. "Who *are* you?"

"A financial visionary and investment evangelist who

can bring the business on a journey of discovery," Avery answered coolly, "At least according to Christopher Sly."

"You're a quick study, Miss O'Toole." Red nodded. "So, here's where we are. We know the DEA buy money was dispersed rather than used for the drug buy. We know someone at DEA orchestrated the 'guns-for-drugs' swap that turned into 'guns take the drugs and shoot everyone in the way.' We know that you two were supposed to have been eliminated in the crossfire, and that either Fuego or Raton are running the damage control since you're both still alive."

"That's about the size of it," I answered, watching Avery. She just nodded, then looked down at her phone.

"We believe," Red continued, "that whoever is calling the shots will inevitably start issuing warrants and subpoenas regardless of your response to Raton's latest text, Miss O'Toole, so our best predictive analysis suggests you both plan on a safe house until we finalize a trip to Banco Delgado. Tu'u?"

"From Banco Delgado we just need routing numbers and a RAT implant," Tu'u said. "If you can get site access at Banco Delgado, we can get both, then we'll start strip-mining their server for transactions. I have a couple of pieces of hardware for you; then after TAG sets up the meeting, you just need to get as deep into the IT portal on site as you can."

RAT—Remote Access Trojan. The hardware was likely a small flash drive loaded with a few RATs, some code, and a bot or two.

"We will force-overlay your banking and investment credentials onto the federal database after close of business east coast time Friday, so you'll have until Tuesday free and clear before the next federal database cyber-sweep. All US banks will be closed, but your Monday meeting in the Caribbean should check out fine from their end."

I nodded. Avery would play the investment banker, and I'd do my best proximity site ingress to implant a few bots and RATs that Tu'u could then take control of.

"I presume you're headed north in the morning?" Red said, putting his pad down. Kind of made sense since south would put us into the Gulf of Mexico, but I resisted the urge to point that out.

"Yes," Avery answered. "We'll be off the roads and headed upriver on a fairly nondescript trawler."

I suppressed a smile. "Nondescript" if you didn't notice the "*Grub Tub*" floating food truck concept, never mind the clumsy pelican who had taken up residence atop the wheelhouse.

Red nodded. "All right. I'll leave you with Dr. Fa'aola to work out the tech requirements, and we'll get back with you with meeting details tomorrow."

I raised a hand in a wave; Avery nodded; then the TAG picture vanished, and Tu'u and Spike filled the whole screen once again.

"So maybe we meet in Baton Rouge?" Tu'u suggested, scratching Spike under the chin. "Or Natchitoches might be even more under the radar."

Avery sighed. "I think we need to spin Audrey up on all of this."

I nodded. I was eager to have Avery inquire about getting evidence to the Baton Rouge DA's office as soon as we had a documented link to Fuego, but I didn't want to be pushy where her sister was concerned.

"Well Big Lou will take us as far as Baton Rouge," I said. "So that's a done deal."

"Okay to meet there, Avery?" Tu'u asked. "Audrey knows me now."

"Just bring Spike," she answered. "Then it's a deal. And speaking of Audrey…"

We exchanged glances, and then Avery continued. "How the hell is this Boucane…*thing* aware of my sister—I've never seen him before in my life."

Tu'u leaned back, puzzled. He sighed. "We haven't figured out what this Boucane is."

Silence held the room for a moment.

"You feel him more than see him," I offered cautiously. "Just not sure…"

Avery stood. "What the hell? I saw him, sort of, heard him, for sure."

"Hologram, maybe," Tu'u suggested. "Double mirror …"

"He sits at the bar, or at least something does," I added.

Tu'u sighed. "Or something paranormal. We can't rule that out."

"You've got to be shitting me," Avery snapped. "A doctorate in theoretical physics, and you…" she pointed at me, "…a doctorate in whatever mumbo-jumbo—"

"The first thing you learn when you get a Ph.D.," Tu'u said quietly, "is how little you'll ever really know."

Avery's phone buzzed angrily, then went silent.

"Text," she said, picking it up. "From Jesse, my partner."

Both Tu'u and I leaned forward expectantly.

"Says Fuego is running Raton from the inside," Avery read aloud. "I'm trying to find Fuego's money trail. He wants me inside with him, needs me to launder some cash for him, to show good faith."

Avery shook her head. "Sly bastard, Fuego."

"Is that it?" I asked.

"No. Here's the rest. 'I'll put him off while I keep pressing. But he did mention a Caribbean bank transfer when I can get my routing numbers. More later. Hope you are okay—I don't need or want to know where you are, just that you're okay. Jesse.'"

She put the phone down and rested her chin on her fist, still staring at the phone. I knew that Red would ask the blunt question, "Do you feel he's playing you?" I knew better than to ask, but still, the question weighed heavily on my mind. I kept silent, waiting.

"So," Tu'u asked gently. "Are you comfortable with his information?"

I suppressed a smile; Tu'u had the same question, but a lot more tact than Red or I could muster.

"I believe so," Avery said after a moment, still staring at the phone. "But from here, at least until I reply, there's no harm he could do either way."

"True enough," I said. "What's your read on a reply?"

Spike jumped off of Tu'u's lap and walked out of the picture. Tu'u remained silent.

"Nothing immediate," Avery said, "because we don't want to get into a real-time exchange."

Tu'u nodded. Very smart and rational on Avery's part, which was a relief. I still didn't trust any of Fuego's federal *compadres* in or out of rehab.

"So, can you get him to route a payment into a federal bait account?" Tu'u asked.

"Too risky," Avery answered. "We don't know who else is on Fuego's payroll. That would expose Jesse."

How about in the state attorney general's office, via Audrey, I thought but didn't say.

"That's something we might work on in Baton Rouge," Avery said at last, reading my mind, "maybe Audrey could reach out to her former colleagues in the state prosecutor's office."

"And one last detail before we head upriver," Avery added, typing on her phone. "There." She handed the phone to me, and I read aloud, "Raton—just tell me what you want to do."

Tu'u nodded. "Good. Measured, receptive, but noncommittal."

Avery took the phone and hit send. "Now, let's get out of this town for a while."

I rolled my eyes. "*Grub Tub*, Big Lou, and that weird pelican. You make it sound a lot more normal than it really is."

Avery folded her arms and cocked her head. "That, Perfesser, is just something you're going to have to deal with."

Chapter Eighteen

"Of course we don't cook the shrimp on the boat, dumbass," Lou growled from the wheelhouse. "It's a trawler, not a floating kitchen." The slate-colored river coursed by smoothly, dully, on either side of the trawler. I never understood the "mighty Mississip'" cliches because, like today, the wide, sullen river seemed just a muddy gray-black, if anything, heartless, dull, and brooding. Lou, ever the skilled boatman, eased us on a tack against the wind, toward a dock on the east bank of the Mississippi about fifty miles north of New Orleans. Our second stop.

"Stupid me," I said, winking at Cassie. Avery laughed, nodding to the bold red letters painted on the side of the deckhouse that proclaimed "Fresh Caught and Fresh Cooked Bayou Shrimp." Beside those letters, in smaller print, a sign on the deckhouse spelled out "GALLEY" in capital letters.

Lou grunted, nodding at the cauldron lashed to a burner on deck. "We buy the shit in five-gallon buckets from Costco. Rice, too. Heat it up, sell it for ten bucks a bowl."

Above us, boom arms strung with nets fluttered in the breeze. Sure looked like an active shrimper.

"About a three hundred percent markup," Cassie chimed in. "Plus the T-shirt sales." She and Big Lou wore matching black T-shirts emblazoned with the *Grub Tub* in cartoon form, including Barnabas, the pelican. "T-shirts are $25, and a picture with Barnabas costs $10."

"The damn bird shits all over the bow," I said.

"Not in the pictures," Cassie said, looking hurt.

"You don' talk shit about a seabird on a boat," Lou grumbled. "Or I tro' your sorry ass ova—bahd."

We eased smoothly toward a heavy, river-worn timber dock near what looked like a city park. A few hundred feet beyond our pointy end—eff Big Lou—a dredging rig on a barge swayed and yawed against its mooring lines; and beyond her, a small, rusty ore freighter sat sullen against the dock, her stack belching black smoke in a thick curl swept off to the west by the prevailing wind. Scruffy dock and boat workers streamed toward the *Grub Tub's* berth. Barnabas squawked, spread his broad, dirty wings, and shit a gush of muck over the starboard gunwale.

"Uncle Lou knows all these ships and sailors," Cassie said, sweeping her hand toward the gathering crowd as Lou eased us toward the dock deftly. "He ferried them supplies at Channel Dock in Nawlins for years and years." That, plus dope, booze, and whatever they were willing to pay for; I remembered that as well.

Lou grunted his agreement. "Now I'm underselling Boudreau Supply Co. by twenty percent, and doing it upriver. Bastard's gonna starve; his customers already fed. They'll skip his shit hole café and go right to *The Owl* or some other sailor bar."

I thought back to our last visit to *Chouette* before *Masperos*. I wondered if the monkey on the high wire was back in operation above the disheveled human tide slopping around inside the dump. I hoped so.

"You going to live aboard?" I asked.

Cassie shook her head. "Lou will, but not me. Just tonight, then tomorrow we do the same stops southbound. Whatever days Uncle Lou thinks there'll be business and decent weather, I'll come aboard, and we'll sail her up and down the river."

That made sense. Back to the Cees motorcycle club and whatever else she did in the swamp. I wasn't sure I really wanted to know.

Avery tossed me an apron emblazoned with a silhouette of the *Grub Tub*. "Make yourself useful, Perfesser." She tied an apron around her own waist as Lou gently docked the *Tub*. Cassie leapt nimble as a cat to the dock and tied the forward, then aft lines to huge metal cleats. Lou killed the motor.

"Don't we have to be in a seaman's union or something?" I asked as Cassie joined me on the aft deck where the enormous, heavy kettle bubbled on the cast iron burner stand.

"You working off your passage upriver, brah," Lou said, grabbing a cell phone credit card reader from the wheelhouse, then he slid down the ladder without touching a step. Barnabas flapped off to the north.

"Well there goes the photo op," I said, watching enviously as Barnabas climb lazily, gracefully into the blue.

"He'll be back," Cassie promised as the big bird soared in a climbing arc to the west. "He likes pictures."

"I'm not sure we do," Avery breathed quietly, untying her apron. She nodded toward a local TV news truck on the dock.

"Get below," Lou said. "Both a' ya. And don't fuck with my stuff."

Cassie tapped on her smartphone, and wireless

speakers mounted aft of the wheelhouse sprang to life with a touristy zydeco instrumental.

"Showtime," she said with a sheepish grin, "We'll cast off in an hour. But TV coverage is good for business." She opened the deckhouse door labeled "Crew Only."

"I'll be in the galley if you need anything," I smarted off, ducking in after Avery.

Inside, Avery stood with her hands on her hips. "You really shouldn't encourage her. You know she has a crush on you."

I laughed. "Give me a break."

"You're so dense, Perfesser," Avery said, trying the door handle near the aft bulkhead.

"Lou said not to mess with his stuff."

Avery held up a hand. "I have to know."

"Avery, you're not on duty—"

"I'm never *off duty*," she snapped back, almost shouting. "I'm not a contractor; I'm not doing a job. I'm living what I believe. I have to know they're straight, that Cassie will be okay, safe."

Our eyes met. "Without a warrant? That's what *we* do—"

"It's nothing *like* what you do," she growled back. "I'm saving lives, taking care of people at risk, even at my own expense. Not a subcontracted, itemized bill of services rendered; I never stop. That's what *we* in sworn law enforcement do."

"Okay," I said. "I guess I deserved that. And I admire what you do, I do—"

"Or you wouldn't be here," she said quietly. "I've given you a dozen chances to walk away."

I studied the deck. "Maybe I'm living what I believe, too."

She nodded, took my hand, and squeezed it. "I know." She looked down at the polished linoleum floor. "I know."

She opened the aft bulkhead door and disappeared down a steep stairway.

People, presumably customers, came and went by the curtained porthole windows on the deckhouse. Lou's boat was spotless inside and come to think of it, so had his gator tour pontoon boat been out in the Lafitte Swamp. Say what you wanted about the coarse, mercurial sawed-off Cajun boatman, but he ran a ship-shape trawler.

Though it seemed like an hour, it was probably no more than twenty minutes before Avery quietly closed the bulkhead door.

"Clean," she said. "And believe me, I've searched many a boat, plane, car, and once, a train. They're clean."

"Good. It's best all-around if they are."

"Get real, Perfesser—it's best for *you*, too. Tell me you're not aware of the enhanced felony this would pile on both of us, plus 'organizing' for the four of us, delivering a controlled substance? You could be Toilet Guy's bitch in Angola for a long, long time."

"Buzzkill," I said, raising both hands in surrender. "I'm thinking more of the *Grub Tub* biz. So they can go straight like they planned."

"May not be that simple," Avery said. "The paper trail that paid for this boat is still dirty."

I laughed. "No. He paid a percentage to Meng for his cut in cash."

Avery cocked her head and narrowed her eyes.

"The paper trail ends with Meng," I continued. "Lou told me it was a cash deal while you and Cassie were talking motorcycles on the way up here."

She nodded. "He's smart. And this *Tub* is clean."

Cassie burst through the deckhouse door. "We need more bowls," she said, breathless. "And the TV truck's gone." She grabbed a box store package of paper bowls then rushed back out on deck.

"I guess here's where 'never stops serving' gets real," I said, tying on the *Tub* apron again.

"Try it," she said, tying on her own. "It'll be a new experience for you." I decided I'd better leave it at that.

I ladled shrimp gumbo atop rice in paper bowls Avery passed my way. Our customers were a mixed lot, from families at the park to crewmen from other, mostly larger vessels alongside the pier, to business people from some offices near the park. Between swiping credit card data for payment, Cassie quietly pointed out people to me, saying in a whisper "they're Skidoo people" or "houseboat folks" or "barge crew."

Lou stood on the bridge when he wasn't ducking below to bring up more thawed gumbo or rice. He seemed to be in his element, at home on his own boat rather than just pontooning gawkers through the swamp for a couple of hours, tossing marshmallows to docile gators who were as much of a commercial contrivance as he was.

Once we were underway again, he put Cassie on the ship's wheel before the ghostly-lit rudder angle indicator, patiently explaining the right of way on the river—"them barges can't stop; we stay well clear"—and how various curves came to be due to freezing of some waterways that inevitably forced the river to carve a new, relentless route to the delta. Barges dotted the shore near cement plants and at least as many sailed up and down the river. The big mag compass in a polished brass stand wavered and swung starboard and port as Big Lou directed Cassie to swing more toward the center of the river, a mile or more off shore.

Then the coastline lost its detail and shrank to a saw tooth horizon of trees, cliffs, cement and power plants, and the occasional anonymous, weatherbeaten industrial works. The blue sky on the western horizon burned with the arcing sun; to the east, haze mottled the ever-changing coastline of buildings, trees, cliffs, then more buildings.

The farther north we'd go, Lou promised, there'd be more refineries, and so we'd avoid the barges and silently running oil behemoths gliding by between *Tub* stops by staying offshore. That suited Avery and me just fine, prizing anonymity over speed or proximity to shore. Lou pointed out spectral radar blips on the side mounted radar screen and like a fortuneteller, his predictions came true as huge tankers, barges, cargo ships, and even a sailboat or two materialized ahead, just as he'd foretold.

Eventually, Avery and I left the wheelhouse and climbed down the forward ladder to the deck. As we walked forward, Barnabas rose, eyed us, then flapped off with an annoyed screech. He flew wide circles around the trawler, never more than a few hundred yards away, keeping an eye on Cassie, or maybe just shrewd enough to appreciate the free grub passed to him on board.

Near the bow, a constant, almost hypnotic splashing of water shoved aside by the boat drowned out the throaty thrum of the motor. We sat on an equipment locker, enjoying the water scent carried by the breeze of the *Grub Tub's* "fifteen or so knots," as Big Lou called his best fuel mileage speed, into calm winds. We leaned shoulder to shoulder.

"I almost wish he'd slow down," I said, not wanting to face the Baton Rouge reality of arrest warrants, the DEA manhunt, the life and death scavenger hunt for incriminating banking data, and whatever ugly traps Fuego and Raton might have set in our way.

"You're the guy who expects bad news on boats, remember?"

I nodded. "I like this one. In fact, I like life as simple as ten buck shrimp bowls, surly pelicans, and wide blue sky over the Mississippi."

We sat in silence for miles, mesmerized by the water, the gentle roll of the boat, the steady forward way she made, and the stately procession of ships passing abeam, north to south, as far as the eye could see.

Hip to hip, I felt Avery's phone buzz. She caught my gaze, rolled her eyes, and stood, pulling the phone out of her back pocket. The spell was broken.

She put her hand to her mouth, closed her eyes, and handed me the phone. A text message, from Jesse, short and sweet; "Raton just blew his brains out."

Chapter Nineteen

The cargo end of Tu'u's plumbing truck was cramped with four of us and a dog squeezed in, sitting before Red who appeared calm on the main screen.

"We have verification," he said, "from two reliable sources. Agent Todd Raton's death was a suicide. Single shot from his service revolver."

Avery frowned, looking down. "Idiot," she said under her breath. "He finally had an original thought. A really bad one."

Audrey looked aghast. "Omigod.You knew him?"

Avery nodded. "Coworker." *More than kin but less than kind* sprang to mind but I held my tongue.

"So, Miss O'Toole," Red continued. "What's your preliminary analysis?"

I hated Red's way of plowing right through any

sensitive issue, but I appreciated it just the same; with Raton gone, the dynamics would change, and likely not for the better. If Fuego got himself discharged from his faux hospitalization, he'd have no option but to come after us. Raton had given him a shield, a dummy to run his posse from behind the curtain of "rehab." This was no time for kid gloves.

"Best guess only." Avery raised a hand as if being sworn in. "But based on knowing Fuego for years, now that his 'shit screen' is gone, I'd expect him to come out with guns blazing."

I cringed at the "shit screen" sobriquet for her dead coworker, but Avery was a hard-nosed federal agent, one whose federal agency had tried to murder her—and me. Spike jumped down from Tu'u's lap and padded over to lay at Avery's feet.

Red nodded. "That's our consensus here as well. Plus, Raton's death leaves Fuego no choice; he has debts he must pay on promptly. Without Raton, he'll need to launder money himself."

That was serious leverage and an unexpected windfall for us; Fuego would be forced to move some of the stolen DEA money.

"Can your partner follow Fuego out of rehab?" Red asked.

Avery pursed her lips but remained silent for a moment. The main electronics cooling fan died, leaving us in silence.

"He could," she said at last. "But I'm not sure we'd want him to."

Red cocked his head but said nothing.

"If Jesse follows him out, Fuego will know he essentially followed him in," Avery continued. "Then Fuego, the heartless bastard, will try to play Jesse like he did Raton."

"Go on," Red said.

"But if Jesse continues what Fuego believes is rehab,

Fuego will reach out to him eventually, to draw him in, maybe to put him to work, if …"

"If what?" I said.

"If Jesse buys in. Meaning, launders some funds, just like Raton must have done."

"How can he accept a wire transfer of dirty money," Audrey said, "And not go down with Fuego when he's busted?" Spike looked at Audrey, then Avery again, and put her head down. *Twins*, I wanted to explain to the dog, *and you'd best steer clear of both—they bite*.

"Maybe the routing number doesn't go to Jesse's new off-shore account in his son's name," Avery mused. "Maybe it goes to the Louisiana State Attorney General's account."

"Go big or go home," Audrey breathed. "Why not the Director of the DEA?"

Once again, the conspiracy of the Irish Sisterhood scared the pants off of me. But I liked their ballsy thinking nonetheless. Another cooling fan near the primary electronics rack kicked back in, breaking the awkward hush in the back of the truck.

"Let's not get ahead of ourselves," Red said, raising both hands. "All good, creative strategy, now we'll start working specifics out of TAG."

"We've got routing numbers inbound from the government transfers for our invoices," Tu'u said. "I can do a little exploratory work."

I smiled at the veiled reference to what, plain and simple, was one of Tu'u's fortes; the DEA financial management division was about to be hacked.

"Now," Red continued, "where are we with containment?"

I expected that, but Avery looked puzzled. Red needed to know how wide our circle of informed actors had become. That loose end, for us, was The Boatman. Big Lou had docked the trawler after sundown on a nondescript, empty wharf just south of Baton Rouge. A swelter of fog, born of the lower dew point as the sun stopped roasting the air and the humidity congealed, shrouded the dock.

"You got my half of the transfer numbers," he growled. "Hook that up with Boucane's and you got what I don't. Then I'm out."

The moon tried, but couldn't shine through the mist and instead, cast a diffused, pallid eye low on the eastern horizon. Lou stood at the aft door of the wheelhouse, one stubby hand on his hip where, without being able to see it I knew, hung the sheath of his ginormous hunting knife. The point wasn't lost on me; he'd carved up gators with that blade—he had no fear of using it on anyone.

Barnabas huddled on the stern, glaring my way. Cassie stood sad-eyed and mournful, hands on her hips, on the aft deck as we gathered our gear and she cast off the lines.

"Hey, we'll ride again soon," I said, thinking back to her smooth, flight-worthy handling of her Harley as we rode with the Cs to the *Dirty Dog*.

"I promise, sister girl," Avery added, pointing at Cassie. She hit a preset button on her phone and conjured an Uber driver as the *Grub Tub* vanished into the mist.

I considered for a brief second not telling Red any of this, but only for an instant. I came clean.

"Big Lou and his niece," I said. "They know what we're trying to do."

"How do we know they're not active man-del CS?" Red asked. Manufacturing and delivery of a controlled substance, Red had said, in a parlance aimed at Avery, and maybe Audrey. Crafty, Red was.

"They aren't," Avery said. "I searched their *Tub*. Nada."

"They only know what they need to know for their own interest," I said, "Which is basically not getting their throats slit by Creed or an indictment from the DEA—"

"In that order," Avery finished my thought for me. That was becoming uncanny. Audrey stared at me with narrowed eyes, then looked away.

"The final tactical move," Red said, "is to pass the money transfer documentation completely beyond federal jurisdiction, into the hands of the Louisiana State Attorney General."

"I have reached out to Emily Bishop, the Chief of the Criminal Prosecution Division," Audrey said. "A trusted friend and mentor. She will act on any hard evidence we bring. But let me warn you; they won't accept nor will I bring them anything half-assed. This needs to be clear links."

"We have located thirteen accounts in Fuego's name," Red said tonelessly. "We've tracked 'structuring' of amounts less than the CTR threshold between all of them."

Avery frowned. "Without a subpoena?"

"Or a search warrant," I added, a reference to her *Grub Tub* search. Pretty sure she got that because she gave me the finger. I smiled back.

Still, the CTR was vital; a "CTR," Cash Transfer Record, is generated any time a total exceeding ten thousand dollars was deposited or transferred anywhere. How Red and TAG dug them up was not my problem, legal or not.

"And," Red continued, "We have multiple CTRs from different casinos showing each time that Fuego deposited ten grand but left with between seventy and ninety thousand a week later."

Avery threw her hands up in the air. "How in the hell does he—"

"Sonofabitch," Audrey breathed. "That's how he used Raton. And why he'll need Jesse out of rehab…"

Before Avery could ask again, Red explained.

"His accomplice or accomplices go in with under ten thousand dollars, put chips down, small bet—"

"Then they collect their chips, give them all back to Fuego," Audrey said, "Fuego cashes out a winner as far as the casino and the IRS are concerned.'

Red nodded. "We need video, which you *can* get with

a subpoena."

"That'll take two weeks, minimum," Audrey said. "More likely a month."

"That's two weeks we don't have," I added. "In case anyone's keeping track."

Audrey nodded. "I can take that account structuring and casino CTR evidence to them, they can open the case. That might buy us some time, at least in this state."

"If the state AG acts," Avery said.

Audrey raised a hand. "Oh, they will. They want this case prosecuted, not buried like 'Fast and Furious,' since it happened in our state, and took the life of one of our troopers."

Red nodded. "Tu'u will get you the files."

"Meanwhile," I said, standing. "We chase the source documents in the Carib."

"That's both ends—where the cash came from and where it's going," Avery said.

"And motive for what went down in the Tombs, and why Fuego wants you dead," Audrey added.

"Whatever we get, we'll pass to you," Red resumed, "when Avery and Ghost send it back."

"Ghost?" Audrey smirked.

Avery shook her head. "Long story."

"All right," Red said. "Tu'u has all the financial intel for you, contacts, and scenarios. Now, you both travel separately to Port au Prince. You have sufficient documentation."

That made sense; better not to be noticed as a pair. I nodded.

"Who has questions?" Red asked, but no one spoke up. "Good. Let's get in and out of Port au Prince undetected and bring back the transfer data to wrap this case up tight."

I stood, waved, and turned toward the back door of the truck. Eventually, the screens went blank, and Tu'u powered down the comm array. After he locked up the plumbing truck, we crossed Audrey's driveway, and reconvened in her kitchen.

"If we can get at least two of Fuego's money laundering pals on a casino video," Audrey said, passing out cold *Voodoo Dreams* longnecks, "We can add 'organizing' to the laundering charges. Every ADA in the Baton Rouge prosecutor's office will be fighting to bring those indictments to a grand jury."

"Which is why," Tu'u said, "your partner needs to not take part."

Avery nodded, sitting with Spike in her lap. "Another reason he needs to not rush out of rehab with Fuego."

"Closet shopping, anyone?" Audrey asked Avery, who nodded, letting Spike hop to the floor. I raised an eyebrow.

"I need biz attire," Avery said, following Audrey. "Which she just happens to have in my size."

"We going to be able to pull all this together in time?" I asked Tu'u once we were alone.

He sighed. "Maybe. I think Audrey's DA connection is the key. That will take the heat off us here. Give us an opening to strike back with hard evidence."

I took a deep draught of my *Voodoo Dreams*. "Well, I haven't talked with Red privately in a while. But I'm guessing Avery and me in the Carib is also an escape plan."

Tu'u nodded. "Yeah, brah. In case the DEA brings down a shit storm, best that you're both offshore in the near term."

That made sense. We could work our way further east, too, easily from Haiti, to maybe Portugal or London as long as our new passports held up.

Avery walked into the kitchen wearing a perfectly tailored and well-fitting business suit.

"Wow," I said, admiring the change. "I like you better in business attire."

"I like you better with a 401-K and less male pattern baldness," she shot back, taking a seat.

"I have a 401-K," I said.

Audrey joined her. "So, take the three suits, leave

everything else here."

"I will," Avery said. "Not playing a part, but *being* the part, as Christopher Sly says."

"I've read some of his stuff," Audrey said. "A novel. Poignant."

"He'll be glad to know that." I stood. I'll tell him if we live through this, I wanted to say. If we can get back from Haiti in one piece, with the fund transfer evidence, then we could fly that big yellow bird up the Mississippi and north over the green, moss-decked trees to Oxford. I'd rather be flying, or even floating down the Cane to sleepy, picturesque downtown Natchitoches or for that matter, riding the big sternwheeler from Crescent City around the mouth of the Mississippi. All of that seemed so long ago and so unreachably far away.

"So, I'll see you in Port au Prince," I said to Avery. She took my hand, squeezed it, and then let it drop. I wrapped her in a hug. She'd fly out of Baton Rouge; Tu'u would drop me off at Louis Armstrong International Airport in New Orleans. Red had routed us separately on different airlines and from different airports to avoid any pairing that could stand out in any advanced traveler database search.

Tu'u studied the floor, and Audrey stared at us, still a little hostile to me, which was good; I wanted her wary and on edge. I still had her business card and number, just in case. Seeing Avery in Audrey's clothing gave me an idea that I would hold in reserve in case of disaster, and I wanted her primed and ready to execute my plan to save Avery, if it came down to it.

I had no such plan for myself. I grabbed my duffel bag and followed Tu'u and Spike to the door.

"C'mon, brah," I said. "Let's make this plan work."

We headed out into the warm, damp night.

Chapter Twenty

Night sounds in the Caribbean, no matter how many times I've been there, always strike me as otherworldly; the breeze, the odd, tropical birds chattering to each other in the darkness, and most stunningly, the sizzling, living, vibrant insect sounds that paint the night in a supernatural cast. The steamy air wafted the honeyed tropical smells of blooms and plants and Hibiscus grown wild on a prodigious scale not possible in the states, the wetness of a recent rain on hot asphalt, and the sweetness of decay and rotting garbage carried on the leeward breeze.

I walked up a hill still glistening from fresh rain, painted a yellow gold by jaundiced street lights. My driver had taken me from the airport to an old section of town that resembled a maze of crumbled old brick and sandstone fortresses. The old, creaky, often gutted shells had been built with the ballast of old sailing ships, offloaded at the port to take on spices and exotic cargo of fruits, sugar cane, and island delicacies to be sailed back to Europe.

I glanced at my phone to check the time. Avery should have checked into the hotel by now, but knowing that she connected through Atlanta, I figured she'd be late, so I had time for the walk through the ruins. I'd connected through DFW and had checked in online and sent my bags ahead with the hotel van. The less I'm seen in public, the better, has always been my policy. The back door and pool elevator would be fine, after picking up a room key.

Before I could put the phone away, a text appeared; "Indie Whiskey all around." Shorthand from Tu'u, using the phonetic alphabet for two words—indictments and warrants. "All around" meant not just me, or if he'd said "double-play," me and Avery. This meant everyone at TAG, including Tu'u, Red, The Maestro,—virtually everyone who'd worked the DEA contract. Avery's prediction had been fulfilled; Fuego was coming out of his feigned rehab with guns blazing.

I sent back a thumbs-up Emoji, with the words, "A clean sweep," a lame attempt at gallows humor. But in a way, there was some relief in the bad news. Now, we'd all certainly hang together rather than just me and Avery alone. Everyone now had a ticket on this thrill ride, so self-preservation would d be a powerful, unifying force.

This also proved Red's decision to take TAG underground immediately after The Tombs massacre was wise, at least in the short term. But Avery and I would need life insurance, fast, and on the island, not an ocean away. I'd had an inkling, maybe just a feeling of impending disaster, for my entire solo airline flight to the Carib. That was another reason for the walk, which I needed to hasten. I flagged down a pedicab.

"Mama Lucia's *Arará*," I said. "Rue Tristesse."

A tall, skinny man with shoulder-length dreads put one foot down, still straddling the pedals and laughed.

"I *know* where *Arará* is, mon," he said in a singsong. "But you don't go there."

"Fine," I said. "I'll find someone else who'll take me."

"No, no, I take you," he said, sweeping a hand with long, spindly fingers splayed toward the tattered back seat under a crude, scrap tin awning. It was beginning to rain, a fine, misty rain casting halos around the few streetlights lit on poles still blown askew from the latest hurricane to make landfall last season. We lurched along over potted streets, squeezing past other traffic, through choking clouds of diesel exhaust, as dread man pedaled strongly, steadily, pedals keeping time with the sway of his rope-like dreads. Fifteen minutes or so later, he pulled to a stop abeam a crumbled curb. The rain ended as subtly as it began, but the halos around street lamps and in doorways remained.

"There mon," he pointed. "Through that doorway, then—"

"I *know* where Mama Lucia is," I said, and handed him some bills. *Arará* was a restaurant but at the same time, it wasn't. The cramped customer area had only a few seats, and there was no menu; Mama Lucia cooked one item a day, and you either ate that or you didn't eat. There was a steady procession of carry-outs but few diners at the few tables and for those who stayed and sat, the focus seemed always to be on anything other than the food. Social deals, business deals, drug deals, always spoken over and consecrated by food.

Through the doorway, ducking under an ancient timber, then over a winding path of broken cobblestones to a small footbridge over a stream of rainwater rushing to the sea, rain or shine, always, it seemed. Then dead ahead, a stout-timbered door with a small, barred window. Suspicious eyes would always meet mine, once I neared the door, then someone on the far side would decide if they wanted me inside, or not. I waited.

A dark face with saucer-like eyes peered out at me, then vanished. Still, I waited, sweltering in the steamy air.

The rain came in swirling misty sheets again, like a Mauka shower in Kahului, and I wished I was on Maui or just about any other tropical island right then. The door creaked open.

"You," a deep voice growled. "The Bondye foretold your visit." The huge black man in a spotless white sleeveless shirt pointed to his left. "The Iwa knows your secrets."

More Voodoo, which like Boucane, I didn't completely understand, nor could I explain, what it was or how exactly it worked.

So I simply nodded as if what he said made any sense and stepped around him. He closed, then bolted the timber door groaning on its hinges as it swung. The fragrance of strong spices, of fresh baking and cooking, grew stronger the farther I walked down the darkened hallway toward the light spilling out of the arched doorway. Voices, some laughter, and the distinctive one-drop sixteenth note of a slow reggae beat echoed down the hall's bare plaster walls.

"You dead," a woman's boomed from the kitchen doorway. "You solid dead."

I shrugged. "Ugly rumor."

The large, doughy black woman with her hair up in a colorful bandana stood with her hands on her hips. "S'what I heard. You and a half dozen others."

"Bondye says different," the big man growled from the darkened hallway.

"I know," she said. "He comes announced."

That was a creepy inference, but this was no time for me to ask questions. Rather, I was there for help.

"I'm gonna need a few things," I said, plopping down on a metal kitchen chair.

"You always need something," she said.

"I always repay, don't I?"

"When you gonna be done, Ghost? When does it end?"

I shook my head. "I don't know."

The huge man who'd opened the door materialized behind me. His catlike ability to appear silently always unnerved me. "You want me to toss his ass back into the alley?"

"Yes, I do," Mama Lucia said without hesitation. "But we're not gonna do him like that on the Lord's day."

That was a relief.

"Thunderheads," I said, using the English version of *Nuage Noir*, the volatile Haitian gunrunners. "Just a whisper."

"No," Mama Lucia stated flatly.

"Hear me out," I said. "If I'm in danger, you know that they're coming for you and Benjo too."

She sat heavily. "Go stir the stew," she said, pointing toward the kitchen. The big man glared at me, then nodded, and trundled off. Trinidad stew, chicken that fell off the bone, tangy spices, red beans—my stomach growled.

Mama Lucia sighed, then slammed her fat palm down on the worn Formica tabletop. "*Every* time I say it's the end," she said, "here it come again."

Benjo, the big man, "Benjamin" by his given name, was mostly what Mama Lucia cared about. I'd been to her for help too many times, and we were too short of time for me to do anything but get straight to the point.

"This would all go away," I explained carefully, "If the DEA was clean. Then we'd all be on the same side."

"Benjo knew," she said. "As soon as we heard what went down, that someone in the DEA set the Tombs deal up not as a bust, but to get rid of evidence."

I nodded slowly. "He was right. A few people inside the DEA pocketed a lot of money. The Tombs was mopping up loose ends, but a few loose ends sidestepped the crossfire. Do the Thunderheads know this?"

"*Noir*. That's your whisper, huh? If I hear, I whisper a warning in your ear."

I nodded again. My immediate concern was Fuego getting word back to his Thunderhead contacts on the island that two of the Tombs targets were loose. My worst nightmare was that he'd suspect we were actually at the money source, on *Nuage Noir* home turf. Then the city, the island, would be too small for us to hide from them. Thunderheads didn't like loose ends.

"You keep Benjo out?" Mama Lucia said, more a statement, a command, than a question, "Right?"

There'd be a "come to Jesus" talk with Red on this later, but he and I had both agreed months ago that Benjo's name would be scrubbed from our database file of known Thunderhead members we'd sold to the DEA. That provided us with a valuable confidential informant—Benjo—and provided Mama Lucia with a way to extricate her son from the gang. But that also eliminated the insider knowledge that would have forewarned us of the Tombs massacre. I wasn't sure now that had been a fair trade or a wise choice.

"You know that I have," I said, "by the very fact that I'm here, not floating face down in the swamp."

I was never certain that Benjo was really "out" of the Thunderheads, or if that was even possible. But in or out, we needed his ears now more than ever.

Mama Lucia narrowed her eyes and leaned back, scrutinizing me. "You protecting somebody."

"Just like you." No need to mention Benjo—or Avery.

She held up a plump, work-word palm. "I know what you need. You'll have it when you need it."

She put one finger to her lips. I took that as a sign that either someone else was listening, or that there was nothing more to be said.

"You got time to eat?" she asked after a moment. That was good news—Mama Lucia sealed a deal with food. That was her word.

"Of course," I said. "I'm starving."

"Yeah," she said, "Me too. Benjo …"

The big man stuck his head out the kitchen pass-through.

"Two, baby."

My phone buzzed, and I hoped that was Avery, saying

she was at the hotel, but I didn't want to check the message in front of anyone. In a moment, Benjo placed two steaming bowls on the counter under the pass-through window. I stood, grabbed them both, and set one before Mama Lucia, the other at my place. We ate in silence.

"Okay," Mama Lucia said at last when she'd placed her empty bowl back on the pass through. "I don't want to know what you're doing or how long you'll be on the island. Gimme your phone."

I handed it over; she tapped in a series of numbers and handed it back. Her phone started playing a reedy thin version of "Don't Worry—Be Happy."

"Seriously?" I asked. She'd texted her phone, so now we both had each other's contact.

She laughed and her stomach, chest, and arms jiggled in time. "No sense dying unhappy."

I stood and placed my empty bowl beside hers on the pass-through.

"So we watch each other's back," I said.

She nodded, walking me down the hallway to the back door. Laughter and deep voices rang out from the small seating area out front.

"Finish this," she said, staring me in the eyes, reading me like a book, I feared. There was no way I could promise we'd get what we needed to call off Fuego's war, but I'd sure try.

"Neither one of us can afford anything less," I said. That much was true.

"Ke Bondye beni," she whispered as I stepped out the door.

"You too," I said, but she'd already closed the heavy door. "God bless us all."

I set out into the misty, dark night, retracing my steps uphill.

Chapter Twenty-One

"Don't get used to it," Avery said, stripping off Audrey's suit coat. The heels had barely made it in the door."

"You look great," I said, stretched out on the queen-sized bed.

"I don't look like me."

"That's the whole point," I said. "We need to be—"

"I know," she said. "We're Christopher Sly's creation, an investment team. I listened to the audio most of the flight. I want this to come off perfectly."

I slipped off the bed and dug in my bag for the secure comm tablet. "Me too," I said, "Ready for an update?"

She nodded, shaking out her hair and combing back it with her fingers. I tapped a few commands into the screen, and we waited.

Avery dug into the fridge and pulled out two cold Red

Stripe beers. She handed one to me. The tablet flashed a register screen; I tapped in the code, and the picture snapped into focus.

"That better not be from the mini-bar," the Maestro said in a dour tone, "Or Red will have a stroke."

"We're about to commit another felony to save all of our asses," I snapped back, "Including yours. If we don't get killed in the process."

"So we win," Avery said, toasting with her open beer, smiling that dangerous smile. She seemed to be right at home in this last ditch, dangerous effort. That was a good sign.

The Maestro grunted, and then the screen split. The left half was blank, but Tu'u and Audrey appeared on the right."

"Hey guys," Tu'u said. "Glad you had safe travels. I have some good news, in a way."

"I'm a big fan of good news," I said.

"Hang on," Tu'u said, altering the feed. A grainy video appeared. A middle-aged man sat at a desk, it seemed. The view sharpened.

Avery stood. "Sonofabitch."

I looked at the screen, then Avery, then the screen again. "What are we looking at?"

"Fuego," Avery breathed, "He's out."

A child, a young boy, wandered into view. Probably his son. He must be at home.

"The good news is, Fuego's cell phone feed's back up," Tu'u said. "He's got it on some kind of dock on his desk. We're getting a good video stream."

That was good news. Sooner or later, he'd say or do something incriminating. I knew that Tu'u also knew the likelihood of Avery's partner engaging Fuego in some incriminating talk would be worth its weight in gold, at least for us. But I knew she'd be reluctant to put Jesse at risk by getting him out of rehab too soon after Fuego. So I said nothing, and I assumed that's why Tu'u hadn't either. Maybe later.

"That's his son," Avery said. "He has a daughter, too. Older, I think."

And a wife, she didn't say, but I thought to myself. *I'm here because I fucked my boss* echoed in my memory, unbidden. I shut it out. Still, I couldn't help hating them both just a little bit, and not just because that bad history had led us here. But the solid reality was that Avery was fighting for her life—and mine—because that was the right thing to do. I cursed such twisted fate, said a prayer of thanks for it just the same, and then put the matter out of my mind.

"Yes," Tu'u said. "The teenage daughter is the one who set up both Meerkat and Periscope. We're watching Meerkat now."

"He told someone on another phone that he's 'working from home,'" Audrey said. "We're recording the feed; sooner or later we'll capture document some organizing."

That would be a windfall, but I wasn't going to count on such good luck. The left half of the tablet screen flared to life.

"Your appointment is confirmed, tomorrow morning at eight," Red launched right into the operation plan. "Meet Samuel Ambroise and Joseph Denard at Café LaRoux. Latest report says no cameras there."

Like it mattered at this point, I thought but didn't say. We'd either be successful within a couple of hours, or we'd fail miserably and egress before anyone could mobilize from either the DEA or State Department. The Thunderheads would be a different story.

"After a brief, and I mean brief working breakfast," Red continued, "move things back to their office inside the Banco Delgado tower, not their downtown office."

"Ghost, you know what to do." Red nodded toward me.

"I'll have the live audio uploading in real-time," I recited, "So Tu'u can update the bots one last time with the names and account identifiers we pry out of Banco

Delgado."

Tu'u nodded. "I will text a code update ASAP."

A well-rehearsed, frequently used plan; whatever intel regarding accounts, investment portfolios, and fund groupings we could dig out of Ambrose and Denard in conversation would fine-tune Tu'u's bots so they could more efficiently zero in on the data we wanted once I got them aboard the Delgado system. We had complete routing numbers after combining the fragment Big Lou gave us with the info Boucane shared. What we needed was a hard ID linking Fuego to the account.

"Miss O'Toole," Red continued. "If you can hold them for at least a half hour."

She nodded. "Do my best."

"We believe that at least half of our bot code will work," Tu'u said. "I overloaded your drives anyway. We'll get enough data and with a little luck, freeze his access."

That would be a stroke of good, but only a temporary stopgap measure. Once Tu'u's bots corrupted the account, Fuego would have no access, but that would get restored within a day or two. Still, if he needed immediate cash, he wouldn't get it from Banco Delgado.

"We'll monitor all of our early warning channels," Red said. "We'll look for even the slightest hint that you two have been compromised, or that any defensive response is evident on the Island.

"Whatever," Avery said. "Just be ready for the data, and then get us the hell out of here."

I smiled. Avery was fearless, smart, and capable. I couldn't ask for a better partner on a deep op, or ever, for that matter. I filed that realization away for later."

"Are you both clear on the egress signals?" Red asked, but he needn't have. "Alas, Babylon" meant bail out now. "Short cake" meant speed things up. And "Tango" meant, "mission accomplished," an old TAG tradition from early ops when we'd say we'd "tango with the devil himself" to succeed. In this case, I wasn't sure that even the devil would dance with us on this, with feds, and worse, *Nuage Noir* snapping at our heels.

"The Maestro runs this op once we go," Red reminded us. "He'll track you both, monitor our early warning channels, confirm the upload when Tu'u gets it, then send the egress code."

I almost felt bad for insulting The Maestro about the mini-bar. Almost. And while I knew how TAG would track me, I wondered how they planned to track Avery.

"Anything else from anyone?" Red asked.

"One thing," I said. "Tu'u, I'm sending you a number to run for intel as well as to intercept."

"Sure."

I typed Mama Lucia's number, with her name and *Arará,* then hit send. "If anything comes from this number, it's a priority warning. We'll both need it if it comes in while we're in Banco Delgado."

Tu'u frowned. "I know that name."

"Mama Lucia?" I asked. "She's—"

"No," Tu'u said, one meaty hand to his brow. "*Arará.* A tribal connotation…"

"It's her kitchen," I said. "Not much to it but she's my connection to a semi-reliable Thunderhead informant."

"Arará*?*" Red repeated. "More Voodoo?"

"I'll run it down," Tu'u said.

"Good God," Audrey whispered. "Listen to this Fuego audio feed."

Tu'u tapped a few keys, and then Fuego's Meerkat replaced Tu'u and Audrey. "Look," Fuego's voice came through loud and clear, "It's a $25,000 bounty on each, so $50,000 for both." He paused. "If I knew where they were, I wouldn't pay a bounty, dumbass." He paused again. Avery's look darkened.

"Him? Dead is fine," Fuego continued. "But her, alive if you can. I want to see her face-to-face."

"Oh, you will," Avery said quietly. "Count on it."

"We have a good capture on this?" Red asked in a

businesslike tone.

Tu'u and Audrey reappeared, Audrey's jaw slack. "Yes," Tu'u said. "All cached."

Fuego's one-sided conversation was plain to decipher and really, no surprise.

"What I'd like to know," I said, "is if he was talking to someone in the US, or here."

"We'd need a tap on whatever phone he was talking on to determine that," Red said.

I shrugged. "Prepare for the worst, hope for the best." *No sense dying unhappy*, Mama Lucia's voice echoed in my memory.

"All right, is everyone ready?" Red asked again.

"Good here," Avery said.

"Let's go." Tu'u nodded, but Audrey stared at the floor.

"I'm good," I added.

Red nodded solemnly. "Before we go, know this. We didn't ask for this fight, nor did we do anything to bring it on. But a corrupt client has left us but one option, and that is to fight back, and to fight back smarter than the criminal who put us in this position."

He let his words sink in for a moment. Truly, we as a contractor, an intel company, a think tank, were way out of our depth. But that, too, was also our strength; we'd fight smarter, and harder, than the rogue Fed leading a blind, dumb, and extremely dangerous law enforcement juggernaut.

"So let's be careful, let's be smart, let's stick together," Red said firmly, "and let's nail the coffin shut on this murderer."

Eloquent, and uncharacteristically heartfelt, from Red, which only served to underscore the grave situation we faced. We'd made a professional career out of being smarter than our prey, and now we faced our biggest test. Again in my mind, Mama Lucia's jiggly laugh and bright, wide smile appeared again. I'd have to get that "Don't Worry, Be

Happy" ringtone. If we survived.

"Well then," Red said with a tone of determination. "I'll be in the full, live stasis, Tu'u's on full tactical and strategic support, we'll live-feed the upload results when we get it and from here, the Maestro runs the show. Godspeed, everyone."

The tablet went dark. I put it on the coffee table, then went to the mini-bar again. I grabbed two more beers, plus the tin of smoked macadamia nuts, just to piss off the Maestro when TAG got the hotel invoice. I tossed the can to Avery.

She laughed, then pulled off the plastic top, and opened the can's pop top.

"I like the way you think, Perfesser."

I sat down again on the love seat, troubled.

"I wish we'd had more time to discuss *Arará* with Tu'u," I said, then took a gulp of cold beer.

"What's up with that?" Avery asked, staring into the darkness and the rain lashing the floor to ceiling windows of the suite.

"I don't know," I said at last. "Something with Boucane?"

She turned from the window, her brow furrowed. "He said 'look for Radaloa.'"

"There's a connection," I said. "It's on the tip of my brain."

She shook her head and plopped down beside me. Rain lashed the window. "Well, Tu'u has research access. Seemed to trigger something with him, too."

"Couldn't be a better support crew than Tu'u working for us," I said. "We can leave it to him."

"Perfesser," Avery said with a deliberate tone that startled me.

"Yeah?"

"I owe you an apology."

I stood. "What are you talking about?"

"Fuego. Which led to all this—"

"No," I said, louder than I meant it to come out, but it just did. I wasn't sure if she meant Fuego as in rogue agent she'd gotten me tangled up with, or as in *I fucked my boss*. And I didn't care.

She stood, face to face. Thunder joined the rain. Lightning flashes illuminated the skyline, and the hills behind them, in ghostly snapshots.

"No. What you owe me, *all* you owe me," I said, more quietly, "Is a good, strong, smart fight tomorrow, and for however long it takes till we put that murdering bastard behind bars."

After a moment, that dangerous smile spread across her face. "Oh, you'll get that, Perfesser." She clinked her cold, wet bottle to mine. "You'll get that, plus much, much, more."

Chapter Twenty-Two

The sun split the flawless cobalt sky like an arc weld. White, puffy clouds stacked themselves far off on the eastern horizon and the Atlantic Ocean spread itself like a perfect deep azure blanket for as far as the eye could see to the west. We walked purposefully down an un-level sidewalk, Avery cursing her heels about every ten yards.

"Shouldn't you be in character?" I asked pleasantly.

"My real life doesn't include heels and a business suit," she muttered, not breaking stride.

My business attire wasn't unfamiliar, really; but I could tell that much longer under the white hot tropical sun, and I'd start to wilt. Today was all about appearances, so we'd sidestep that risk; the small French patisserie where we'd meet Ambroise and Denard was less than a block away.

We hadn't checked out of our hotel rooms, but I'd had all of our belongings sent by car to a chain hotel closer to Toussant Louverture International. We needed to be near to the airport to quietly leave the island early the next morning; plus there was no point being found downtown that night, because there were only bad reasons why anyone would be looking for us.

I carried a thin leather business case, Avery a slightly larger leather valise case slung over her shoulder with a strap. In her business attire she looked purposeful and attractive and the last part, though I wouldn't say it aloud, was as much bait as anything. She'd turn heads, both at Café LaRoux and later, at Banco Delgado. I needed heads turned in order to accomplish my goal of inserting at least three of the five thumb drives I carried.

At the few steps up to the Café LaRoux patio, Avery didn't hesitate and sprang up all three. She looked the part of the investment banker, walking with a determined stride, and didn't even look back at me. She opened one of the heavy glass French doors and waited. I caught up with her, then followed her through the doors.

Spare, white-washed walls, dangling halogen lights, and modern furnishings on a marble slab floor telegraphed nouveau Paris café. One long, chrome-trimmed counter with a curved glass face displayed confections arranged neatly on lacy paper doilies spanned the width of the cafe. On the far end of that bar, against the wall, the tubular metal apparatus of exotic coffee brewing gave off a pungent, delicious odor of java brewing. My stomach growled.

At a chrome and glass table near the back, a thin, middle-aged man stood as Avery clacked across the marble with confident strides. He wore a tailored dark suit, a white button-down shirt with cufflinks, and accessorized with an immaculate white pocket square. Light-skinned for a black man in the Caribbean, I thought; and he wore a neatly clipped mustache under a thin nose.

"Ms. Hatcher?" He extended his hand. The stocky,

Eastern European-looking man next to him stood, but did so just a fraction of a second too slow to be anything other than a statement of reluctance, if not disapproval, of the requirement to stand when a woman approached. I instantly took a dislike to him.

Avery extended her hand. "Molly Hatcher, The Sly Fund." Had to love Christopher Sly's sense of the absurd.

"And this is Christian Moses, my chief analyst and technical director," she said, nodding to me.

The man with the clipped mustache nodded and said, "I'm Samuel Ambroise, president, and this is Joseph Denard, head of capital."

Denard eyed me warily, and though I could appreciate the irony of his position, this was no laughing matter. We already knew that the firm handled dirty money and the fact that he and I both were not what we appeared to be seemed glaringly obvious to me. I hoped it was clear to Avery as well.

"A pleasure," Ambroise said, shaking Avery's hand, then mine in turn. I shook Denard's hand next but avoided eye contact. If my instinct was correct, he was the Neanderthal type, a Baltic version of Toilet Guy, and there was no point in starting that bull moose mating dance. I'd save it for later in case I needed to push his buttons. We sat and a waiter in a starched white shirt and pressed black pants scurried over.

"I've read your vitae, Mr. Denard," Avery said abruptly. "What was your reason for leaving Marcus Capital after only a few months?"

I suppressed a smile. Avery clearly had sized things up the same way I had and was wasting no time backing Denard down.

"Well," he answered in a surprisingly high voice for such a burly man, "I was—"

"We hired him away," Ambroise interrupted gently. "We needed his acquisition talents here, and we appreciate his abilities more than they did."

Denard nodded and looked down. I tried not to guess at his "abilities," although I did check him for any telltale tattoos or other gang markings. I couldn't see his forearms, but I wanted to know if the Thunderhead lightning bolt was on one or the other.

"Coffee all around?" Ambroise asked smoothly, as if no one had challenged anyone, but we all knew different.

"Espresso Romano," Avery stated flatly. "With a shot of Grappa."

"Cappucino," I added.

Ambroise nodded to the waiter, who backed away with our orders. Denard studied his hands on the table.

"We appreciate you flying in on a Sunday night," Ambroise said pleasantly. "Especially knowing that today is a Monday holiday in your country."

No problem, I wanted to say, *because this was the only way our fake credentials would hold validity long enough to hack your database*. I said nothing.

"Our clients expect us to move on every opportunity, three-day weekend or not," Avery answered with a pert smile, pretending to take Ambroise's words as praise.

"Then let's enjoy coffee and croissants, and get down to business," he answered with a similarly pert smile that turned up the clipped edges of his mustache.

After a few moments of idle chit-chat about last night's storm, plus the relative merits of French versus Italian coffee styles, the waiter approached with a glass-topped tray laden with china serving pieces and a polished pewter basket of croissants nested in a white linen cloth. He placed each drink before the right person, placed the basket in the center, and withdrew.

Avery tipped her shot glass and poured the clear liquid into her espresso cup, then stirred. We made more idle conversation, and Denard tore up pieces of his croissant and dipped them in his coffee. I'd thought he was perhaps Ukrainian, but crude table manners fairly screamed Russian, probably from the north. I wondered what type of dangerous arrangement Fuego had gotten himself into.

Amboise lifted his espresso cup with an exaggerated flourish, inspected it closely then offered a slight toasting motion to Avery.

"The British have a saying," he said. "Fortune favors the bold. You are bold for choosing to place your investors' portfolio with us. We have more freedom to operate, to accelerate your returns, even beyond the considerable tax savings we'll provide instantly."

Avery cocked her head. "Actually, the tax savings accrue to my firm for taking the funds offshore. And the bold favor the wise, which is why our investors entrusted me to seek answers to every question regarding whom and what exactly we're dealing with here."

Denard flinched at the "every question" part but said nothing. He studied Avery, and I almost laughed out loud. He'd likely never met a woman like her, whether he realized that or not.

"Certainly, but," Ambroise said, raising both hands as if in defense. "We are nothing if not discreet concerning our clientele, you included."

"Well," Avery smiled, "then you'll have the discretion to share the information we need to feel confident in what will amount to our co-investors, given the size of our fund."

"One point nine million," Ambroise said, "I believe was the figure."

"No," Avery said. "The peripherals we bring will boost that figure by at least twenty-five percent. And my word to others in my wealth management community will underwrite future earnings for you."

She paused to let that sink in. Denard paused in mid-dunk, a chunk of buttery, flaky croissant hovering above the crumbs floating atop his black coffee.

"If," she finished, "you can give me the reassurance we require to commit our assets."

"That you shall have," Ambroise promised. "That you shall have."

Denard's paw moved downward like a giant steam shovel, and the croissant dipped into the dark brew then spread outward as it wicked coffee upward.

Talk shifted back to the news of the market, of SEC heavy-handed bond market oversight, and intrusive investment regulation. I glanced at my watch. Red had said brief, and we'd been here barely thirty minutes. Right on schedule.

After the waiter had cleared the table, Ambroise stood. There was no bill, so no opportunity for Avery to insist on paying. How very French of Ambroise.

"And now," he said with a flourish, "To our new office downtown."

"No," said Avery, gathering her leather valise. "I prefer the private conference room at Banco Delgado."

Ambrose and Denard exchanged glances, and then Denard spoke. "We have a very impressive, fully equipped conference room in our downtown office we'd like to show you."

"Fine," Avery said, turning on her heel toward the door. "We'll go there after we conclude our presentation at Banco Caribe. That's our security policy."

There was nothing either man could say without seeming unduly defensive. Back on the sidewalk, we walked in silence the long block to the bank building, the blue sky now more intense and the humidity rising with the sun. Sunlight glinted off the glass face of the towering Banco Delgado building. Guards in paramilitary gear, one with a leashed German Shepard, stood on either side of the main doors, acting as if they weren't scrutinizing everyone who came and left the building. Inside the cavernous lobby, more uniformed guards stood beside a reception desk. They looked us over carefully, but the receptionist just smiled and waved Ambroise through to the glass elevators on the back side of the lobby.

The lobby floor seemed to drop away as the glass elevator rose smoothly. Despite the strong-following air conditioning, sweat trickled down the small of my back.

"I suppose you'll want to visit the IT and mainframe floors, Mr. Moses," Denard said in his oddly squeaky voice as the floor numbers flashed on the panel above the door "Fourth floor for both, if you do."

Of course I did. I needed to launch a squadron of code bots and digital Trojans flying into the digital stream, half to ferret account transfer information, plus a handful to corrupt and lockout the fund transfer capability of assholes like Fuego.

"No," I lied. "I'm just here to ascertain your transfer and access protocol requirements to transfer funds to you, as well as to support Ms. Hatcher's technical requirements." And I knew from poring over the building blueprints with Tu'u that the IT floor was actually ten, not four, but more importantly, now I knew what I suspected at Café LaRoux; Denard was baiting me. I smiled, knowing that two could play that game—and I sure would.

The elevator eased to a stop, and the doors slid open. Ambroise stepped out, then stood aside and motioned us forward. We followed him down the hallway to a set of frosted glass double doors. Between us and the door, I noticed a janitor's cart with the word "Radaloa" stenciled on the trash bin. Avery gave the faintest nod toward the cart, telling me in the subtlest way that she had noticed the name as well. *Look for Radaloa,* Boucane had said. Loa, the constructive deity of Vudon, or Voodoo, as most say. Not the capricious Loki or worse, the Gede family of death. A janitorial service? Could Boucane have been referring to *that*?

We took another left turn immediately after entering the offices. A secretary at the main desk stood as we entered, but Ambroise breezed by her and led us into the conference room. A long mahogany conference table dominated the room. Avery strode confidently to the head of the table where a handful of remote controls lay.

I followed her, ever the dutiful assistant, then focused

on the audio-visual control module in a wood-paneled case as she poured herself a glass of water from a pitcher near the center of the table. I selected a remote source, then plugged the first of our flash drives into the port on the side of the screen. I'd attached a fire engine red lanyard to the drive, making it obvious; here's what I'm doing—here's the presentation you're about to see. No extra code, no bots or Trojans—just a boring old Powerpoint developed by Christopher Sly and Avery back in Oxford, Mississippi a thousand miles and seemingly, as many years ago.

I set up my place at the table, centering a legal pad in front of me, two pens, a phone and a keychain with at least three thumb drives off to the side, a few Manilla folders of spreadsheets, a small notebook, and spare pencils. I wanted to look the tech support part.

"Shall we?" Avery said, standing and clicking a remote that dropped a screen from the center of the far wall. A projector suspended from the ceiling whirred to life, and deep blue claimed the screen, then the "Sly Investments" logo faded in.

"By all means," Ambroise said with a grin that once again tipped up the corners of his clipped mustache. Denard struck a pose that might have passed for polite interest, maybe in the Gulag or whatever hellhole he was from, but that was clearly nothing more than a pose.

My phone buzzed in my back pocket. Right on schedule, but I wouldn't pull it out and let Denard know the phone I'd placed on the table top with all of my assorted crap was just a decoy, one that could easily get left behind later.

Avery launched into her preplanned spiel, and once I was sure the slides were advancing as planned, I tuned out. Go time. I left everything spread about my seat, including my jacket. This reminded me of college, of even grad school, when at times it was necessary to present the façade of attendance while making a necessary side trip elsewhere. I stood, nodded to Ambroise, then left for the men's room.

The secretary outside the conference room leaned over her desk, looking at me as if to say, *where the hell are you going?* At least in my mind.

I smiled. "Too much coffee."

Once out the double doors, I made a left and headed for the stairwell. I paused at the Radaloa cart, then pushed through the stairwell door, just praying that Tu'u had read the schematics correctly—no alarms. I ascended two flights of stairs to the computer and tech floor, leaving the stairwell quietly and walking casually toward the men's room near the elevators.

Inside, I checked my phone. A green light from The Maestro, meaning there were no threats and we were on schedule. There was an urgent message from Tu'u, so I clicked on it, of course.

Arará, Tu'u wrote, *is Radaloa.* Mama Lucia? I scratched my head. How could that be, but then I realized the significance. One was generic Vudon—Radaloa—and Arará was Haitian for the same family. How could I have missed that? So Boucane was pointing us toward Mama Lucia and…Benjo? But how? And why?

Before I could consider an answer, a meaty hand reached over my shoulder clamped over my mouth, and then a giant arm wrapped around my chest and dragged me to the floor.

Chapter Twenty-Three

I twisted one shoulder, then the other, trying to loosen the giant bear hug. The hand stayed clamped over my mouth.

"Be still, mon," Benjo's deep voice came through in a whisper. "Be still."

I stopped struggling, and Benjo eased the bear hug, then the meaty hand inched away from my mouth but hovered, ready to clamp back on.

"Benjo?"

We stood up, face to face.

"Yeah," he answered, looking sheepish. He flung a shirt and pants at me. And an ID with a magnetic strip attached.

"What the hell?" I asked.

He shrugged. "Orders."

"Orders? From whom?"

Benjo crossed his arms and leaned against the main door, preventing anyone from going in—or out.

He rolled his eyes. "Boucane. Word a' la boucane."

"Wait," I said, checking out the shirt and pants. A uniform, just like Benjo's. *Radaloa.* "Are you saying 'boucane" with a capital 'B' as in a person's name, or a lower case 'b' as in the French word for smoke?"

"You one crazy dude," Benjo said, shaking his head. "It means what it means, mon."

That was a non-answer, leaving me in the dark still.

"Don't just stand there," he said, shooing me with his hands. "Put on the uniform, stow your clothes in the cart, and go."

So, I was to be Rada Loa. I nodded, then sprang into a stall while Benjo held the main door closed. I stashed my drives in a pants pocket, my phone in the shirt pocket, and put the tiny Bluetooth earpiece and mike into my left ear.

When I emerged, Benjo was gone. I slipped out of the men's room, placed my dress clothes inside the metal cabinet in front of the trash drum and wheeled my way toward the IT entrance, pulling on a pair of plastic cleaner's gloves from the box atop the cart.

"Tango," I called quietly, as if talking to myself.

"Got you weak but readable," Tu'u answered in the small speaker.

My phone's camera poked out from the shirt pocket, and I had Periscope rolling, sending video on the secure channel.

"Getting video now," Tu'u said. "The video's actually clearer than the audio."

"Lowest bidder," I said, knowing both Red and The Maestro were listening. Ever the budget slashers, they'd gone for the cheaper mike. But the video was more important today anyway.

I held the ID card up to the small panel near the access door. The light changed from red to green, and the panel buzzed. I pushed the door open then rolled the cleaning cart inside. The door closed securely behind me. The room was warm despite equipment fans and the odor of hot electronics mixed with stale vent shaft air. That couldn't be good for sensitive digital components, which I took as a plus.

"Access," I confirmed quietly. I knew Tu'u would want to know how I'd gotten into the server center, but I also knew we had no time for discussion. I checked my watch. I'd been gone from the conference room for three minutes, going on four. We'd plan the tech insertion for no longer than seven minutes.

"Find the trunk rack," Tu'u said. I knew he was viewing an overlay of schematics on the largest screen in his truck, monitoring my position on another.

"Four minutes," The Maestro said calmly on the mission frequency.

"Left another five feet," Tu'u called.

I found the trunk rack, then circled around the shelf to the back.

"Backside," I answered, telling Tu'u I was a step ahead.

"CRU-60?" he asked.

"Yup," I answered, telling him that the port was standard, although we'd brought a metric dongle in case. "Rack labeled 'OC3-P.'" The prime interface.

"One through four," he said.

"Roger." I plugged three units into the parallel ports.

I moved inboard of the main rack. I checked for "visitors," but the room was empty.

"Dealer's choice," Tu'u said, meaning the last drive could go anywhere I saw fit, with an eye toward an obscure port that would be difficult to detect. I got down on my hands and knees.

"Four minutes," The Maestro said quietly. "Egress at five," he reminded me.

I slid a hand under the bottom edge of a thick rack, probing ... *there*. The bottom rack had a taller lip and between two units, I found a connector line with an empty port I only detected by feel. There'd be hell to pay for whomever had to find this circuit of nastiness I plugged in securely.

"Thirty seconds," The Maestro called matter-of-factly. I surveyed the rack area, double-checking the drives I'd implanted.

"Egress," I said quietly, pushing the cart toward the door. We were a few seconds early.

"Roger," The Maestro noted calmly.

"Valid data stream," Tu'u said, mostly for my benefit, because there was no time to return anyway. "Decent cache already. Bots away."

That was a good feeling. I grabbed my business clothes from the bin then dragged the cart across the bathroom door as if to suggest that cleaners were inside. I dressed hurriedly, then stuffed the janitor's uniform in the trash bin but pocketed the ID—Ain't Bee could use it later, if there were a "later."

I pushed the cart toward the far end of the hallway, then headed in the opposite direction toward the stairwell, stashing the Bluetooth and my phone. I slipped into the stairwell and descended the stairs two at a time.

I opened the corridor door carefully, checked both ways, and then moved quickly toward the frosted double-doors. I paused, took a deep breath, and then stepped inside.

Denard bustled out of the conference room then froze, fists bunched but trying to appear calm.

"Better cordon off that men's room," I said, slipping past him into the conference room. "I just shut it down," I said, fanning the air.

Inside, Avery had a wall of pie charts and graphs projected on the large screen. She nattered on about "yields" and "structures" and even "a canary in the mine," but again I tuned out. I surveyed my spot at the table. The cell phone was gone. Good.

When Avery finished her presentation, she passed the remote control over to Ambroise. I retrieved the flash drive and lanyard and left them carelessly near my legal pad. Denard walked over to the wall switch and dimmed the lights. Music began to swell from hidden speakers—sounded like a movie soundtrack, perhaps the opening credits—and a video that must have been shot from some type of aircraft flying low towards the beach claimed the screen. I tuned out.

Nearly an hour later, Ambroise concluded his pitch. I'd caught snatches of his lengthy infomercial explaining why our fake investment consortium should transfer capital to their control, including an organizational chart listing "Fire" as one of their key investors. Avery looked duly impressed.

"Well," she said. "I believe we may be able to conclude our business today, rather than having to make a return trip after conferring with our investment group."

Ambroise steepled his fingers and smiled.

"Excellent, Ms. Hatcher," he said with a grin so wide his eyes nearly closed. "Let us adjourn now to our corporate office on LaSalle to initiate the transfer details."

"First," Avery said with a fake smile. "I must have a conference call with our trustees. We'd planned to take a meeting for the go ahead, but I think we can do that on a call and save another trip back and forth to this fine island."

Denard's eyes narrowed. He glanced back and forth between Ambroise and Avery. Ambroise seemed unconcerned.

"Very well," the thin man said. "Shall we expect you at two?"

"Three," Avery said, extending her hand, "Would be more realistic given the time delay—it's still early in the central US time zone, and it is a federal holiday."

Ambroise shook her hand, then covered their clasped hands with his left hand. "Three it shall be. And afterwards, perhaps you and I could meet for drinks and dinner, and toast what I believe could be a very satisfying partnership." He winked.

"That would be lovely," Avery purred. "We could make an evening of it, if you're up to that."

I stood and gathered most of my things hurriedly, clumsily. Denard pushed himself up from his armchair and jammed his hands into his pockets. He frowned.

Avery snapped her leather case shut, turned on her heel and strode confidently toward the conference room doors. I nodded to Ambroise and Denard, then followed.

"Do you have everything?" Denard asked.

Everything that matters, I wanted to say, *except for whatever you think you've stolen, or I've forgotten.* I smiled. "I believe so."

"Will you require any assistance setting up the conference call?" Ambroise asked. "I can speed things along."

"Thank you, Mr. Ambroise," I said as warmly as I could muster. "We'll do a Google hangout. Simpler than a conference call. Shouldn't take long once we gather everyone."

Avery and I rode down to the lobby in a half-full elevator.

"There's so much macro volatility given the EU situation," Avery parroted Christopher Sly's script convincingly.

"That's why we're here," I adlibbed.

"Our back-testing says we can outperform the market," Avery continued. "If we can get a segment of this fund flow."

"We're just a conference call away," I said, checking my watch.

Finally, as our cab pulled away from the curb in front of Banco Delgado, I checked my phone. A green light and a thumbs up, plus a reminder; an ant Emoji appeared on the screen. I put my index finger to my lips briefly and looked at Avery. She nodded.

From my valise, I pulled a travel clock. In the bottom left corner, a red hourglass appeared.

Bug sweep, I texted to Avery. I ran the fake alarm clock case over my belongings. The hourglass turned green. I passed it to Avery.

She skimmed her jacket, then her valise. The hourglass turned red. After digging into her bag, she pulled out what looked like a dry erase marker.

"Crude tracker," she whispered, holding it low behind the driver's seat. "Russian model."

"Like Denard," I said.

She nodded. "No doubt. No audio, just a weak GPS track."

I took the marker and examined it closely. The word "Erase" was misspelled, the pen felt excessively heavy for a marker. I handed it back to Avery.

"Russian bug," I said, "Russian thug; anybody wonder where the arms sale originated?"

She took the marker and stuffed it deep into the crack between the seat bottom and the back cushion.

"We need this money trail," she said, "not only for Fuego, but also for the guns."

I nodded. "We got decent fund data, at least initially. But we're out of here, never mind the arms deal or the Russian angle."

She held up a hand. "I know. Just saying. There may be a bigger fish than Fuego to fry in this."

"Once we're out of the frying pan, maybe," I added. "We'll get a debrief from TAG as soon as we're secure."

"But the initial report is success?"

I nodded. "Right away, Tu'u said good data." We'd have to leave it at that for now.

"I'd say Ambroise was just like you and me, only worse."

I laughed. "No doubt. Good actor, poor script. Denard didn't really even try."

"Well Ambroise is going to be stood up tonight," Avery said. "But Denard, we might have a second date."

I gave her a pointed frown. She held up a hand.

"I know, first things first. I'm just saying; I'd like to explore the Russian connection, including the dullard Russian."

The cab pulled up near baggage claim at Toussant International. Avery opened the rear passenger door and swung her legs out, then stood. I scooted across the seat and put one foot out the door. I handed the driver some bills as I made a last minute check of the car to be sure we hadn't left anything behind save the crude Russian tracking pen.

I followed Avery through the main doors of baggage claim, past several crowded luggage carousels, and around a throng huddled near the bags riding the trundling conveyer belt. We walked past the rental car desks and out the side door, out into the hot, wet air again.

Avery put two fingers in her mouth, took a deep breath, and let loose a whistle that shrieked and echoed off the concrete walls. I'd always wanted to be able to do that but never could.

"Well, that was subtle," I said as heads turned and another cab pulled to the curb.

She yanked the door open, then stuck her face a couple of inches from mine.

"I'm just about done with this act," she said, then slid into the back seat.

"Ms. Hatcher has left the building," I muttered to no one in particular. "And Molly Hatchet is back." I ducked into the cab.

The driver took us the short distance to the airport hotel, and I had him drop us off on the back near the pool. I'd already checked in online, so when we reached the hotel desk, it took only a minute or two to get two card keys, then walk to the elevator. Same room, since no one knew we were staying there anyway.

Once inside, I bolted the door shut, and Avery went straight to the mini bar. I pulled off my tie, and she handed me a cold beer.

"To The Maestro," she said, raising her beer. "And

Red, who will pitch a fit about the mini-bar bill."

"Hear, hear." A cold, fiery swig felt good going down. I dug my smart pad out of a duffel bag and turned it on.

"So," Avery asked, sitting heavily on the sofa near the wall of windows. "Did you get in, and were we successful?"

I nodded. "The Radaloa connection?"

"Right—the janitorial firm?"

"Yes—my CI on the island works there. Out of the blue, hooked me up with an ID." The smart pad booted up and went into its secure link search.

Avery stood. "What?"

"I know," I said. "I was dumbfounded. He said 'orders from Boucane.'"

"Here? Boucane's here?"

I took another deep, cold swallow. "I don't know; I don't completely understand it, and there was no time to discuss."

The pad screen flared to life and the Maestro's scowl sharpened into focus.

"The mini-bar?" he said with a distinct edge to his voice. "Again?"

"Good to see you too," I said. Avery smiled sweetly, toasting the scowling image on the screen. The screen split and Tu'u appeared in the left half, squeezed in between Audrey and Spike, who looked bored. The dog slumped down and closed her eyes.

"Good job, brah," Tu'u said. "Actually, maybe too good."

Red appeared in the right half of the screen.

"Too good is right," Red said, "But the mission is an overall success."

Too good? I'd figured the report would be that we were on-target, or maybe "barely but adequate," given the challenge. But "too good?"

"First off," Red continued, "How did you get access to the secure server room?"

"No," I said, "first off, what's the 'too good' thing?"

Avery sat down next to me, staring intently at the screen. Audrey seemed to avoid her eyes. Something was going on between them, but I couldn't quite make out what.

"We got a positive, unmasked ID on Fuego's account," Tu'u said, "But..."

I stood. "But what?"

"The Banco Delgado server crashed before we could get specific transfers and quantity numbers," Red finished Tu'u's report.

Avery stood. "What the hell?"

Red raised both hands. "It's a temporary setback. And we wanted to freeze his access to funds anyway. That objective has been met."

"Placing our bots inside the mainframe was a brilliant move," Tu'u said. "And I still want to know how you got in there. But we think the OC-3P input crashed the whole bank."

The "dealer's choice," as Tu'u had termed it while I was in the secure server room. Not only had I done too good a job placing the drive, Tu'u had gone way too far in the bot design.

"So we don't have total dollar amounts of deposits or transfers," Tu'u continued, "Though we have a positive ID on Fuego's account."

I sat. This was not in the plan and given the arrest warrants hanging over our heads; there was no time for a delay.

"The stasis group has already hashed out a contingency plan," Red explained. "It depends on two key factors."

Avery sat again, peering at the screen. That dangerous smile began to spread across Audrey's face, and to me, that was a very bad sign.

"First," Red continued, "tropical storm Faith is bearing down on Louisiana. That will divert law enforcement efforts to find you two, especially if Faith becomes a hurricane."

"Here it comes," I whispered, to Avery. She looked at

me with a furrowed brow, then back at the screen.

"What's the second factor?" Avery asked, her arms folded across her chest.

Audrey looked directly at the camera in Tu'u's truck.

"The second key factor is," she said, still smiling the patented dangerous grin of the Irish Sisterhood I'd come to love and fear, "I'm going to jail."

Chapter Twenty-Four

"The hell you are," Avery growled, standing bolt upright.

"Hear me out," Audrey said, also standing. Spike looked up at Audrey, then at the camera. The dog padded off, which I envied. I wanted no part of this firefight either.

"No," Avery snapped back. "I don't want you involved in this mess."

"I already am," Audrey shouted, then in a lower voice added, "and the key is to outsmart the bad guys, not hide from them. Right, sister?"

Avery sat again but frowned just the same.

"I'm going back to the DA's office, back to my old organized crime and racketeering division, starting next month."

"Your practice," Avery said. "What—"

"My partners are buying me out." Audrey held up a

hand. "The Chief of the Prosecution Division is on board with this case. The DA is aware of the entire story that you—*we*—allege regarding Fuego and the DEA."

I stared at my beer bottle intently, listening carefully to Audrey, but admiring the cool rivulets rolling down the smooth, dark glass. I'd almost wish to be back aboard the *Grub Tub*, feet propped on the bow, watching the muddy Mississippi sunset after a day of ladling reheated gumbo into disposable bowls. Almost.

"Can you think of a safer place for Audrey to be…" I interjected quietly. "…than in state custody while both Creed and the DEA hunt for her face?"

"You don't talk," Avery snapped at me, holding up a hand but still staring at the screen. "Why in custody?"

"Trojan horse," Audrey said, both hands raised palms up. "A misdirection. We'll very slowly leak that Avery O'Toole is in custody, then let the media take photos and video."

"That will take the heat off of you, Avery," Red said. "So you can go back after the DEA corruption."

I stood bolt upright.

"No," I stated flatly. "That's way too dangerous."

"The State of Louisiana has gone to war with the DEA over this case," Audrey continued. "We lost a trooper in the LaFitte operation we wanted to run, but the federal agency muscled in despite state opposition. So you'll be safe working that angle here in state."

She let that sink in; a civil war between the federal government and a very strong-willed, capable southern state. The classic, throwback irony would enjoyable if the key players in the crossfire weren't people I cared so much about.

"We'll drag our feet on the extradition, using that to leverage a few conditions the State Attorney General will demand, like local custody for state prosecution first."

Playing with fire again, I thought, shaking my head. This was a game of chicken between government agencies, between the state and federal law enforcement. A dangerous gamble, an all-in bet.

"We're talking about a temporary strategy that only needs to hold long enough for us to get what we know to be damning evidence on Fuego," Red said. "Audrey is safe," he added, ever the shrewd negotiator, "And if all goes as planned, you get to make the arrest on Fuego yourself."

That sealed the deal; I'd have to bet. As I'd said, there was no safer place for Audrey than state custody—she even had Avery's clothes to complete the illusion—and the thought of arresting Fuego herself would be too great for Avery to pass up.

"No," Avery said. "I won't go along with this plan. Run the stasis group again till you have a better strategy, one that doesn't involve my sister."

"It's too late for that now," Audrey said, holding up a *USA Today* newspaper. I could barely make out the small headline in the bottom corner of the front page, but the bold-face words were clear enough; *fugitive federal agent arrested in Louisiana.*

Avery put a hand over her face. "Shit."

"The DA had a news conference early this morning," Audrey said.

"Was this before or after the Banco Delgado crash?" Avery asked quietly.

"After," Red said. What he didn't say was that it had probably been Plan-B all along. And though I'd mentioned the possibility to Tu'u, I was deliberately unaware of anything else, knowing I'd answer to Avery eventually.

"You knew?" she asked, looking at me.

"First I've heard of it," I answered, mostly honestly. "I don't like it either."

That part was true; this operation was originally designed to simply monitor and report on minor drug deals in an obscure corner of Louisiana. That mission had spiraled out of control, spilling over into Haiti and now, Russian arms. We were outmanned, out gunned, and hopelessly underpowered against all the threats that seemed to multiply daily.

"This is way out of our league, Red," I said.

"Yes," he answered. "It is. But what choice do we have?"

The top headline on the newspaper Audrey held was promising; "Tropical Storm Faith Bears Down on Bayou States."

"The nature of federal and state bureaucracy will slow this process down," Tu'u said, "both the manhunt and the extradition."

Good point—the manhunt for Avery might end, but there were still warrants out for me and most of TAG, or at least the parts the Feds knew of.

"And this tropical storm will become a hurricane within hours," Red added. "There's a natural governor slowing this engine of prosecution."

I recalled the old days, the early days of TAG. *What we lack in money and power,* Red used to say; *we make up for in smarts and luck.* We'd need an overdose of both, and the stakes today were higher than we'd ever dreamed then.

"So we seize the opportunity," Red said. "Because there's no other choice."

Avery sighed. "Give us a minute."

I looked at Avery, then at the screen again. I wasn't sure what exactly Avery had in mind, but whatever it was, gave me a feeling of dread. Because one thing was clear; we were alone on the far end of a long, dangerous continuum of threats, what-ifs, danger, and risk. The rest of the cast in this sad morality play were a thousand miles removed from the battlefront, leaving just the two of us to bear the risk. I nodded.

Tu'u gave me a thumbs up. "Call us when you're ready, brah."

The screen went dark.

Avery stood and walked toward the wall of windows looking out on the pool and beyond that, the ocean.

She turned and looked me in the eye.

"I want out."

I cocked my head. "Out? What's out?"

She turned back to the windows. A storm gathered itself near the eastern horizon, piling up angry stacks of cumulus, threatening lightning.

"Out of this; my sister in jail, Russians, Fuego, you."

"Me?"

"I dragged you into this," she murmered. "You're over your head. My sister goes to jail. We have nothing going for us, all because I—"

Because I fucked my boss.

I grabbed her shoulders. "Don't," I said. "Just don't."

A flight of gulls winged by, then a pelican flapped lazily west to east. The spirit of Barnabas, I thought to myself. And Cassie, and Lou, and the freedom of the river, of better times.

"There is no out," I said. "You run, we run, and it's over."

She nodded, looking down.

"We fight, Avery," I said. "We're fucked, maybe. But we don't quit, because we can't."

She faced me, eyes narrowed, anger mostly gone, but wounded just the same.

"We have forces on our side," I said, trying to think on my feet. Because she was right, we were screwed. She raised an eyebrow. That was a good sign. Maybe she'd hit bottom; maybe she could pull us both back up when I sank.

"We have people like Tu'u, and Audrey," I said. "Not only with us, but depending on us. And," I paused, groping.

"We have Faith," Avery said.

"Faith?"

"The hurricane," she said.

"It's a tropical storm."

She raised a hand. "Will be a hurricane. And we have Boucane."

She was back, I decided. I was floundering, but Avery

was back.

"Whatever the hell Boucane is," she continued. "And we have each other."

I nodded. "There's no out, Aivs," I said. "Only through."

She took a deep breath, staring at the relentless surf beyond the seawall, wave after wave, rolling toward the break regardless.

"I had a moment," she said, "I'm back."

"Then we stand and fight," I said, only half believing my own words.

She tapped a few keys, and the smart pad came back to life. Red sat on the left half, scrolling through something on his own pad. Tu'u and Spike appeared on the right.

"Let's have it," Avery said. "What's the new plan?"

Red looked up. "You two may need some down time. Why don't you just chill tonight as we analyze the data we did capture then—"

"No," Avery said. "Let's keep going."

I nodded.

"First," Tu'u said, "You need to know about Fuego's feed."

"The phone, and the Meerkat feed?" I stated the obvious.

"Yes. He needs to pay some gambling debts now that he's out."

"So?"

"His funds are inaccessible, thanks to your excellent work," Red picked up the narrative. "So we expect to see him organize another casino laundering operation."

"He's planning some type of group effort," Tu'u explained. "We anticipate another 'organizing' trip to launder cash at a casino. We're monitoring ten of his bank balances and three showed multiple withdrawals under the CTR threshold."

That meant Fuego was drawing out funds just under the reporting limit of ten thousand dollars, then combining them. His crew would each take small individual sums to buy chips at the casino, which he could cash out later as "winnings."

"He also realizes that Tropical Storm Faith will disrupt his access to both banks and the casinos he normally uses to launder money," Red continued.

"So you're figuring there'll be a major move on his part," I said, trying to hurry this along. Really, what could that have to do with Avery and me, with a thousand miles of ocean between us and the United States?

"The same urgency applies to you two," Red continued, as if reading my mind. "If you don't get back here before the storm hits, you're likely to be stuck in different cities on the east coast until the airports reopen."

That was a dismal prospect, especially given the law enforcement manhunt in progress, at least for me.

"There's a Russian connection in this Thunderhead arms deal," Avery said. "That part bears further investigative work, probably right here."

"We agree," Red said, and my heart sank. I wanted off that island before *Nuage Noir* got marching orders from Denard or worse, picked up our scent.

"But," Red continued, "That's another whole project. We do have preliminary data that shows Russian funds co-mingled with their firm's accounts."

First things first, I wanted to say; get us back on American soil, closer to our assets, and finish off Fuego. Never mind widening the scope of an operation already spilling way over the boundaries of our normal operations.

"So we may pitch that project," Red said, tossing Avery a bone and easing my concerns. "With ATF and DOJ when we shut down this DEA witch hunt."

Avery nodded but said nothing, which I took as a good sign. That meant Red was reading her just right, even baiting her; she had to be considering the possibility of life beyond the DEA, given what they'd done to her at The Tombs. Red would love to have an experienced ex-DEA agent on staff, especially to pitch that Russian arms intel contract. Of course, that all depended on us living through this intel contract run amok.

"So," Red said carefully, "Let's get you two back here safely, then let's finish this mission successfully. Agreed?"

"Yes," I said. Avery nodded.

"I'll go back into custody now," Audrey smarted off, probably for the benefit of her Irish sister. "And you have safe travels."

"We'll slip under the radar and grab dinner, and then we're out of here at the ass crack of dawn," I said firmly. I wanted this conference over before anyone had other ideas, none of which would be good news for us.

Red stood. "That's it then. We'll track you off the island and through U.S. Customs. Meanwhile, we'll pull data out of Banco Delgado as the bot and their server comes back on line. When you're back on friendly soil, we'll update. We need to hear from your partner, Miss O'Toole."

"We'll be waiting for him, too," Avery said. "If I don't hear from him by tomorrow I'll reach out."

Good idea, since he'd likely know what Fuego was up to and maybe where he was.

Once everyone had signed off, Avery sank onto the sofa. She tipped her beer up and drained the last of it.

"Grab me another, would you?" she said with a long sigh.

I shook my head. "No."

"No?"

"I have a better idea."

"I'm all ears."

I took her hand and pulled her up from the sofa.

"I think you need Trinidad stew. And there's someone I want you to meet."

She looked at me sidelong, her eyes narrowed.

I grabbed a card key and stood by the door.

"Oh, what the hell," she said and followed me out.

Chapter Twenty-Five

"What kind of man drags a lady out in a thunderstorm like this?" Mama Lucia said, pulling open the steel door. "Get your bad selves in here and dry off."

I followed Avery through the heavy door into the darkened hallway.

"Yeah," Avery threw over her shoulder, "What kind of man?"

We took seats in the same small alcove off the kitchen where I'd sat with Mama Lucia when I arrived in Haiti, not only on this trip, but so many years ago and a world away.

Mama Lucia handed Avery a clean but worn dishtowel. Avery bent over to the side, shook her hair out, and then dried it with the towel.

Mama Lucia trundled laboriously back to the table

with a tall bottle of Rhum Barbancourt 3-star and three empty water glasses. She poured three fingers into each glass carefully, then sat.

"So," she said at last, seemingly sizing Avery up. "This is the one?"

Avery looked back and forth between Mama "L" and me but said nothing. Laughter and loud voices tumbled down the darkened hallway from the small eating area.

"Today, how did Benjo know?" I asked, ignoring her first question.

She laughed a booming laugh that shook her wide belly and breasts under a worn apron.

"How does anyone ever know?" she asked through her own laughter. "Easier to say what you don't know."

"Does anyone here do normal conversation?" Avery asked politely. "Because I'm not following any of this."

The wafting smell of spices, of tender chicken, and savory broth, made my mouth water and my stomach growl. I sipped the rum carefully, letting the hundred-fifty proof gold burn slowly downward, warming me from the inside.

Mama Lucia wagged a finger at Avery. "Not so fast, friend of the ghost."

I couldn't be sure if she meant me, or another spirit, but there were no simple answers to be had. She toasted Avery, then swallowed a healthy dose of her rum with closed eyes.

Avery knocked back half of her drink, then extended her hand.

"Avery," she said, "pleased to meet you."

The big woman put her flat palm on her chest. "Mama Lucia. And I already know who you are, child."

"Boucane," I said for Avery's benefit. A ghost, sort of, I had to admit. *One thing you learn when you get a doctorate,* Tu'u's voice echoed in my mind, *is how little you'll ever know*.

"What is all this," Avery said, raising her hands as if in consecration. "Voodoo? You're all talking in riddles; you make no sense."

"Oh it makes sense," Mam Lucia said, splaying her plump fingers on the table.

"How did Boucane know about me? My sister?" Avery asked. "How did *you* know about me?"

"*Hounfour*," Mama Lucia said. "The prophet. Told me. The prophet knows."

Mama Lucia slapped a fat palm on the clean, worn tabletop and rumbled with laughter, then refilled all three glasses. Rain clattered on the corrugated awning above a propped-open window. A cool breeze swirled in.

"Vodou, child, is not about questions," Mama Lucia said with a broad, toothy-white smile, her eyes focused elsewhere. "It's about answers. It's not about finding; it's about being found."

Avery knocked back the golden rum then poured herself another. Her eyes began to narrow, a look I'd seen a few times before an epic drinking session at The *Ole' Saint* in the French Quarter. I knew we'd soon reach the point where I'd either have to pump the brakes and drag her home, or hop on for the ride, hell be damned. I poured myself another drink.

"I don't know what to believe in anymore," Avery said, her eyes grown as distant as Mama Lucia's. I studied her face, which I could normally read pretty well, but there were no answers to be had there. The past? Was she seeing and regretting the miles and mistakes that had led us here? Was she looking at our cloudy future, wondering? Not fearful, because if anything, Avery was fearless. So, what then?

Mama Lucia laid a hand on Avery's forearm and patted.

"Child," she said. "It doesn't matter what you believe in anyway. What matters is what believes in you. That's my Vodou."

Avery cocked her head. "Spirits, what … *believe* in you? Us?"

"Speak to you," Mama said. "If they believe in you, they speak to you, for you."

Now I wasn't following. I knew Mama Lucia mostly as a Catholic—there was a statue of Mary at the window, a rosary neatly placed at her feet.

"Boucane," Avery breathed the word like a prayer.

Mama Lucia nodded. "Smoke. You see truth in the swirls, the way it rises, turns, flies, a face in the glass, the cloud, the rum; everywhere. Yes, child. Yes."

"We've seen him," Avery whispered, taking Mama Lucia's hand.

"No child," Mama said, "You've *been seen*."

She refilled Avery's glass.

"He's seen you, the smoke god," Mama Lucia continued. "So he looks out for you."

"Benjo?" I asked. "He appeared out of nowhere today."

Mama Lucia nodded. "Hounfour last night. Benjo listened, Boucane carried the message."

Was that Boucane with a capital "B," I'd asked Benjo. *You one crazy dude, mon.* I decided to say nothing, to not ask Mama Lucia.

Mama Lucia's face darkened as if a cloud had crossed the moon. "But boucane didn't tell you everything, did he?"

"What more is there?" I asked.

"About your sister," Mama Lucia said tenderly to Avery. "About your family."

"No," Avery said, eyes wide. "Tell me."

Mama Lucia held up her hands. "I would if I knew. You ask him. Go to the slave market. Back in Moisant."

"Nawlin's," I said for Avery's benefit. "*Masperos.*" The old slave market in the French Quarter.

I groaned, but no one seemed to notice or care. But more Boucane, *Masperos*? I put a hand over my face, which neither of them seemed to notice either. What was the connection to the spirit of smoke and Avery's sister, or family?

"You go ask him," Mama Lucia urged. "He's Hounfour. He's the prophet. You ask *him*."

"What..." Avery tried to form a question, then stopped, mouth slightly open, the thought suspended somewhere.

"You don't ask, Avatar," Mama Lucia said. "You just listen."

"Avery," she murmured. "My name..."

"Avatar, your name is here. Avatar is what you are," the big woman said, then crossed herself. "You are what is to pass. You are what is to come."

The sun fell toward the Atlantic, and the light from the propped-open window sighed from light blue to dark, then burned light orange. Glasses were refilled. Stew appeared, not too hot, but perfect, tangy, warm, all the way down. The rum burned steady like a pilot light, taking the edge off, as Mama said, while she poured again and again.

"No more questions, sister girl. You listen for answers, for truth," Mama Lucia said. "You don't find truth—truth finds you."

Avery nodded, as if she understood, and maybe she did, or maybe she'd just come with more questions than I had. For me, the answers were simply in the sky beyond the awning that had gone to blue-black, flecked with crystalline stars between cloud schooners riding the breeze west to east. That would have to do.

"So, Avatar child," Mama Lucia said, standing. "You live without fear. You live out your truth. That's your life. Why God put you here."

Seal the deal with food; the thought burned slowly like an ember; then I realized we already had. I stood.

"Jesus, Mary, Rada Loa, and the saints go with you child," she said, putting her plump hands softly on Avery's cheeks.

Avery stood, nodded, and arm and arm, we walked to the door. A pedicab, bright and loud as a carnival ride, waited outside in the steamy mist. Mama Lucia leaned against the heavy timbered door jamb under an electric sign that seared *Arará* into the darkness like the beacon atop a lighthouse. I steadied Avery, helped her into the back seat, and then fell onto the bench beside her. Rain dripped off the awning, the roof tiles of the low stucco building, and ran in dark rivulets down the potted, crowned, narrow back street.

"Ke Bondye beni," Avery said, her voice throaty. A full moon mustered strength as it rose, solid as a promise, sure as the truth.

"And with you," Mama Lucia said, still in the doorway as we eased away from the curb and into the moonlit night.

Chapter Twenty-Six

Morning sunlight spilled through the windows on either side of a seemingly endless corridor crammed with moving, struggling bodies, all trudging resignedly to the far end. I could barely see Avery's head of jet black hair about ten yards beyond me. She held her position, walking, in the sea of passengers just deplaned from international flights like our short hop from Port au Prince to Miami International. After we landed, I'd counted at least three international wide-body jets on the taxiway also lumbering to the terminal, headed to U.S. Customs and Immigration, each with several hundred passengers who'd have to line up there just like us. That was good news; better to be a pair of small fish in a big pond, swimming unnoticed in a huge school of like-minded fish.

I kept my distance from Avery in the human tide rolling towards Customs officers waiting in booths, ever mindful of pattern analysis and facial recognition software pulling images from the ceiling-mounted cameras stationed seemingly everywhere.

No need to worry, or as Mama Lucia would say, no sense dying unhappy; the ubiquitous cameras were a numbers game. They'd manage to capture maybe a third of the crowd and of that number, maybe half of the images would be of a quality that facial recognition software required. One-half of one-third, in a crowd like this, was decent odds. Besides, what choice did I have? I kept an eye on Avery, maintaining our separation for safety's sake. We'd meet on the far side, if our Ain't Bee credentials held up.

I was beginning to sweat and not because of the stress, or even last night's bucket of Barbancourt Three-Star Rhum still vaporizing from my pores. The terminal's air conditioning was weak, likely only turned on an hour ago when the Customs area opened. That plus the crowd of huffing, sweating, long-traveling bodies made for a stifling hike. Welcome to Miami International.

The alcohol was a factor, but the rejuvenating effect of Mama Lucia's Trinidad stew, the herbs, spices, the magic, was a legendary post-rum elixir. Still, I outweighed Avery by a good ninety pounds, and she'd actually downed more Barbancourt than I did, so I wondered how she was holding up. Her head bobbed steadily, resolutely marching toward the line of Customs officers seated in glass booths ahead.

I chose a line and stood behind a raucous family of four pushing a cart piled high with shrink-wrapped luggage. My choice was between them and a seemingly reserved, dignified British couple off one of the two British Airways jumbo jets that had passed us on taxi in. I decided the contrast for the Customs Officer dealing with the chaotic family, then me, would be more a bit of a relief, which would be a half ounce of subliminal favor I might need.

Maybe that was wishful thinking, an illusion, or just more "intel overthink," as Avery called it. We inched forward.

I was still about four people back when Avery approached a Customs booth a few columns to my left. She was in full Christopher Sly character, her business suit immaculate, hair, makeup—very much the weary business traveler who'd lost a holiday weekend to work-related travel. The agent smiled, seeming even to try chatting her up as her scanned her fake passport, but like the real Avery, she'd have none of that. He had no idea that the prim business woman could deck him, or take him down and disarm him in a heartbeat, and would do it with a wicked smile. After a moment, he waved her through.

Just like at the grocery store, I was in the wrong line but this time by design, behind a price check, a "manager needed," and probably a "wet cleanup," judging by the youngest child's sagging diaper just ahead of me. A perfect workday sine wave for the beleaguered Customs guy wading through their documents and assorted Duty-Free purchases; I'd be unremarkable, and a relief by comparison.

At last, the family straggled through the narrow lane from the "Show Passports Here" station and the pudgy Customs Officer wiped his brow and waved me forward. I presented my passport and Customs declaration. He eyed me up and down, then opened my passport, and placed it face down on the scanner without really looking at it. He stared at the computer screen.

"What was the purpose of your travel to Haiti, Mr. Moses?" he asked, still focused on the screen in front of him. A fly whizzed by, then landed on his arm.

"Business," I said without inflection, as if I was talking with Red and didn't want him to read my mind, like I was worn out, actually, which I sure was. I stared at the fly taking jerky steps towards the agent's collar.

The Customs officer clacked a few keys, glanced at me, then back to the screen. The fly vanished.

"Nothing to declare?" His eyes fell on me again, but

only for a moment.

I frowned. "No. Costco liquor prices have pretty much made that not worth the effort."

He laughed. "I hear ya."

He scribbled something on my custom's dec with a fat felt tip, stuck it in my closed passport, and handed both to me.

"Welcome home, Mr. Moses," he said, then waved the person in line behind me forward. I said a silent prayer of thanks to Ain't Bee for our safe passage through U.S. Customs and Immigration, then strode purposefully toward the exit booth, dodging slower moving travelers weighted down with luggage and hand bags. There another agent took my form, glanced at it, then waved me through. Done.

Avery walked out of a restroom as I made my way towards the domestic flight terminal.

"Fancy meeting you here," I said.

"What was in that stew last night?"

I shrugged. "Stew stuff. Plus a little Mama Lucia magic."

"I guess so," Avery said, shifting her valise from one shoulder to the other. "I feel much better than I should."

"Business trips are tough," I said idly, typing our flight number into the Google search window on my phone. "Hmmm."

"Hmmm, what?"

"Says our Nawlins flight's on time, which is surprising." A wide screen suspended over a moving walkway proclaimed what Avery promised yesterday; Faith was a hurricane, a Category 2 at that, gathering strength in the Gulf of Mexico and bearing down on the bayou.

Avery yawned. "So we have over an hour."

"*La Caretta*," I replied. "We'll need Masitas. And café Cubano."

"Lead."

We made our way to Terminal E and stopped by *Café Versailles* for espresso on our way to *La Caretta*. Avery staked out a table in a dark corner of *La Caretta* where we could sit with our backs to the multiple security cameras mounted near the ceiling as I went through the cafeteria line.

I joined her at the table, and we huddled over a Styrofoam container of steaming pork. I plugged a splitter cable into the earphone jack of my TAG phone. Avery plugged in her earbuds, and I tuned up a secure video.

After a moment, the compact screen came to life with The Maestro's dour image.

"Immigration went satisfactorily I presume?" he droned as if inquiring about his dry cleaning.

I nodded, my mouth full, chewing.

"Props to Ain't Bee," Avery said, stabbing a piece of meat with a spork.

The Maestro nodded. "I'll pass that along. I expect we'll complete the final leg of your egress without delay in deference to what is shaping up to be a direct hit from Hurricane Faith."

"Well," I said, motioning with my tiny espresso cup, "They're offering a $500 voucher for those willing to take a later flight. Figured we'd grab that and head to the Caribbean."

"Barbados," Avery chimed in. "Beach time."

"I'll get Red," The Maestro sniffed, shaking his head.

Red appeared on screen. "We have new contact with your partner, Miss O'Toole. We'll have Tu'u fill you in."

Nice to see you too, I thought but didn't say.

"Good data mining at Bravo Delta," he said, and it took me a moment to realize he was talking about Banco Delgado."

"Wouldn't 'Banco Delgado' be easier to say?" Avery whispered to me.

I shrugged. "Saves a syllable."

"But the data download's slow," Red continued. "We have account IDs, but not transfer totals. Yet."

"We left the island clean," I said, getting back to

business. "And should have no further complications from here to New Orleans." I didn't mention Boucane and hoped Avery would let the visit to *Masperos* wait till after Faith passed through.

Red nodded. "When we have full comm, we'll brief you up on the next steps. Might be facing a time crunch depending on how fast the storm moves. But we also got a windfall; the governor declared a state of emergency—that puts the LEO manhunt on the back burner."

Avery shook her head. "Faith'll slow down. And weaken."

I glanced at her. She'd clearly left Haiti with a bit of Mama Lucia's ability to "just know," or at least she believed she did. What *was* in that Trinidad stew?

"We'll hope so," Red concluded. "Anything else?"

Yes, I wanted to say. We needed to pin down the loose ends with Boucane that Mama Lucia had alluded to at some point, plus corral Fuego before he did the same to us. And maybe there'd be some way to squeeze in a trip to Strawn's in Shreveport for pie.

"Is my sister okay?" Avery asked.

Red nodded. "You'll see video on cable news of her behind bars being interviewed by detectives, but there's no audio, of course. Tu'u says the discussion is mainly Audrey and her new boss discussing how to access *Grey's Anatomy* on Netflix for free."

"Free on Amazon Prime," Avery said.

"Anyway," Red said. "Glad we're clear of Customs. Keep us posted."

"Will do," I said, then tapped the window closed.

Avery unplugged, wound her earbuds around one hand then stuffed them into her valise. She stabbed another piece of spicy pork with her spork. After a moment, she spoke.

"Go ahead, Perfesser, say it."

This was one of those hypergolic moments that I knew too well could burst into flames if I said the wrong thing, or if I said nothing. But I had to. Carefully.

"Well," I sighed, thinking fast, "I'd say we track Fuego as priority one. *Masperos* and Boucane have been there for two hundred years—they'll keep."

I let the words float, scooping up some sauce-drenched meat.

Avery looked up and away, as if thinking, then back at the nearly empty Styrofoam container. She nodded.

"Yes. I'm afraid you're right."

"Afraid I'm right?" I asked, pausing with a spork midway to my mouth. I'd let her have the last bite and likely, the last word.

"I have questions for Boucane. About my sister, my family."

I nodded, tipping my espresso cup one way, then the other, watching the remaining bit of deep nut brown java coat either side then slip towards the center. Like a pendulum, everything comes back to center. Eventually.

"But we have Fuego to put down first," she said, "to be safe enough to go forward and ask those questions."

I looked up from my espresso. The remnants were cold now anyway.

"Spend tonight at the Haunted Mansion?" I suggested. "Then tomorrow, Baton Rouge?"

"Faith?"

I smiled. I'd spent years in the Pacific as an Air Force pilot. On islands, and typhoons were a way of life.

"Trust me," I said. "The best weather you've ever seen precedes a monster like Faith. We get our act together, then make our way north."

She raised an eyebrow.

"Vulgar, foul pelican," I said. "Grub tub, sawed-off boatman."

Avery dug her phone out of her valise and dialed.

"Cassie will be ecstatic."

I sighed again. I wasn't sure I would be. But knowing Lou, he'd be sheltering his boat up north, past the worst of the storm. And any evacuation from New Orleans, especially with still-fresh memories of Katrina in the public consciousness, would be glacial in speed and supervised by law enforcement for whom arresting me would be an added bonus.

"Sister girl!" Avery chirped into the phone. I picked up the now empty Styrofoam container and stood, looking for a trash container. If nothing else, I knew I'd sleep in my own bed that night, which was worth a lot to me. Beyond that, the future, like the hurricane gathering strength over the Gulf, would be bad news we'd deal with when it got here.

Chapter Twenty-Seven

"There's where Jimmy Swaggart got blown," Gibby yelled over the slipstream raging through the open windows in her pickup. Airline Highway, south and eastbound toward the city we flew, hell bent for leather as if Gibby only knew one way to drive, and that was full-throttle on a chopped Harley.

"Who's Jimmy Swaggart?" Cassie asked, sitting next to me in the back seat, her hair wild in the wind.

Avery turned and leaned over the front seat.

"He was a televangelist back in the day," she said.

Gibby nodded. "Got busted with a hooker in a cheap motel on this here road."

Having Gibby pick us up at the airport was Avery's idea, and bringing Cassie along was Gibby's idea. Or maybe just Cassie's. But we needed Uncle Lou to ferry us upriver in the morning ahead of Hurricane Faith, and for that, we'd need Cassie's intercession with her flash-tempered uncle.

Just as Avery had foretold, Faith had slowed, and she'd been downgraded to a Category One storm as well. Still, any hurricane commanded respect when you lived in the bayou lowlands and especially, in the Crescent City itself. I couldn't help but notice the sparse traffic in our lanes headed toward downtown New Orleans compared to the outbound lanes full of those wisely evacuating the city before the storm.

We flew down the highway toward the city on the elevated concrete slab past strip malls and hotels and cemeteries with dome-like crypts and mottled concrete crosses in row after row. Gibby blabbered, Avery nodded, and Cassie chimed in now and again but mostly, sat there quietly, seeming as if she'd rather be elsewhere.

"How's the *Grub Tub* business?" I asked her. She seemed to brighten.

"Good," she answered. "Uncle Lou says we could actually run two boats, one for lunch, one for dinner."

"I hadn't thought of that," I said, flying my hand out the back window in the slipstream like a bent wing gull. "I guess you'd have to spend the whole day on one dock to work both times."

She nodded. "Later is actually the best, because we're selling beer now, too."

She went on to describe the sales numbers and the new stops, finishing with, "When my pop gets out of the workhouse, we can maybe run another boat."

The sun burned bright in the late afternoon, ideal weather, with uncommonly low humidity for a summer afternoon, driving with the windows rolled down. The high pressure that dragged the hurricane with it as it melted away to the north brought a spectacular blue sky which before weather satellites, disarmed folks, especially fishermen and other mariners.

I couldn't help but see the similarity to our present

situation, living on sunshine and borrowed time till the shitstorm of arrests and indictments swirled howling out of nowhere. We were forewarned, something we couldn't forget. That may have been why Avery seemed subdued.

"But," Cassie said with a wide-eyed, forlorn frown. "Barnabas is gone."

The gangly, flapping, constantly shitting pelican. Suddenly I liked the idea of traveling on the boat northbound a lot better knowing the foul bird wouldn't be glaring at me the whole voyage.

"Don't worry," Avery said, leaning over the back seat. "He probably just found himself safe haven from the coming storm. Animals instinctively know about these things."

I wondered if that prediction was more of Avery's seemingly newfound "knowing" she'd taken away from Mama Lucia, or if she was just trying to brighten Cassie's spirits. And maybe we too should seek a safe haven from the coming storm.

"Barnabas is a big part of our mojo," Cassie said, her eyes a thousand miles away. "Uncle Lou says it's a bad sign if a seabird abandons a sailing vessel."

I suppressed a laugh, and Avery shot me a look that made me glad I had. But seriously? Like we'd worry about that stupid bird, maybe add his mangy carcass to the growing pile of real threats stacked before us?

"Well," I said, watching a flight of four gulls winging lazily over a crowded graveyard. "After the storm, I bet he'll be back."

"Uncle Lou wants you to ask Smokey about Barnabas."

Avery shot me another look that said *you'd better not say anything smartassed,* so I didn't. But the fact was, Big Lou thought Voodoo was all bullshit—he'd said as much—but of course to him such ridiculous sailors' superstitions were sacrosanct.

"What's that look for?" I asked Avery as the hump-backed Superdome rose from the jumble of buildings below the elevated concrete slab like a colossal grey Quasimodo.

"It's an 'I told you so' look."

"Really? What did you tell me?"

"You damn well know," Avery said, propping her chin on her fist on the seatback, "I need to ask Boucane a few things myself."

Ah, Mama Lucia; *Hounfour*—the prophet—and truth from the lies of a Rhum Barbancourt tankard. Audrey, her parents, and more, Mama Lucia had said. *Ask the smoke.*

"Not tonight," I said, waiting for Avery to protest. But she didn't.

"When we do," Avery said to Cassie, "You come with us, ask him yourself."

"If Barnabas doesn't fly back after the hurricane," I said, fighting the urge to say I can't believe I'm going along with this, "We'll all go to *Masperos* and seek answers."

That seemed to satisfy Cassie and Avery both, at least for now. I glanced at my watch and sighed. The afternoon was halfway gone, and we had yet to switch out clothes and bags for a quick trip north first thing in the morning. Plus, we were still in the dark about several important issues, like Avery's partner's latest report and Fuego's moves that TAG would provide via secure comms at my place. A north wind swept the sky of clouds for as far as the eye could see, but I knew better.

Because soon, the tide would drag itself out and away, as if snatching itself clear of the storm marching relentlessly our way. The fickle wind would become still, then shift to the south; mild at first like a smooth, subtle entreaty. But then, as I'd seen in typhoon after typhoon in the South China Sea in a previous life, a fortress of dark, angry clouds would stack itself at the far edge of the southern horizon, brooding.

Then the wind would take on a raggedy, unstoppable force, easy, light, but constant in the beginning, a down payment on the gale to come. An unexplainable, sparky energy would charge the air; a potential, an urge toward strength and violence you could feel in your bones. Shelter, the urge would whisper as the flat cloud deck drew near, looming larger heartbeat by heartbeat. From a clear spot on the coast, you could see the saucer-like curve of the crumbly cumulus lip on the smooth decked cirrus tower climbing into the heavens. Then it would be too late, if you were at sea, on the Gulf, or even the Mississippi once the storm drew near. Maybe Barnabas knew that, maybe he was smarter than I gave him credit for. Maybe he was simply wiser than all of us.

I knew this storm truth, had lived this, felt it playing out again in my bones as Avery and I walked the few blocks from *Café Dumonde* where Gibby had dropped us at last. Avery agreed; no one needed to ever know where the Haunted Mansion stood tall, morose, and somber against the furious blue of the pre-storm sky, waiting to shelter us as it had me so faithfully for years. Arm in arm in silence we walked.

I resisted the urge to walk down Pirate's Alley, past Meng's barbershop. I wanted to see what had become of the place, and what had become of Meng. By now I figured she was either long gone, back up north where she'd come from, or if the Creed tracked her down, probably dead. There'd be too much DEA scrutiny watching my old haunts, so we walked a more circuitous route to the back alley entrance of The Haunted Mansion.

Inside, we grabbed cold drinks and sat down on the love seat while I fired up the TAG comm on the big screen.

"Alright," Red said, "Let's fill in some blanks. First, we got a video intercept sent to your old phone, Miss O'Toole. Date-time group was yesterday."

Avery held up her phone. "I have one here, just haven't had a chance to open it yet. Let's see if it's the same."

She hit play at nearly the same time as Red did. The two recordings echoed each other.

Tu'u nodded from the other screen.

"Same SIG-MSG tag," he said, scanning data on another screen.

Avery tapped her phone, which then fell silent, and we watched the larger video Red projected.

"Avery," the large, shaggy-haired man on the screen said, "I don't know or need to know where you are; don't call me back, just listen."

We both leaned forward, listening closely.

"I was discharged today," Jesse continued, "Now en route to meet Fuego for an op he has planned. He says once federal authorities in Baton Rouge verify reports of your arrest, he's free to move."

"Move?" I asked quietly.

"He plans to drag out your extradition until he can wrap up some loose ends."

He paused, looked over his shoulder, first one, then the other.

"My guess is he's trying to close some bank accounts he doesn't want anyone to know he has, but I think he's having some kind of technical problems doing so."

Avery nudged me with an elbow, and I smiled, silently taking credit—with Benjo's reluctant help, of course—for the "technical problems" that were making it difficult for Fuego to manipulate his Banco Delgado accounts.

Red hit freeze on the video. "Fuego will have trouble doing anything with his BD accounts."

"Even as Banco Delgado gradually recovers cyber-function," Tu'u said, "we now have a lock on his accounts."

"But even if he could close those accounts," Avery said, "He won't necessarily be able to hide his links to Ambroise, will he?"

"No," Red said. "In fact, we see Ambroise and Denard—whoever is really in charge—taking defensive measures, partitioning off their shared funds, which include Fuego's 'Fire" fund."

My heart sank at the thought of having to return to Haiti to extract that data from those two any time soon. Red tapped play again.

"Looks like we're headed to a casino, for some reason, on The Plantation Road," Jesse continued in a low voice.

I wracked my brain, trying to decide where they were headed. There were several casinos near Baton Rouge, but "Plantation Road" suggested one in particular.

"Plaquemine," I said. *Casino Colossus*, on the levee near a river bend north of Oak Alley.

The video resumed.

"I'll report when I can, in the blind if I have to. If you're in custody," he paused, groping for words, "All the more reason to have the truth about Fuego on record with your attorney."

"Or with whatever prosecutor gets a search warrant for this phone," Avery said.

"I only went into rehab to uncover Fuego's real motivation, to exonerate you—and me. Fuego's laundering money and I'm going to nail his ass. Take care, Avery."

The screen went blank.

Avery shook her head. "He just needs to come out. Report back to the DEA."

"Do you think he's worried about the DEA turning on him?" I suggested.

She sighed. "There may be players above Fuego with dirty hands," she said at last. "Or maybe Fuego's the top. I guess staying undercover on this is the safest move for him."

"If he's sincere about wanting to be on the record as being on the clean side of this," Red said, "We expect to hear from him regularly."

That would be more early warning that we could certainly use, but a Hobson's Choice for Jesse, trying to play Fuego. Raton had ended up dead trying.

"Meanwhile, you two are the closest operational assets we have," Red stated flatly. I'd expected that. I waited, but I knew what he was going to say regardless.

"We need a similar cyber-ingress, placing a bot

package into their server," Red continued.

Here we go, I thought to myself. I couldn't help adding, in my mind, *just one last time*. That thought surprised me, but there it was. I said nothing.

"We've got withdrawal data from eight of Fuego's many bank accounts," Tu'u said. "We need his Colossus PCTD data."

Avery looked at me quizzically.

"Preferred Customer Transfer Data," I explained.

"Guys like Fuego who buy and cash out tens of thousands of dollars of chips sometimes prefer an electronic transfer of their funds rather than walking out with six figures in cash," Tu'u continued.

"You want documentation of what he's doing," Avery concluded.

"Yes," Red answered. "But That's not all."

A smile spread across Tu'u's face.

Avery stood. "No way."

"No way what?" I said, looking at Avery, then the screen.

"We're going to send the money elsewhere," Red said quietly.

The Irish Sisterhood; I recalled our last TAG session…*send Fuego's money electronically to the Director of the DEA*. The Director would wake up to discover a few hundred thousand in casino cash payout from Fuego sitting in his personal account. Which he'd have to explain—to the world.

"We'd also Tweet documentation, plus all of the video we've cached from Fuego's phone tagged to every media account, hashtagged DEA."

"Before we get too excited," I chimed in, "It's probably more difficult to get into a casino server in the United States than a bank server in Haiti."

"You've done so many more difficult implants, Ghost," Red said. Ah yes; Mexico City, one in Japan, and even a savings and loan in Cleveland. All to document similar money laundering and fraud.

No one spoke for a moment. Outside, the wind had shifted from a gentle promise to a steady threat; I could hear it press against the French doors. Traffic noise below confirmed what I already figured; people were leaving town, evacuating in the face of the hurricane

"It's the final piece of the puzzle," Tu'u said.

"We'll have Fuego's Caribbean accounts, his structuring accounts in the US," Red said, "Plus his casino-laundered cash, dumped on the DEA doorstep, and broadcast with supporting evidence worldwide on social media."

"Plus a felony charge of 'organizing' for the casino money laundering," Avery added.

One last time echoed in my mind, unbidden but there it was. Maybe it was finally time, as Mama Lucia said, to be done. Sail up the Cane to sit in the sun on *Maglieaux's* deck in Natchitoches. Maybe Ain't Bee's big yellow Air Tractor was ready to fly north to deep green Mississippi. Me and Avery in a cool, cloudless sky, quiet air miles. I sighed.

"All right," I said. "Let's hear the plan.

Chapter Twenty-Eight

Like a dragon's breath, steady, unflagging, hot, sighing, a relentless wind rushed across the deck of the *Grub Tub*. Big Lou strutted, scowled, muttered, and cursed as the throaty diesel below decks grumbled idly. Lines were singled up, and then Cassie grabbed the aft rope from a dock cleat and hopped nimbly aboard from the pier.

The arch of the sky had lost its furious summer blue to a gauzy veil of cirrus arching out south to north from the center of Hurricane Faith who wandered out of the Gulf at her own regal, deliberate crawl. Like herald angels, the high-altitude bands of ice clouds proclaimed the coming tempest; never mind the blue sky, Faith's on the march, and she's about to remake the world in her own stormy image. Lou swung the stern of the *Tub* away from the dock abeam the New Orleans Aquarium, then out into the channel.

I counted out five twenties and held them out to Lou as Avery laughed. We both secretly savored the likelihood that

Red and The Maestro would freak over the budget on this operation run amok.

"Don' want yo' money," Lou growled. But, we needed speed, and on a trawler, that meant fuel costs driven through the roof. As I'd explained to Avery, the drive to Baton Rouge was largely direct, whereas the river meandered many more zig-zagging miles between the two cities. And time was something we just didn't have.

Cassie snatched the bills out of my hand then logged them on a ledger app on her phone.

"I do," she said. "We make no revenue stops today."

Cassie too seemed grim, maybe due to the lost Barnabas, maybe due to the tension of the storm against the backdrop of the Crescent City under siege, all roads out of town jammed with cars and people who should have fled yesterday. The local and national news showed the northern arteries clogged and creeping, and I was grateful for the waterway and Big Lou's proud trawler splashing forward against a muddy dark tide.

"Spaghetti plot shows Faith all over the place," Cassie said, referring to the television weather charts with squiggly colored lines predicting hypothetical storm tracks overlaid on a map of the Gulf coast.

"TV weather's all bullshit," Lou growled, spinning the wheel to starboard to line up alee of a squatty tug shoving a barge down river. "A boatman feels it in his bones."

I cast a sidelong glance at Avery. She seemed focused on the darkening blue lip beginning to bruise the southern horizon.

"I just hope Barnabas feels it, knows it in his bones," Cassie sighed.

I said nothing but still believed Cassie's gangly, flappy friend was likely hunkered down among the ilk of waterfowl nested in the reedy delta shoreline. Unlike us, resisting the instincts of common sense and self-preservation, heading once again into a set of law enforcement jaws that even a dumb water bird could see plain as day. I wished that my focus could be narrowed to concern for a bird or a boat or even a spaghetti plot rather than the arrest warrants and indictments hanging over my head.

The *Tub's* single stack belched gouts of black smoke, and the deck vibrated as Lou angled us north at what I judged to be a good twenty knots.

"Goddam storm," Lou grumbled, "She's blowing steady enough to push the river north. Going to be hell to pay once the backwash starts."

"Wetlands are doomed," I said idly, watching the New Orleans skyline recede as the river spread wide before us.

"We gon' shelter tonight at West Pointe a La Hache," Lou said, squinting into the afternoon sun, one eye on the horizon, one on the GPS navigation system pointing the way north. "I got blood there with a potato levee big enough for two shrimp boats."

"I gotta plumber there," I said, "With a truck. Picking us up."

Avery snorted, then grabbed my arm, and pulled me toward the stairs aft of the wheelhouse. I followed her down the steep stairs, then forward. I paused.

"Feel that?" I asked.

"Feel what?"

I held up a hand. "The wind, from the south." We were headed north.

"So?"

"We're making at least twenty knots, northbound," I said. "Your friend Faith is catching us—has to be more than twenty knots and growing, which means she's pushing thirty knots."

"Thanks for the science lesson, Perfesser," she said, watching the *Tub's* prow split the muddy green-blue splashing to either side. "Is there a point to all this?"

"Just that time is compressed and getting even more so. I'm feeling the squeeze."

She turned to face me, shading her eyes with one hand.

"Yeah, it is. So?'

The eastern shoreline etched a jagged horizon; to the west, more water and a hairline of brown and green. I could see where this was going.

I sighed. "You're loving this aren't you?"

"Maybe," she said, not even trying to be subtle. "Maybe this is where my good old fashioned law enforcement trumps your brainiac think tank."

Maybe it did. We at TAG weren't fast on our feet; outthinking complex problems took time, a luxury you didn't have in a fast-unfolding, treacherous situation like we were in now.

I nodded. "We're don't adapt quickly or work well on the fly," I said, dodging a gale of spray flung off the rising bow. Just thinking about that—was the wind changing? Why the leeward spray? Was Faith tracking more westerly? That would make a big difference in our timeline, and our options.

"Yeah," Avery said, squinting into the wind. "I notice Red isn't quite as cocky as things have unraveled lately."

I laughed. I'd noticed that too.

"So we make a good team," Avery said, sidestepping the gloating I expected and maybe, she'd earned. Her type of law enforcement handled things in real time, met direct force with equal measure. "You with the skull session assets and me with the street level smarts."

I thought back to Lurch—Toilet Guy—and how she'd taken him down in Krotz Springs. She was right, but…

"True," I said. "But…"

I lifted my sunglasses—getting darker to the south and it seemed, the west—and put them on my head. Avery folded her arms across her chest and said nothing.

"But maybe it's time to be done with this game," I finished.

She eyed me for a moment, then shook her head slowly.

"No," she said. "It's not. When we're both in the clear,

maybe we rethink."

Now the bow started to rise ever so slightly, falling gracefully. Every dip tossed a fine mist our way. On the nav bridge, Lou scowled, and his lips moved, but I couldn't hear the curses he must have been tossing at the weather.

"Overthink, in your case," she added. "But not now. We're neck deep in this. Let's see it through, then decide what's next."

I noted the "we" in that. I nodded.

"Speaking of over-thinking," I continued, "Faith moving northwest works in our favor."

"What does her direction have to do with anything?"

"Plaquemine is the Iberville Parish seat," I explained. "Part of the *quid pro quo* for allowing the *Colossus Casino and Resort* tax abatement deal with Iberville was that the whole facility would be designated a hurricane shelter."

Avery cocked her head, then steadied herself as the *Tub* pitched to starboard. Faith was tracking more westerly. "Say more, Perfesser."

"I'm thinking maybe Fuego needs to know that *Colossus* will be powered and open despite the storm."

She nodded slowly. "He needs the money. We get hurricane refugee access."

"Jesse," she said, pulling out her phone and typing, "Can pass that along."

We did make a good team; I had to admit. The rising swells and waves of spray forced us aft, but that was fine. We had a plan, and a commitment. We sailed north.

As we rounded the cabin on the leeward side, Cassie met us, standing with her fists on her hips, blocking our way.

"I know what you're going to say, but hear me out," she said, looking me in the eyes. Avery smiled thinly but said nothing.

"Sure, Cassie. What's up?" I said, trying to mask the note of resignation I felt.

She took a deep breath. "I need to go with you guys."

I raised a hand and started to speak, but Avery interrupted before I could.

"We're a little shorthanded, in case you hadn't noticed."

"I know, but," I fumbled for words that wouldn't hurt Cassie's feelings. "Is this the best way?"

"No," Avery said. "Let's call HR, have them do a job posting. We'll select a few candidates, bring them in for an interview."

"All right," I said, "point taken."

"Let's hear what she has to say," Avery said calmly.

"I don't want to be penned up with Uncle Lou and his cuz drunk and crazy for however long the storm takes to pass," she said, "They'll be outside shooting off guns and running wild."

That was an ugly specter I wouldn't wish on anyone. And I could see Lou and whatever "cousin" was also sheltering a boat, running amok inside and out.

"No one knows me in Plaquemine," she continued, still looking at me, "and my face isn't plastered on handbills in every post office in the state."

"Like some people we know," Avery added. Thanks a lot, I thought but knew better than to say. And I had to admit; Cassie was right. The advantage of Avery manipulating Ambroise's libido in Haiti was leverage we wouldn't have in *The Colossus* since Fuego would recognize Avery immediately. Then the ruse of Audrey pretending to be Avery in custody would unravel and a real arrest—or worse, another shootout like the one that was to have eliminated us at The Tombs—would be the final act of this morality play gone wrong.

I leaned against the bulkhead. "How old are you, Cassie?"

"Twenty-five."

"Really?

"Almost twenty-five."

"*Really* really?"

"Okay, I turned twenty-four last month."

"You sure you want to get involved in this mess?" I asked cautiously.

"I already am. Until we call off the rogue arm of the DEA, I'm half owner of a business they will confiscate."

Lou eased the boat starboard, tacking to parallel the coastline as Faith's westerly vector pushed us further from shore. I guess a course correction was the natural thing to do, and to do without a conference call to TAG. As Avery had said before, we're pretty much on our own on the battlefront. We'd make our own call on this.

"I just want to be sure this isn't some type of revenge thing between you and Fuego," I said.

"Gimme a little credit, Perfesser," she said with a dark look. "And he's not worth it. But we could use some insurance."

"What kind of insurance?"

"His one lifeline," she continued, "And it's pretty lame, is to say he was coerced. Video of him bragging to a beautiful young woman in the casino pretty much rules that out."

"Is that objective something you think manageable," I asked Avery, "And constructive?"

She looked over the starboard rail, her hair blowing.

"We don't have much going for us, Moses." At the use of Cassie's unorthodox nickname for me, they both smiled. This was probably their plan all along. "Better use all the help we can get."

She looped an arm around one of Cassie's and pulled her toward the stern rail where the big diesel churned a luminescent wake that trailed behind the *Tub* in a curved line angled to the southeast.

"Sister girl," Avery said, "Let me fill you in. I know exactly how you can lead our wayward DEA man around by his nose."

Clearly, Avery knew that much firsthand, but was just being polite to Cassie by not saying "lead him around by his dick." I climbed the ladder back to the wheelhouse then stood by Lou.

"They're plotting against us," I said, scanning the GPS plot on the screen near the big, wooden wheel.

"Mutiny. S'what women do," Lou grunted. "Learned long ago to stay out of their line of fire." He adjusted the tiller slightly to port. We motored on at the *Tub's* top speed, outracing one storm, flying headlong into another.

Chapter Twenty-Nine

"She's fine," Tu'u said. "More in protective custody than under arrest." A gentle rain patted the roof of the truck, and I wondered if that was the early bands of rainsqualls flung out like tentacles from slow spinning, powerful Faith.

"Is she not in a holding cell?"

"No, she is," Tu'u continued. "She—we, the DA—want no chance that anyone in the 19th Judicial District Courthouse thinks she's not who we're saying she is."

That seemed like a wise move, and I was reassured that at least this very crucial part of our strategy was guarded closely. But for Avery, the image of her sister in a cell only added more urgency to an already volatile situation. That type of thing could rush decisions, maybe make someone overlook important details. That made me second-guess myself about agreeing to bring Cassie in on this operation.

But as Avery said over and over, Cassie had handled Creed and the motorcycle mob successfully, although Avery hadn't seen the part of the *Dirty Dog* men's room adventure where the big, ugly gang thug threw Cassie across the room with one hand. Of course, Fuego wasn't Creed.

Tu'u had picked Avery and me up at Lou's "cousin's" dock near sundown. We made plans for an early pickup of Cassie the next morning so she and Avery could make a quick blitz through a twenty-four-hour *Super Target* store to assemble the appropriate casino-vamp look for Cassie. Now it was time for one last TAG session in the comm center in the back of Tu'u's plumbing truck. Spike sat at Avery's feet, looking forlorn, pretty much displaying the dread I felt but hid about the upcoming video conference.

"She doesn't like anybody in her seat," I said. "Remember?"

Avery picked up the poodle who then curled up comfortably in her lap. The main screen buzzed to life.

"Are we all present?" The Maestro asked in a bored tone. "If so, I'll summon Red."

Spike barked once, then laid her head down.

"I'll take that as a yes," he sniffed, then stepped out of camera range. The truck rocked in a wind gust.

"If you missed the Fourth of July fireworks," I said under my breath, "This will make up for it."

"All right," Red entered the picture talking. "Let me say from the start that the Stasis Group doesn't like this strategy."

"Power and satellite coverage in a hurricane are tenuous at best," I said, trying to save Tu'u from having to defend what was essentially my decision. "It's imperative that we have tactical control in the field on this."

"We agree on that," Red said what I already knew. My comment was an attempt to deflate his opposition to Cassie. "We'll be in a backup mode here in case field comm fails for any reason. But…"

Here it comes, I thought.

"We definitely oppose your use of an outsider in this op."

"Duly noted," I said.

"I'm an outsider," Avery reminded Red.

"You're trained in law enforcement, self-defense, and undercover ops," Red said. "Has anyone vetted this person? Background check? Drug test? Gang affiliations?" Red asked. "Any of that?"

"Nope," I answered flatly. I thought of mentioning Cassie's all-female motorcycle gang watching me relieve myself on the side of the hangar in LaFitte, but decided that snark would be like striking a match in a tinderbox.

"The one element we need, Fuego coordinating the money laundering," Avery said, "she can get. Her involvement will be minimal, and she's not aware of any TAG organization or operation beyond what we're asking her to do."

"In a casino money laundering op, Fuego will likely never show on the gaming floor himself," Tu'u said. "We need simple smartphone app audio and video that puts him at the casino, in charge."

"Plus anything else he may let slip," I added.

Red shook his head. "I have a twenty-four-year-old daughter. I would not send her in there. You're risking a sexual assault or worse."

"She can handle herself," Avery said, more confidently than I felt. What if we were pushing her into a dangerous position beyond her ability to control? I took some comfort from Avery knowing Fuego and what he was capable of from firsthand experience, but for God's sake, he'd signed a death warrant for Avery and me.

"And I'll be on site to exfil her if necessary," I said, leaving out the fact that Tu'u would be on site at the Colossus, and Avery running the op from the plumbing truck. No sense in sandpapering the lion's ass with that new tactical decision the three of us had already made.

"Let's move on," Red said, all business. "Miss O'Toole's partner confirmed this morning that Fuego is en route now to *Colossus* with several others; two DEA agents and two of unconfirmed affiliation."

Avery raised an eyebrow; I guessed at the non-DEA involvement. Could that be someone to whom Fuego owes money? A Haitian or Russian connection?

"After they conclude their cash-out there, they'll proceed directly to the Baton Rouge 19th Judicial District Courthouse to interview what they will insist is rightfully a federal prisoner."

No one spoke aloud the looming deadline in Red's last statement; this was our last shot. We needed the racketeering and money laundering evidence to go with the documentation of Fuego's offshore accounts. By first thing in the morning.

"I know there's no ambiguity in anyone's mind about our present situation," Red said in a hollow voice, "But here's the feed from Fuego's smartphone." The screen blurred, then displayed a grainy but distinct picture of Fuego's home office."

"Look," Fuego's voice could be heard off camera. "We've got her in custody. I'll personally verify her prints then stay at the 19th till someone from the U.S. Attorney's office gets there with a judge's order to take control."

A shadowy figured walked past the camera, then faced directly into the lens of the phone seated in the recharging dock.

"I don't give a shit what happens to her accomplice," Fuego barked into the phone. "If Thunderheads want the undisputed bayou badass title, find the bastard, then chop him into gator-sized pieces that will be digested by the crocs in the swamp."

He paused, and the realization that he was referring to me in bite-sized pieces only strengthened my resolve to outthink him. Plus, this audio and video just confirmed the link between Fuego and the Haitians as well as the

Russians. And Fuego was an idiot; there were no crocs in the swamp, as I'd heard Big Lou explain to countless touristas a world away and an age ago on his pontoon boat.

"Gators, crocs," Fuego snarled into the phone, "I don't give a fuck; if you want to show Creed who's the new sheriff in the LaFitte, feed Dr. Mosby to the swamp wildlife." Clearly, he'd been corrected by someone on the other end of the call. Chilling, but I still allowed myself a wry smile.

"We have a surveillance team watching his condo in the Garden District," Fuego continued. "When they spot him, and they will, I'll alert you, then pull them off. The rest is up to you."

I'd have been surprised if they'd found the Haunted Mansion, which they clearly hadn't. That was a relief, although my neighbors at my Garden District faux residence were in for a nasty surprise when a gang of Haitian gunrunners showed up. But, if our plan worked, that wouldn't happen, and if we failed, it wouldn't matter. Rain poured insistently on the metal roof of the truck.

"Once he's disposed of, and we have O'Toole in custody, we'll shut down the rogue intel subcontractor who started this mess. Pick 'em off one by one."

The grainy video vanished, and Red reappeared.

"There's more, but you get the point. This is an all or nothing gamble."

No one spoke for a long moment. I tried not to be subjective about our chances, knowing that wouldn't help.

"Since you're running this op from there, brief it, Ghost."

I took a deep breath, then started.

"It's simple. We'll infil early, using the hurricane shelter volunteer check-in at *Colossus* as a way into the service portion of the casino. Tu'u's got Fuego's comms and location updates from Jesse and his smartphone. I'll use the *Colossus* food service ID Tu'u just downloaded from Ain't Bee," I said, holding it up for Red, "And work as deep into their tech center as I can. We have current building schematics and Tu'u will track me and send comm and vectors to the right area."

A civil defense alert buzzed all of our phones. I glanced at mine—a flash flood warning for the entire southern portion of the state.

"Avery's off the property, but she can go in after Cassie if things blow up. Cassie will simply get as close to Fuego as possible, while Snapchatting Spike," I patted the dog's head, "And streaming Periscope and Meerkat to the comm truck."

I glanced at Tu'u, who picked up the briefing.

"Once we cache enough audio and video from Fuego via Cassie, we pull her out. Ghost plants the bots we need to reroute Fuego's payout; we confirm the group chip cash-out in Fuego's name, and then we all vanish. End of story."

That sounded simple enough. If you didn't count the infil obstacles, my challenges getting into and out of the IT area, and Cassie's risk with a homicidal egomaniac. Plus, a hurricane bearing down on the site.

"National Weather Service says Faith will veer west," Red said. "So you'll have a ton of rain, which is good cover, but not the brunt of the wind."

Okay, we'll count the hurricane on our side. For some odd reason, Avery already had. The wind leaned on the truck, causing a slight list to starboard. By morning, we should have quite a gale.

"Make no mistake about this," Red said at last, "We disagree with elements of this plan. We also acknowledge that we're now well beyond the boundaries of what a private intel contractor should ever attempt, and we're both outmanned and outgunned."

Another alert vibrated from our three phones, as if in a dismal backup chorus for Red's song of woe. *Hurricane warning, all counties, seek shelter immediately...*

"But here's what matters," Red continued. "We're fighting for our very existence against a juggernaut hijacked by a handful of thugs. We will prevail because we're smarter, more dedicated, and ultimately, aligned with the truth and what's right."

Silence, except for the rain, the wind moaning and sighing as if Faith was as troubled as we were, huddled the comm compartment.

"Here's how confident I am of that," Red said, with perhaps the barest hint, yet unmistakable edge of emotion. "I've scheduled a meeting with the Justice Department in Washington, DC for Wednesday."

Even Tu'u's eyes widened. Red was agreeing to walk into the DOJ in mere days from now.

"I'm sure they anticipate I'm going to surrender myself and Tactical Analysis Group for prosecution. But what I am one hundred percent confident I will do," he paused, settled himself back into his more typically taciturn demeanor, "Is dictate to the Attorney General what TAG will require to seal the evidence we have regarding the DEA's corruption after Fuego's arrest tomorrow."

A slow smile spread over Tu'u's face; mine too. *Once more unto the breach*, the mythical king's voice echoed in my mind, which then added, *one last time*. I glanced at Avery and thought of our pact; we see this through and then decide what's next, or if there'd be a next time. She simply looked resolute, calm. Avery seemed at her best under fire.

"Sealing" the results of our investigation would include the hard data about a rogue DEA agent with financial ties to a Haitian gang connected to a Russian arms supplier; a group DEA money laundering operation and ultimately, dead bodies in the LaFitte Swamp. We could all read between the lines; a fat government contract to pursue the Haitian and Russian connection would be the bare minimum.

"Now," Red said, "Let's be smart, be safe, execute the plan, and finish this operation."

There was nothing more to say. After a moment of heavy silence, Red nodded, and the screen went blank. I stood.

"Well," I said, stretching, then steadied myself as a gust of wind-lashed rain rocked the truck. "You heard the man. Let's make this happen."

Chapter Thirty

The woman seated before me in the chaotic banquet hall-turned-hurricane shelter had florid hair nearly the color of her Red Cross volunteer T-shirt. She scanned a long computer printout with a squinty-eyed befuddlement.

"You're with, you're with," she mumbled. "Did you say—"

"Smith," I repeated.

"Oh, with the First Savings Bank group?"

"That's it!" I said with mock enthusiasm. How fitting; I'd play a volunteer from a bank civic group to work a money laundering sting. I'd figured there'd be a "Smith" on the list somewhere. Tu'u had already cleared the volunteer check-in security desk with the unlikely last name "Jones," apparently volunteering with his Rotary Club colleagues to man the rapidly filling hurricane shelter.

"Grab a T-shirt," she said, nodding over her shoulder to a pallet of ripped-open cardboard boxes overflowing with red T-shirts like the one she wore. She slapped a volunteer nametag and a fistful of coupons labeled "free pizza" ("You'll need these for lunch") down before me, then turned to the next volunteer in the growing, slow-moving check-in line behind me. I moved past the tired-looking police officer standing by the roped-off volunteer entrance, grabbed an extra-large volunteer shirt, pulled it on, and then pinned on the nametag.

"We're in," I said under my breath as I spotted Tu'u towering above a group of volunteers stacking shrink-wrapped pallets of drinking water.

"Copy," Avery's voice came through over my Bluetooth. "Cassie's on her way up to the executive lounge."

I breathed a silent prayer that Cassie hadn't been drenched by the lashing rain coming in regular waves as Faith swept by just to the west. But like the many loose threads in this operation, we each had to just do our part smart, efficiently, and confident in each other's ability do the same.

"You're a go, Ghost," Tu'u's voice spoke softly through the audio channel. Meaning, he'd been watching the service door to the catering facility, and there was no police presence, simply one casino security person posted there. I pinned my "Colossus Catering" picture ID onto my t-shirt and walked a zig-zag course around several rows of cots set up on the broad ballroom floor towards the back of the room.

"Volunteering on your day off?" the security guard asked, eyeing me up and down, as I approached.

"You heard Mr. Abignale." I shrugged as I stepped around him to the propped open door. Ain't Bee had sent the *Colossus* internal memo from owner Bubba Abignale urging casino employees to volunteer at the casino shelter "to foster good will in our community."

The swarthy man checked my ID and laughed.

"Like you'll see Bubba's fat ass here today," he said, waving me past. "He's probably on his private jet fleeing the goddam hurricane at this very moment."

"No doubt, brother," I laughed, then strode purposefully down the brightly lit service corridor.

"All the way down on the right," Tu'u's voice came over the comm channel. I pictured him sitting on a folding chair in the volunteer break area, scrolling through his phone like others "on break," except he was tracking my progress on Glympse.

I found the exit to the east side of the casino.

"No good," I said, "It's alarmed."

I moved on. We needed an emergency access point for Avery in case Cassie needed her, and a propped-open exterior door was our best option.

"First left," Tu'u said."

There. The door was barely cracked, held open by a smashed paper cup. Cigarette butts littered the floor. Perfect.

"This one's good," I said. Tu'u would screenshot the location and text it to Avery in the truck. If Cassie sent the duress signal, Avery could get in quickly.

I retraced my steps, heading for the food service facility. I pushed through two round-windowed, double-doors into the steamy clamor of the dishwashing area. I grabbed a clipboard off a rack on the wall and flipped through the papers. Supplies, requisitions, orders. That would do.

I edged past a cart stacked with trash bags, through another set of swinging doors and down a hallway.

"Should be about ten yards, on your left," Tu'u said. "Their terminology is 'drop deads,' and 'the vault.'"

I entered a small anteroom labeled "Quick Serve." Two uniformed waiters wheeled a cart laden with canapes and fruit bowls through plastic strips hung above a walk-in freezer room, trailing a blast of frigid air.

A harried man in a parka followed them out, marking items on a handheld wireless device with a stylus. His glasses immediately fogged up in the warmer air. He flopped his hands to his side in disgust, then removed his glasses.

"What?" he said to me with a huff. He squinted at my volunteer shirt, then my catering ID. "You taking Hors d'oeuvres to the trailer trash in the ballroom?"

"Hell no," I said with a smirk, "Taking drop deads to the vault."

I held up the clipboard. He squinted, then waved a hand.

"Bubba needs his money counters well-fed," he said, "with the leftovers."

Drop deads, the catering leftovers from past week's banquets headed for the trash next.

I pushed through the plastic strips and called over my shoulder, "Nothing's too good for *Colossus* employees."

In the freezer, my breath showed as I grabbed a wheeled cart. I pulled a pair of disposable gloves from a box by the door and stretched them on. Then I loaded up trays of appetizers; deviled eggs arranged in overlapping arcs, two shrimp cocktail platters, and three cheese trays. On the far wall, desserts; I took two trays of decorated brownies and cookies plus a container of chocolate mousse ramekins. When I pushed the cart through the plastic thermal barrier, the parka guy was yelling at someone on his cell phone, back turned. I wheeled past.

"Cassie's got a visual on Fuego," Avery said. "In the executive suite, stuffing his face."

Free food for high-rollers. Probably not drop-deads either.

"I've got two of his accomplices," Tu'u said, probably crosschecking the screenshots Jesse had sent Avery. "Burly guy with a crewcut, with a skinny Asian guy. But no Jesse."

The lights in the corridor flickered, dimmed, and then came back to full strength as thunder echoed overhead. The casino had ginormous backup generators, of course. Gambling, like a surgical suite, was too important to interrupt because of a blackout. But we needed the lights on at least until Fuego's team had finished their scam.

I trundled slowly toward the service elevator on the far end of the corridor, trying to appear bored. A security guard sat before the elevator, tapping his phone with a fat finger.

"Fucking Q," he muttered. "Always needs a goddam U."

I stopped by the elevator control and swiped my Tulane faculty card through the reader. A red light glared on the panel.

"Excuse me?" I replied to the muttering security guard. He looked up.

"What? Oh," he stared at his phone. "Words With Friends."

I squinted at the screen.

"Quid," I said, pointing. "Right there."

I swiped my card again. No dice.

"Yeah," he poked the screen with fat fingers, then smiled. "That'll set him back."

"Fucking computer card," I sighed. "This stuff's supposed to go up to marketing."

The portly guard looked up, as if seeing me for the first time, then his gaze fell on my food-laden cart, and his eyes widened. Thunder rumbled overhead.

I pulled back the cellophane wrapper on a tray of delicately decorated press cookies.

"Go ahead," I said. "The marketing staff won't miss a few."

He palmed a half dozen cookies, then reached his own card key idly toward the elevator control box. With one swipe, the green light glowed, and he let the card dangle from the lanyard around his neck.

"Buncha fatasses anyway," he muttered, returning to his phone.

I punched the "up" button. A chime rang, and the doors

slid open. I rolled the cart into the beat-up interior then pressed seven. Coincidence? That the "vault" in a casino was on floor seven? The doors slid shut.

The elevator rose grudgingly, grinding and chafing against the shaft as it ascended. Nothing's too good for *Colossus* employees; I murmured to myself.

"Getting a clear Periscope feed from Cassie," Avery said. The plan was for her to stash her TAG phone in the side pocket of her cocktail purse, camera eye out. "Cache is on."

"Perfect," Tu'u said. I wasn't sure I had the tech savvy to work the truck's cyber tools, but I was glad Avery had learned. "What about audio?"

"Intermittent," Avery said.

"Switch to the B channel," Tu'u said.

The elevator shuddered to a stop then the doors slid open. Another security guard at a desk by the locked IT door raised a hand.

"Where do you think you're going with all that?" he snapped.

I pushed the cart right up to his desk. I nodded at the door.

"In there," I said flatly. I put a latex-covered finger to my lips, then pulled out a platter of shrimp cocktail. I placed it quietly on his desk. He looked at the platter, then me, then the platter again. He pushed a button and the door buzzed.

"Go on," he said, unwrapping the platter.

I rolled the cart around him and was halfway through the door—

"Wait," he barked.

I dropped my arms to my side and cocked my head.

"Can I get some more cocktail sauce? Please?"

I bent to the cart, unwrapped another platter just enough to slip the cocktail sauce out and placed it on his desk.

"You can come by here any time," he said, smiling at the shrimp.

I pushed through the door into a room of stuffy, electronics-smelling air. Bright florescent lights overhead bathed the room in a bluish tint that spilled over racks of servers and drive cabinets. A man in a white coat put down a tablet device and walked my way.

"All right!" he chirped, ogling the food piled on the cart.

"The inner door is fourteen feet to your left," Tu'u said in my ear.

A shorter black man with thick glasses appeared from behind a tall router rack. He flashed a toothy smile.

"Yeah baby," he said. He nodded toward the inner door. "Should I take some into him?"

Another card key lock sat waist high on the inner door.

"Lemme see," said the taller man, pawing through the food. He looked up at me. "Take him some of these brownies."

I was ready to play my part, having been thoroughly briefed by the Stasis Group. *The key,* Red's voice reminded me from that memory, *is to make them think they thought of this themselves.*

I shook my head.

"Can't," I stated flatly. "I'm not allowed in there."

The man grabbed a platter of brownies and shoved it into my arms.

"I don't want Brunson eating shrimp or eggs on my shift," he said as his partner dipped three shrimp at once into the cocktail sauce. "He farts like an old brown mule as it is."

He followed me to the locked door, held his card up to a reader and the door unlatched.

"Just tell him this is all you have," he said, then shoved me through.

"Getting clear audio now from Cassie," Avery said. "She's pouring Scotch down the asshole's throat at a pretty good rate."

The inner room was more dimly lit, just as Tu'u had

predicted. Advanced data transfer, beyond wireless; ZagBot. Infrared. This would be easy.

A tall, gangly man with tufted, unkempt hair and wearing safety glasses approached me from behind a chest-high counter of monitors.

"What the hell?" he asked, then noticed the tray of brownies.

"They weren't going to share," I said, nodding toward the closed door. "But I saved you some."

"Assholes," he said and strode to the glass window. He pulled down a mini-blind slat with one finger.

"Assholes!" he roared, watching the other two eat. "Don't move."

ZagBot boasted 128-bit encryption at a 182 MBs transfer rate, Tu'u had said, but not using Wi-Fi; rather, using light. The inner room, he promised, was full of infrared sensors shuttling data from the gambling floor and a thousand gambling devices, at the speed of light, into the mainframe. Hence the dim, greenish lighting.

"The sonofabitch is hitting on her," Avery said, and I wished the comm frequency had more than one secure channel. I didn't need the distraction as I placed two silver-dollar shaped disks atop the highest cabinet.

"Midlife crisis," I said. Those were the only two Zags we had, and Tu'u had spent hours refining them for TAG's purposes. But all or nothing, Red had said. If we succeeded, he could afford to buy a few more. If we failed, it wouldn't matter anyway.

I was sure Red was smoldering over Avery's editorializing, which made me smile. And I relished the discomfort the use of both ZagBots—they were cutting edge and expensive—would cause for Red and The Maestro. Quickly, I seated two thumb drives into a floor level cabinet, just in case.

"We've got two green Zags," Avery said. That I needed to hear; both devices were transmitting to the truck.

"Upload cued," Tu'u said. "Do it."

"Data streaming," Avery said after a moment. We were in; Tu'u code was pouring into the *Colossus* mainframe, changing commands, gathering data.

The door burst open, and the rangy-looking guy returned with a tray of deviled eggs.

"Leave the brownies, too," he said, seating himself at the console again. "Assholes weren't gonna share."

I have free pizza coupons, too, I wanted to say, but instead, I walked silently to the door.

"Still no sign of Jesse," Tu'u said.

In the larger IT room, the shorter man sat with his feet propped on the table, scooping mousse from a ramekin. I grabbed a rolled up ham slice with Boursin cheese in the center and chewed it thoughtfully.

"Not bad," I said. *For leftovers*, I thought but didn't say. "It cries out for a light Sauvignon Blanc."

"Hey, see if you can get any of those crab legs, wouldja?" he said pointing his spoon at me for emphasis.

"I'll see what I can do," I lied, pushing the empty cart through the door. I wheeled toward the elevator and tapped the down button.

When the elevator reached the ground floor, I pushed the empty cart past the security guard. Once out of sight, I stuffed the latex gloves into a dumpster and abandoned the cart.

"Cassie's with Fuego, heading back to his suite," Avery said.

Here's where all my earlier worry came back to roost; I hoped she's be strong enough to fend Fuego off, to resist whatever bad ideas he had planned.

"All of his guys here left the floor at least twenty minutes ago," Tu'u said. "You have video feed from her?"

"Yes," Avery answered. "Very Blair Witch; they must be walking. Or … staggering."

Dammit, I swore silently. He got her drunk? Now, he'd drag her back to his room? After a moment, Avery continued.

"They're in his suite now, I think."

If Tu'u was in the truck, he could check to see if all the chips had been cashed out to Fuego's account. But even if they hadn't been there was nothing we could do about that now. We had his players all on video; now the Zagbots just had to do their job.

"We've got a problem," Avery said.

I stopped in my tracks. Our plan was for me and Tu'u to exfil after he'd gotten video of Fuego's designated gamblers and I'd placed the devices. But with access to the service elevator, I'd be in the best position to help Cassie if she needed it.

"Standing by," I said.

"What's the plan, brah?" Tu'u asked quietly.

"Get ready to ex-fil, Tu'u. Avery," I said, "Can you patch through Cassie's audio?"

"How?"

"We'll do it from here," Red's voice spoke over the comm freq.

"You ruffied me, didn't you?" Cassie's voice came through, shrill, angry, and scratchy, though distinct. "Sonofabitch ruffied me."

"Yah," Fuego slurred. "For your own good."

I heard a crash, then a thud.

"Shit," Avery's said quietly. "She just punched him in the face.

"On my way," I said, turning back toward the elevator. I broke into a run.

Another crash; angry words and the sound of breaking glass, then silence.

"Pretty sure," Cassie's voice said after a long moment, her voice hushed. "Pretty sure I just killed Fuego."

Chapter Thirty-One

Thunder boomed overhead; the lights flickered then came back on. I bounded down the empty hotel corridor to the single door held open by the deadbolt.

"I'm at Fuego's suite," I said for the group comm. I pushed the door open gently, just wide enough to slip through, then worked my way flat against the wall carefully into the suite. In the sunken main room, carpeted with a tacky shag, Cassie stood over a crumpled Fuego, swaying slightly, holding the broken-off neck of a Scotch bottle.

"Cassie, you okay?"

She turned, standing awkwardly in a black cocktail dress, shoes in one hand, broken bottle in the other. She nodded.

"He tried to ruffie me."

I knelt next to Fuego, a stocky, swarthy man. How had

he managed to talk Avery into anything physical? I shoved the thought aside and put my fingers to Fuego's carotid.

"He's alive," I said. I turned to Cassie. "He ruffied you?"

"Tried," she said. "I got woozy halfway through my first drink, so I switched mine with his."

I stood. "So, he ruffied *himself*?"

She nodded. "Stupid sonofabitch."

"You throw a good punch," I said to Cassie. She swayed slightly. "Pretty sure you broke his nose."

"That's my sister girl," Avery's voice came through on the comm freq.

I took what was left of the bottle from her hand. "You smashed this over his head?"

"Damn right," she said with a nod. "He put a hand on my boob."

I smiled. "Awesome. And he's an ugly little troll, isn't he?"

I guess I mainly wanted Avery to hear that. But there was no time for conversation—we needed to make a hasty exit.

"Let's get her out of here," I barked on freq. Fuego began to stir. His nose leaned askew and blood trickled from one nostril.

"Friggin' monsoon out here," Tu'u's voice came in weak over the sound of wind and rain. Thunder boomed overhead.

Cassie clutched her purse and fumbled with her shoes, still swaying a little.

"Forget the shoes," I said, leading her toward the door, "We need to move. *Now*."

"No," she snapped, standing up straighter. "I like them; they come in narrows. They're hard to find.

I rolled my eyes and moved us both towards the door, but heavy footfalls thumped down the hallway.

"We've got company," I said, peering out the door. Two men with drawn guns stood outside.

"Go for the stairs," I whispered to Cassie. "Four floors down, then out the exit that's propped open. Avery's there in the big plumbing truck."

She nodded.

"What about you?" she asked. "I'm not leaving you here."

Lightning strobed from the curtained window; then thunder shook the building.

"You're no good to me drugged. Go—I'll hold them off, and then I'll be right behind you."

She nodded.

"Count of three," I said. "One…two…

I yanked the door open then cross body blocked the first hulking guy into the skinny Asian man behind him.

"*Go*," I shouted to Cassie. Her footsteps receded, and then I felt a boot in my ribs. Skinny man fumbled his gun, which clattered off, to his left. I aimed a knee into the groin of the burly guy. He folded, avoiding most of the blow, then brought the butt of his handgun down on my head.

I'd leaned so the blow glanced off, but I saw stars. The big guy tried to draw down on me, but I sidestepped him and put a knee on the skinny guy's back then twisted his head with a forearm under his throat, my other hand pulling his chin around to his shoulder.

"I'll snap this fucker's neck," I promised. The big man lowered his gun, but looked over my shoulder. Shit.

"I'll take it from here," Fuego said weakly.

I turned. He leaned against the door jamb, and held a nine-millimeter level with my head.

"Game over," I said resignedly into the group comm.

I released the thin man's head but shoved it hard enough to bounce it off the floor. I stood.

"We've got good tracking from your chip, brah," Tu'u's voice came through the comm freq.

"Jesus, Moses," Avery said. Even in such dire straits, I still appreciated the Old and New Testament juxtaposition.

"You see who this is?" Fuego asked the pair holstering

their weapons. The skinny guy had a wiry mustache and saggy, sad eyes. He shook his head.

"He's O'Toole's goddam accomplice," Fuego roared. "Cuff him."

All of this would go out over the mission freq, I figured, at least until they snatched my Bluetooth. The big guy grabbed a pair of cuffs from the back of his waistband. Were these the two DEA agents Jesse had warned of? Rogue accomplices, with Fuego? And where was Jesse?

"You send a whore up here to bait me," Fuego seethed. "Think you're going to just walk in here and take me down?"

"Aggravated sex assault," I said to no one in particular, but hoped to jar the legal sensibilities of the other two law enforcement officers. "That's your style, Fuego?"

"Your nose is busted, chief," the big guy said.

"I *know* that, Butler," Fuego hissed between clenched jaws, touching his left-leaning nose gingerly.

"The little girl beat him up," I said casually. "The little girl he tried to ruffie."

The skinny guy cringed and looked sidelong at Fuego.

"Shut the hell up," Fuego snapped as Butler cuffed my hands in front of me.

Hail clattered against the windows in Fuego's suite as they prodded me inside.

"Futenma," Fuego pointed to the skinny guy, "Go get the car. *Now*."

He nodded and dashed out the door.

"Butler," Fuego snapped. "Are we cashed out?"

"Yes," the burly man said, nodding. "All clear. And, you said—"

"*Not now*," Fuego shouted, glancing at me. "First, we're going to get in the car and—"

"Might need a quick stop at Redi-Care," I added. "That little girl made your nose turn the corner."

"*You shut up*," Fuego spat, "Or I'll gag you."

Butler eyed us both, his brow furrowed. He studied the

floor.

"Now," Fuego said, steadying himself. "We're going to take this fugitive with us to the Baton Rouge District Attorney." He spat a bloody glob on the shag carpet.

"We'll wait for the US Attorney I've already prearranged to meet us there," Fuego continued. "Then we leave there with both of them in custody. Got it?"

Butler nodded, then flinched—I did too—as a clap of thunder exploded right outside the window.

"We've got Cassie," Avery said. "Stay strong, perfesser."

"No worries," I lied, worried as hell. A lot could happen between here and Baton Rouge, most of it bad.

Butler shoved me down into an overstuffed chair. Warmth trickled down the nape of my neck, probably blood from the gun butt. I was confident that TAG was still getting the audio.

"He's wearing a wire, Chief," the big guy said.

I sighed. "It's a Bluetooth, genius."

"Well then get it the fuck out of his ear," Fuego ordered. "And take his phone."

Butler picked the miniature mic and speaker combo out of my ear, then stared at it like it was an alien artifact. His phone buzzed, and he glanced down.

"The car's ready at the south entrance."

Fuego snatched the Bluetooth from Butler and held it up to his face, staring at me.

"Red," Fuego spoke into the mic, "I know you're listening. Your contract is hereby terminated. And I'm coming for you with warrants, you and your whole raggedy-ass gang, after I deal with your two sorry ass felons in Baton Rouge."

"Butler and Futenma are the DEA agents with Fuego," I yelled loud enough for everyone on the comm loop to hear. "Wipe the phone."

Fuego backhanded me with his pistol across my left cheekbone. Stars exploded before my eyes and a heat welled up in my nose. Warmth trickled down my cheek. Fuego crushed the Bluetooth with his heel and ground the fragments into the carpet.

"Our names," Butler said, eyes wide. "They've got our names."

"*So what?*" Fuego hissed. "We're three federal agents bringing in a fugitive. *We're doing our job.*"

I wanted to believe Fuego had backed himself into a corner with Butler; now they'd have to deliver me right into the US Attorney's hands. And TAG would track me every step of the way.

"Let's move," Fuego ordered. "*Now.*"

Butler looped an arm into mine and whisked me toward the elevator.

"How is it as a sworn officer of the law," I asked him, "working for a sexual predator like Fuego?"

"I'm warning you," Fuego growled, punching the "down" button. "Not another word."

Fuego stood on my left, Butler to my right with a firm hand on my bicep as the elevator sank. Two floors later, the doors slid open. An elderly couple peered in; then their eyes grew wide.

"C'mon in," I chirped. "The water's fine."

There must have been blood and a gash on my cheekbone, judging by their startled looks. Both Fuego and Butler flashed badges at the couple who stood frozen, mouths agape. The doors slid shut, and the elevator sank once again.

Once the elevator doors opened on the ground floor, Butler fairly dragged me in a rush toward the main exit. Lightning flickered, rain poured, and thunder boomed as the plate glass doors whisked open. Futenma stood beside the government issued black sedan, its trunk bristling with antennas, doors hanging open.

Butler shoved me inside, then squeezed in, pushing me sideways against the left passenger door. Fuego ducked into the front passenger seat then slammed the door. Futenma rounded the car to the driver's seat. He cranked the engine, and we sped off. As soon as we left the cover of the entrance awning, rain and hail hammered the car.

"Pull around to the back," Fuego ordered.

Futenma turned to Fuego with an inquiring look.

"Do it," Fuego barked.

Futenma changed lanes to the right then veered onto the service road. I searched for the plumbing truck, wishing it was still back there, but hoping it wasn't. I took solace knowing Avery, Cassie, Tu'u, and even Spike were safe. But a cloud of doubt about my own immediate future began to engulf me.

The car rounded the far side of the *Colossus* near the loading dock. A torrent of rain poured down the truck ramp.

"Stop here," Fuego ordered. He drew his gun then cracked his door, splashed around to mine and yanked it open.

"Out," he ordered.

"Kinda wet," I said. "You have an umbrella?"

Fuego yanked me out, then ducked his head inside, and barked some orders I couldn't hear. He slammed the door shut.

"I could put a bullet in your head right now," he yelled above the wind and rain. Rivulets streamed down his face, slewed sideways by his broken nose like a rudder slung hard to port.

"You won't," I shouted back. "Because you can't explain that to Butler, who you assured you're 'just delivering a fugitive,' remember? You think he isn't already having second thoughts about that—and you?"

Fuego pulled the slide back on his nine-millimeter.

"Go ahead," I said, looking him in the eye. "And there goes your big moment in front of Avery."

The wind-driven rain felt good, actually. Fuego's eyes narrowed, then he dragged me to the back of the sedan. He beat on the trunk until it popped open, released by Futemna in the driver's seat.

"If I get even the slightest moment with you alone," Fuego hissed, "You get a load of lead in the head. Understood?"

I said nothing, staring him down as rain poured over us both.

"Get in," Fuego ordered.

"Fuck you."

He put a forearm into my back and shoved me into the trunk, then slammed it shut. His footsteps splashed around the car; a door slammed then we started moving again. And all at once, the darkness seemed huge, dark, hopeless, and all too familiar.

Chapter Thirty-Two

If you're going to have a flashback, I forced myself to acknowledge, you know you must craft it yourself before it runs out of control. My mind reeled unbidden back to a certain hellish darkness years ago; *resistance school.* If you bail out over hostile territory, it's vital to your survival that what you encounter in captivity is not new to you; that you're ready for and familiar with the physical and emotional stress, that you develop resistance ahead of time, not on the fly as interrogators and captors beat you down.

A secret base in Idaho. Standing in darkness, in a coffin-sized box, alone. All night. Grown men breaking down, losing it—you'd hear the wails—but you steeled yourself, bore down, resolved. There was a peephole at waist level, but the box was too narrow for you to bend down and peer out—but guards peered in. If they caught you leaning, stooping, anything but upright, the door flew open and a bucket of cold water splashed in, drenching you, then the coffin door slammed shut again.

So you stood. You saw the light change near the coffin door hinge and by the peephole. You knew they were there. *Fuck them.* You'd stand. All goddam night, you'd stand. They wouldn't break you.

Walking for days, little or no food, evading capture, before the round up, *kneel, fucker*; hosed down, thrown in a cage with others. Then, one to a coffin, *march.* Time fled in the sensory deprivation; how long had it been? An hour? A day? Hallucinations came—were you asleep or awake?

You'd stand no matter what. Was that the metaphorical lesson? That you could *stand* it? You'd make yourself? A slop bucket rested at your feet, and God knows you wanted to use it, to pee. Needed to, but would not. There would be no humiliating trudge in front of The Hostiles, you dragging your own waste. Nope—you stand.

You thought of other things, reviewed places you lived, friends, people; every girl you'd ever fucked, every shred of life's details you could muster in the darkened coffin; enduring the misery of now through vicarious memories of then.

Been here before, I told myself in that darkened trunk. I can endure. I can use the darkness and, as I learned in the coffin and later buried in a trash can, I can use that as down time, as rest for my body—even though I had to be extricated from the trashcan by my compadres with a strap slung under my legs which had lost feeling. But I had slept some. I had recharged an iota. *I had resisted.*

Anything, anything to fend off the dreaded crate flashback; a smaller box, like a big cooler, wooden, chicken wire sides. You can see out; they can see in—*get in.* What could you do? The Weasel had four thugs. Get in, scrunch, squeeze, door shut—*padlocked.* Can't move. Fight down the panic.

Haul you out of The Crate, thugs, three of them. Rush

one—the other two deck you. Beat you—*they use soap bars in a knotted sock, hurts like hell, leaves no marks*—then stuff you back in The Crate. Fight the panic as the padlock clicks shut.

This was the trunk of a car, not The Crate. Drag up the coffin from the memory banks, the trashcan; *this was not The Crate.* This was not The Weasel; this was Fuego. And what did we learn, plunging a thousand feet straight down with a tangled chute, green fields below zooming up—you can make out cows below—just seconds from certain death? *You'd rather be dead than afraid.* A bullet in the head from Fuego? *Fuck him.*

Unreel a bit of now in the stuffy, humid trunk; darkness, the roar of floodwater against the tire wells, medium speed probably due to Faith's gale and rain. The rear tires slid some, shimmied, and then regained traction. Do the math; hydroplaning occurs at nine times the square root of the tire pressure. Normal tires at 35 PSI, means six times nine equals fifty-four miles per hour the prime skid zone—*slow down, Futenma, and control will return.* Just slow the fuck down.

Still standing, you can embrace the dark. Focus on controlled, measured breathing. Replay more endurance lessons—you don't have to run twenty-six miles, just have to run this next mile; then the next, just one mile. Just one more. Then before you know it, there's less running ahead than behind.

How long to Baton Rouge, given the storm? A couple of hours? Maybe they stop at least once? Don't panic—a bullet in the head; *fuck Fuego.* Rather be dead than afraid.

These US-manufactured sedan trunks could be unlatched from the inside—I'd done it—but stay calm. Won't be worth the struggle handcuffed, plus I was the tracking beacon, the chip in my arm, *like a dog* Avery said. They're delivering me to their own ambush. Stand up, stay straight. Another mile, another hour.

Trade now for then; Avery and me on the deck of the

Natchez, the rail lined with drinks, the breeze, the sunset, the city. Natchitoches sunshine in your face on Magliaeux's deck, the Cane rippling sedately below; Cassie gushing over her diarrhea bird talisman as the *Tub* sails upriver; a windblown night ride on her Harley; a perfectly calm sky and a slow roll in the big yellow Air Tractor; *we need to discuss your previous life*, cool and collected Avery had said. An adult beverage outside on the square in Oxford, Christopher Sly bitching about popular fiction.

The car slowed, then stopped. Doors opened, then slammed. Rain steady on the trunk. Muffled voices. The trunk popped.

Butler.

"Get up," he ordered. He dragged me upright, then pulled me out of the trunk. Steady rain, but not the deluge like down in Plaquemine. We'd gone east, and north, while Faith fled northwest. But how close to Baton Rouge? Looked like a shabby suburb, maybe the outskirts of a town. My legs and hips protested the movement, cramping, and stiff.

"Where are we?" I asked.

"It's some kinda 'Doc-In-The-Box," Butler answered, pushing me toward the passenger door of the car.

I might need something to close the laceration on my face, maybe the one on my head. But damned if I'd accept anything from these thugs.

"I don't need it."

He paused, smirked, and then opened the door.

"Get in," he said. I ducked into the passenger seat, and he smashed in beside me. "This stop ain't for you."

That figured; Fuego needed to have his nose fixed for his big show in Baton Rouge. *They're driving you to their own ambush*. I was still wet from the rain at the *Colossus*, which hadn't dried much in the trunk sauna.

"Chief is inside," Butler said. "And we can't drive into the courthouse with you in the trunk, now can we?"

So maybe we *were* close to Baton Rouge? I couldn't

read the dashboard clock from where I sat.

"You got duct tape?" I asked.

"Of course. Why?"

"I want to make a splice for this cut on my face."

"You shitting me?"

I shook my head. "You ever box?"

He nodded.

"Well, haven't you ever cut one out of tape? Saves time."

Butler looked away as if remembering. After a moment, he leaned over the seat, popped the glove box, and pulled out a roll of utility tape. He tossed it into my lap.

Boxing was another lesson, like the parachute fiasco; you could and would, if you stayed on the fight card, eventually get the shit beat out of you in the ring. You wouldn't die. Might hurt, might need to tape shut a gash. But you heal, then fight again. I pulled off a small piece of tape, no easy task in cuffs, and then bit a notch to tear it off.

I stretched my neck to see my face in the rearview mirror. I tore the tape into a butterfly bandage shape, maybe an inch long. I squinted into the mirror, then pressed the top part of the tape above the gash. I pinched the cut together, pulling up the bottom, then pressed on the tape. *Voila.* I suppressed a smile, thinking, *what a dumbshit, still taping your face back together at your age.* It really was time to be done with the fight game, despite what Avery might say. At least I was out of the coffin, for now.

"Where'd you box?" Butler asked.

"College."

"Were you any good?"

"Nope."

Butler laughed. "Me neither."

We sat in silence for what seemed like almost an hour, interrupted only by Butler's disjointed announcements related to his text messages. He scrolled through his phone.

"US Attorney will meet you at the Baton Rouge courthouse ASAP."

I suppressed a smile. I allowed myself a ray of hope that TAG had forwarded his name and Futenma's to Audrey's new boss, the state prosecutor.

"Oh, this is muy bueno. The Deputy Director of the DEA has driven up from New Orleans, wants to see all three of us personally."

"At the courthouse?"

Butler looked up with a grin. "Yup."

"Gonna be crowded." And an amazing shit show; I hoped for a front row seat. *One mile more, then another*.

"Plus the Commander of the Louisiana State Police," Butler said, stuffing his phone back into his jacket. "They must want you two really bad."

"On with the show," I said with a fake smile.

"You're pretty chipper for a guy facing a needle and a gurney."

I pictured Mama Lucia, the flash of her white teeth, that electric, soul-warming smile.

"No sense dying all tensed up," I said.

"Yeah, we'll see."

The door on the squatty building ahead flew open, and Futenma trailed Fuego, splashing to the car. They piled in.

"That was quick," Butler snorted.

"Amazing what you can get with a badge like this," Fuego tossed over his shoulder, his voice all nasally.

"Sometimes more than you bargained for," I said in an offhanded tone.

His head whirled around. A piece of white tape over a plastic support held his rearranged nose in place, although it still seemed lopsided. And swollen.

"I told you to shut up."

I held up my hands, but they were cuffed, so the gesture was lost.

"I'm just saying," I let my hands drop. "Don't say I didn't warn you."

Butler and Futenma exchanged glances and for a moment, I thought I caught a flash of unease shoot between them.

"*Drive*," Fuego commanded. Futenma cranked the engine, then craned his neck over the seatback to reverse out of the parking lot.

The rain poured steadily, but the wind seemed to have lost its hurricane mojo. We stuck to main roads, mostly, slowing now and again for spots where the water stood nearly an inch deep and swerving around tree branches and debris on the road. Big Lou was right; the flooding, storm surge, and backwash would devastate the wetlands.

As we neared the Baton Rouge suburbs, Futenma did a double-take in the rearview mirror. Butler turned in his seat and peered through the fogged up rear window.

"Looks like we've got a tail, Chief," Butler said, leaning forward.

Fuego twisted in his seat, looking out the back window, then in his side mirror.

"Fucking local goons," he sighed.

"State Police. Actually, two units," Butler said quietly.

Fuego waved a hand.

"Like I said," he groused, "Barney Fife and Podunk PD."

"Looks like Podunk PD wants you to pull over," I said pleasantly.

All three heads whipped around. Both State Police cars had the red lights flashing. One passed us, then pulled in front of us.

"Probably just want to escort us in," Fuego said.

"Please pull over," a voice boomed over the loudspeaker.

"God*dammit*," Fuego cursed. "How far are we from the courthouse?"

"Google Maps says about ten minutes," Futenma said. "Maybe longer depending on road conditions."

Fuego bowed his head. "Could this get any more difficult?" He sighed.

I held my tongue. Yeah, it could. And with any luck, it

would.

Futenma eased us to the right, then into a gas station parking lot. He pulled under the awning. A nice gesture, at least for the troopers.

After a minute or two, the trooper parked behind us was joined by the one in front. They walked together in matching rain gear to Futenma's window. He hit the auto open, and as the window whispered down, all three DEA agents held up their credentials.

"Gentlemen," the taller trooper spoke. "Can we be of assistance?"

"Why yes you can," Fuego said in a terse voice. "You can get the hell out of our way so we can get to the courthouse to meet your commanding officer."

"I see," the trooper said. "Is that a detainee you have in the back seat?"

The trooper poked his face in the window, looking at me, and Futenma's eyes grew wide.

Before Fuego could answer, Butler said, "Yup."

"Well then, we need to do a welfare check," the trooper said in a bored tone. "State procedure. Avoiding subsequent misconduct claims and all."

"I assure you, he's fine," Fuego snapped.

"I'd like to hear that from him," the trooper said, looking at me. "He doesn't look fine."

"He's just clumsy, if you know what I mean," Fuego said with a smirk. "Now, move aside, and we'll be on our way."

"I could use a vodka tonic," I sighed, "But otherwise, I'm just dandy."

The troopers nodded, exchanged looks; then the taller one walked back to his car. The shorter, Cajun-looking trooper stood next to the open window.

"This will only take a minute, sir. Please wait."

Fuego huffed but said nothing. In my head, I urged the trooper back in his car to be radioing my response to a law enforcement and state justice department conference in the courthouse. Let Red, Tu'u, anyone confirm the code word "dandy," meaning no imminent threat. *Just another mile, then another. Almost there.*

The taller trooper returned. He held his fingers together as if in a salute but aimed at the road instead.

"Please proceed, sir," he said briskly. "We'll be escorting you to the courthouse."

Bookended by state police cars, we eased towards the courthouse. We rode in silence, except for in my head. *Stand, still standing. We will stand.*

Chapter Thirty-Three

This wasn't how I envisioned the ending of this hellish Odyssey. The streets of Baton Rouge were largely empty, odd for a weekday, as Faith fled west leaving behind rain-lashed, flooded roads, blown debris, and empty city blocks. My spirits sagged.

I felt soggy, tired, my head throbbed from dehydration, most likely, plus the knot on my head from Butler's gun butt, and I really needed to pee. Just like the coffin, except there was no bucket. Which I wouldn't have used anyway.

Like every high-stress endurance contest, this one was becoming a struggle for survival, never mind "finishing." We approached the massive gray courthouse from the west side, turning left down a ramp to a gated corrugated metal door. The final irony; we were driving into The Crate. Sheriff's deputies scrutinized Futenma's credentials; then they raised a gate. We pulled forward; the gate lowered then the corrugated door clattered open slowly.

As soon as the car's antennae were clear, Futenma eased us forward, up the ramp till the cavernous garage swallowed us up. The metal gate rolled down behind us, and Futenma followed the hand-signals of more sheriff's deputies who directed us to a loading dock. We stopped.

Deputies pulled open the back door. Butler sprang out, nodding to a US Marshal who ignored him, pulling me by my outboard arm. I struggled to my feet.

Fuego opened his mouth to speak, but another Marshal handed him a clipboard and a pen.

"We'll book the prisoner and bring him up to the arraignment," he said.

Fuego looked around nervously. His mouth opened, closed, then opened again, but no sound came out. He nodded, signed the form on the clipboard, then two state troopers and a half dozen deputies walked him and Butler and Futenma to double doors at the end of the ramp.

The Marshal holding my forearm barked at a deputy, "Get these cuffs off of him."

I held up my hands and after fumbling for the correct key, the deputy swiftly unlocked the cuffs. I wasn't exactly sure what was going on, so I wasn't about to let down my guard—yet.

A water bottle appeared out of nowhere. I drank it all down without stopping.

"How about a bathroom," I said.

The Marshal nodded, pointing the way. "Let's go."

Inside, I relieved myself, then at the sink I stood and blinked at the reflection staring back at me; I looked like I'd been in a car wreck, with matted hair, dried blood on my neck and my cheekbone, an angry, swollen gash under my crude, makeshift butterfly, and two tired eyes. I shrugged. Might as well look the part for the arraignment, because it would take more than splashing water on my face to fix this mess anyway.

"We'll get you some medical attention," my tall escort—Lanigan, his nametag read—said in a booming, drill sergeant voice.

"But," he added, "The US Attorney has asked if you'd mind waiting till after the arraignment."

"Sure." I waved a hand, too tired to ask why.

"If you wouldn't mind, sir," he said with a touch of apology, "The State Attorney General would like you to put this on."

I looked down at the jail jumpsuit folded neatly on the sink. Even through my fatigue, the patterns of a strategy began to form. My spirits raised; could this be?

"Thank you, sir," he said once I'd changed. "I'll log in your belongings, and you can pick them up after the arraignment."

My spirits soared, as the reality of the situation became clear; if I was to pick up my belongings after the arraignment—*then the charges weren't for me*.

"This way, Dr. Mosby," he said. I followed him out of the men's room, then stopped dead in my tracks.

Outside the door, wearing an identical prisoner jumpsuit; Avery.

"God almighty," I said. "You're a sight for sore eyes."

She looked me over, then put both hands gently on my cheeks.

"You, Perfesser, are quite a sight. Looks like there's been a war somewhere."

We hugged.

"You okay?" she asked, leaning back, looking at me intently.

"Yeah. Everyone else? Cassie? Tu'u? Audrey?"

"All fine," she said.

"You look damn good, even in a jailhouse jumpsuit," I said.

"You must have a concussion," she said, flashing that dangerous smile I'd missed so much, that I'd focused on in The Coffin.

"Folks," Lanigan said. "We need to move along. I'm sorry."

"Sure," I said. "Let's finish this."

He hesitated, then spoke.

"We'll need you both in cuffs for the arraignment," he said sheepishly.

I held out my hands, wrists together. Avery did the same and a deputy cuffed us both.

"More judicial theater," I sighed. "Let's get this over with. I need some sleep."

Avery tossed her head, then followed the officer to an elevator.

"This will be the good part, Perfesser," she said. "You'll want to be awake for this."

The elevator rose, packed with us, plus more US Marshals, and a half-dozen state troopers. I was beginning to get the picture. The troopers had lost one of their own, and the Marshals worked for the US Attorney waiting upstairs. I allowed myself an inward smile, having "warned" Fuego.

Lanigan led the way to a cavernous courtroom only half full, but there was the tail end of a hurricane just now leaving town. The gallery was mostly empty, probably only ADAs and staff required to be on duty during the weather emergency. I spotted Audrey, seated next to Tu'u. We exchanged nods.

Lanigan led us up front, past the bar, into a holding area behind a low rail against the side wall. Bailiffs stood on either side. At the front of the room, two large wooden tables faced the towering bench and witness stand. The state seal graced the back wall, above the empty bench. At the tables, men and women in business attire milled around. Fuego stood next to a man in a suit who I didn't recognize, with Butler and Futenma to his right. Futenma had a wide-eyed, deer-in-the-headlights look, while Butler studied the tabletop and frowned.

"All rise," a bailiff finally barked, and there was a brief

shuffling of feet, then silence.

Justice Karnes, a tall, thin, distinguished-looking black man towered not only from the height of the bench but also from his own impressive stature. He had a long face with serious frown lines, and enormous, long hands. Must have played basketball in college, the stupid thought formed in my head. I dismissed it.

"Be seated," he commanded in a deep voice, seating himself. "This has to be a scary important matter to get this many bigwigs together in a monsoon. So let's get on with it. Madam prosecutor."

A tall, trim, elderly woman stood up from the table on the left.

"Thank you, your honor." She held up a piece of paper. "Here's the docket for this hearing, sir. I realize this is unorthodox, but we're going to accomplish several necessary motions in the least amount of your time if you will allow."

Justice Karnes leaned his head into one large palm. "Proceed."

"First, for the record," she continued. "Here are the relevant parties present today for these proceedings. I am Kelly Bishop, Chief Prosecutor. To my left, Mr. Stanbridge, the state attorney general. To his left is Commander Evans of the state highway patrol. To my right is Mr. Davis, Deputy Director of the Drug Enforcement Agency, Southeastern Division. Next to him, Special Agents Fuego, Butler, and Futenma."

At the mention of his name, Futenma flinched. Butler stared at the state seal above the judge's head on the back wall, his face stone. A burly court reporter beside the bench clicked away silently, taking down every word spoken.

Bishop extended her hand toward our pen. "Here we have two individuals under arrest, Dr. Jay Mosby, and DEA agent Avery O'Toole."

"Former agent," Fuego interrupted.

Bishop turned to her right and leveled her gaze coolly

on Fuego.

"Actually," she said, "We checked and her credentials and thus her powers of arrest were never rescinded by your organization."

Fuego leaned toward Butler, whispering angrily. Butler just shook his head and stared at the state seal again. I liked him. A regular guy, probably, doing his job but somehow, derailed along the way and regretting that now. Plus, a crappy boxer, like me.

"Now," Bishop continued, "To the charges against these two prisoners."

Fuego straightened, and his smile returned under his knobby, splinted nose. He shot a wicked glance our way. The rough fabric of the jail jumpsuit scratched my neck, but at least it was dry.

Bishop read off a typed sheet of paper. "Based on a preponderance of exculpatory evidence recently discovered by this office, the state requests you drop all charges."

Fuego's eyes grew round, and his jaw sagged.

Karnes eyed Avery, me, and then let his gaze rest on Bishop.

"I have read your motion," he said in a rumbly, distinguished baritone, "And I've reviewed the evidence and find it to be convincing. Does the US Attorney concur?"

The man in the dark suit with a broad, black push-broom mustache stood.

"We do, your honor."

"Then all of the charges against Dr. Mosby and Agent O'Toole are hereby dismissed. You are both free to go."

Fuego's eyes closed, Futenma dropped his head, and Butler stared straight ahead. *Stand tall*; I willed for Butler. *Just stand.*

Bishop turned to us.

"The state requests that you both remain to answer any questions that may arise," she said as the bailiffs removed our cuffs.

"That is," she added, "if Dr. Mosby's obvious injuries

allow."

I may look like hell, I wanted to say, but I feel better than ever.

"I'm fine," I said and sat down. Wouldn't miss this shit show for the world.

"All right," Bishop said. "Agent O'Toole, if you will."

Avery stood, pushed open the gate to our dock, and strode to the front of the state's table.

"This won't take long, your honor," she said. "Just a brief show up."

A "show up," meaning a victim visually identifying an assailant.

Karnes nodded. "Proceed."

A bailiff entered from a side door, followed by Cassie. She stood next to Avery and pointed at Fuego.

"That's him," she said simply.

"Him who?" Avery asked.

"The sonofabitch who ruffied me and tried to rape me."

Fuego pounded a fist on the table, I smiled, wanting to applaud, but I knew better. Avery was all business. The bailiff escorted Cassie back out the side door.

"Let the record show that the injured party has positively identified Agent Fuego as her assailant. In addition, the state has audio and video evidence the court has already seen supporting this accusation."

"Based on that evidence which I have reviewed," Karnes said with a deliberate edge, "I believe that probable cause exists to issue a warrant for the arrest of Mr. Fuego on one count of aggravated sexual assault, and an additional count of aggravated kidnapping, and official oppression."

"The hell?" Fuego muttered, glaring at Avery, then Bishop, then me. I rested my chin in my palm, my middle finger across my gashed cheek, giving him the finger, and smiled.

"The state has security camera footage from the *Colossus* loading dock in which Mr. Fuego has been positively identified putting Dr. Mosby forcibly into the trunk of a government vehicle against his will then driving off," Bishop stated for the record.

She turned to me.

"Dr. Mosby, were you forced against your will to get into the trunk by Mr. Fuego?"

"Yes, I was forced against my will," I answered firmly, "At gunpoint." Hence the "aggravated" enhancement, which everyone there already knew, but I wanted the words to add to Fuego's ass-pucker. He avoided my eyes.

Davis, the DEA Deputy Director, standing at Fuego's elbow, cleared his throat.

"Effective immediately," Davis spoke, "Fuego, Butler, and Futenma are placed on indefinite suspension and all federal authority granted to them is herewith revoked."

Bishop nodded at Avery, who took a step toward Fuego.

"You are under arrest," she said staring Fuego down with that dangerous smile. "For aggravated sexual assault, aggravated kidnapping, and official oppression. Stand up and put your hands behind your back."

Four state troopers moved toward Fuego, cuffing him, as Avery moved towards Butler and Futenma.

"Based on the law of parties," Bishop stated coolly, "Agents Butler and Futenma are charged with all three counts as well."

Troopers cuffed them, then stood behind them. Karnes eyed them coldly.

"Based on the evidence presented to this court on this day, I hereby order you remanded to the custody of the state pending a bond hearing and trial," Justice Karnes ordered. "Are there additional charges?"

"Yes your honor," Bishop continued. "The state will add counts of racketeering and money laundering for all three." She held up a sheaf of computer data. "Documents from *Colossus Casino* confirm a money laundering operation directed by Mr. Fuego and executed by Mr. Butler and Mr. Futenma."

Fuego slumped in his seat.

"In the matter of bond," Bishop spoke up, "The state maintains that Mr. Fuego is a flight risk, having uncovered evidence of several off-shore bank accounts in his name."

Fuego sat bolt upright, then glared at Avery who'd returned to sit next to me. I winked at him and mouthed *don't say I didn't try to warn you*.

"Based on the overwhelming financial evidence," Bishop continued, "The state will be requesting a ten-million-dollar bond for Mr. Fuego."

Fuego's trembling anger turned to fear. He tried to talk, his jaw working, but no words came out.

"The court recommends you don't speak, Defendant Fuego," Karnes boomed from the bench, "Until you have legal counsel."

He turned toward Bishop.

"And on the matter of bond," he said, "Ten million may be a bit excessive." He paused. "But five million we might consider."

A slam dunk, for Avery, for Bishop, and me.

"The final matter for this hearing, your honor," Bishop spoke, "Is one additional charge based on evidence presented to the court this morning."

The commander of the state police walked over to Fuego.

"Stand up."

Fuego shuffled to his feet, his hands cuffed.

"You are hereby charged with the murder of Louisiana State Trooper Arlen Stennis at The Tombs in the Lafitte Swamp."

Fuego looked around wildly, but deputies grabbed both of his arms. Avery stood, arms across her chest, and glared at Fuego as they led him out of the courtroom.

"I will hold your plea in abeyance until you've had time to consult legal counsel," Karnes called as he went.

"Are here any other motions you wish me to hear

before I go and see if my house is still standing, Ms. Bishop?"

"No, your honor," she answered. "Not at this time."

I stood. "Can we get the hell out of here now? I really need to be done with this."

"Me too," Avery murmured. "Me too."

Then, like a summer storm or a faithless hurricane, it was over.

Chapter Thirty-Four

Late morning sunshine spilled over the patio at Coffee Call. A single teenage boy wearing a paper hat and an apron swept away debris from far-away Faith, now tormenting Texas and Arkansas as a tropical storm. Two other bored-looking teens, also in paper hats, dragged wrought iron tables back onto the patio. I grabbed two chairs and placed them at our solitary table on the outer edge of the wide, flat tiles.

"See?" I said to Avery who took the seat I proffered. "I can always work as a busboy if I decide to leave the intel biz."

Avery sat, joining Tu'u and Audrey, pulling up chairs themselves. Tu'u placed a tray of café au laits and beignets in the center.

"I think you'd do better at the nerdy professor gig,"

Avery said. "Less manual labor."

"You could always work as an investigator for my office," Avery said. "You all do amazing work."

"Even if it's not admissible in court?" Avery asked.

I bit into a beignet—burned my mouth, it was so hot—and a cloud of powdered sugar rained down on the freshly swept patio. Like the tiles, the streets of Baton Rouge gleamed not only from the welcome sunshine, but also from Faith's power wash, which nonetheless left behind a scattering of debris everywhere.

"Doesn't matter," Audrey said. "You've saved us months of investigative work; we're headed straight to subpoenas, and we know exactly where to go and what to ask for."

"Schrödinger's Cat, intel edition," I said, sipping the velvety, rich café au lait.

"In plain English, please, Perfesser," Avery said, pointing the butt of a beignet at me for emphasis.

"Quantum mechanics," Tu'u said.

"*Verschränkung*," I said. "The problem of simultaneous but opposite outcomes. The evidence we gathered isn't admissible, but the facts remain true. All the DA has to do is 'discover' what we already have through orthodox legal protocol, and then the inadmissible truth is admissible."

"Seriously," Avery said, setting her coffee cup down, "I think you've spent too much time with Christopher Sly."

A humid breeze blew in from the west. Small birds alit on the edge of the patio, anticipating table scraps now that the patio was opened again. The bayou was slowly returning to life after the crisis of Faith. The hop-stepping, twittering birds reminded me of slobbering, gangly Barnabas and I hoped for Cassie's sake he'd returned to the trawler from wherever he'd weathered the storm."

"There another dimension to that," Tu'u offered between bites. "The DEA and our cache of incriminating evidence. The only way to avoid our exposure of their criminality is to deny our evidence exists—which means they can't go after us for the way we gathered it."

"The DEA and really, Justice Department," I said, "Is mulling over a very unique pre-Snowden 'Wiki-Leaks' opportunity."

Avery nodded and laughed. "If they want all the files sealed, they'll offer Red a contract for more work."

"Right," I said. "TAG has inroads into what is likely a Russian guns and drugs operation in Haiti that's spilled over into the United States."

We owned that, I thought to myself. It wasn't like Mama Lucia was going to chat with Feds about her beloved Benjo.

Tu'u nodded. "TAG can in good conscience seal the incriminating information so as not to impede or expose our new undercover work on such an important case."

"Important," I added, "As in high-budget contract."

Tu'u shrugged. "We're a business."

"But continuing with your simultaneously live and dead cat," Avery said, "Red can't use any of the damning evidence against the DEA or he's liable for prosecution for the way he obtained it."

"Yes, and no," I said. "He might have to be Snowden's roommate in Moscow for a while, but no one in either the DOJ or DEA would survive what would be a massive congressional investigation into their inept leadership and egregious corruption if Red fired all the evidence off on social media before he left the country."

Avery held her phone up to me, showing me a text from Cassie; "No Barnabas."

I sighed. Add one more ugly loose end to tie up with Boucane I'd hoped to sidestep. I already knew that was a slim chance after Mama Lucia planted questions in Avery's head about her sister and even her family that I knew she'd not forget. But I'd promised Cassie, so *Masperos* was inevitable.

"Cassie," Avery said for Tu'u and Audrey. "Her

faithful pelican is still missing in action after the storm."

"Guess you'll have to do your séance or smoke or whatever it is thing," Audrey said, and the Irish Sisterhood exchanged dangerous smiles that sealed my fate. They'd already discussed Boucane's allusions to their past. Well, Avery and I were headed to New Orleans straightaway after Coffee Call anyway.

"They sailed all the way back to Nawlins and still no idiot bird?" I asked.

"Nope. And you only say 'idiot bird,'" Avery added, "because Cassie's not here to punch you in the face."

Tu'u laughed. "I'm glad she doesn't know we have her slugging Fuego and breaking his nose on video or she'd plaster that all over Facebook and Instagram."

"Well," I said. "He had it coming. And I guess what I have coming is another smoky séance, as you called it."

Either way, we were talking about a beating, and that once again turned my thoughts to walking away. Maybe Avery was right; the academic gig made more sense. I could see teaching as an adjunct at a venerable Eastern European university in Hungary or Romania, a place with classic old world charm and no one there who wanted to arrest me or worse.

"Don't be such a wuss," Avery said, laying a hand gently on my cheek below the real butterfly bandage holding the cut closed as it healed. "I won't let Cassie mess up your pretty face any more than it already is."

Audrey stood.

"Well, thanks to you two," she said, looking at Tu'u and me in turn, "And I do thank you both, I have a mountain of subpoenas and indictments that aren't going to prepare themselves."

We walked toward the parking lot in silence till Tu'u stopped before his truck. Avery reached into the open window to pet Spike who sat behind the wheel as if ready to drive the truck herself.

"I'll patch you guys in with TAG for the wrap up while

you drive south," Tu'u said. "You can hear from Red firsthand about his DOJ meeting."

I nodded. "Fine. She's driving."

Avery cocked her head. "You sure about that? Last road trip we did from here was kind of sketchy."

I held up a hand.

"I'm turning over a new leaf," I said, "No more worry about boats or your driving." Or The Crate, the coffin, The Weasel, or balky parachutes, I thought but didn't say. I pictured a university in Budapest, maybe teaching two classes. At most.

"Let me know what you find out at *Masperos*, if anything," Audrey said to Avery as they hugged.

Audrey's car pulled out of the lot first, and then Tu'u and Spike followed us. We all went our separate ways at last.

We both would have preferred a lazy drive south on the windy, two-lane Plantation Road that in many places hugged the levee's west bank. That route, thanks to Faith, would be largely impassable for a few weeks, so we found ourselves on the Interstate speeding south towards Nawlins.

About an hour out, I plugged my phone into the USB port as Avery drove and within a minute, her car speakers chimed with the TAG conference signal. Avery tapped a switch on the steering wheel.

"I trust everyone is now here?" The Maestro's dour tone came through the car's audio system.

"Here," Tu'u said.

"We're up," I said.

"Very good," The Maestro droned. "I'll go get Red."

The tires thudded over slab breaks on the miles-long bridge span, so I turned up the volume.

"The Attorney General was in a very solicitous mood," Red stated without any time wasted on pleasantries. "First, Miss O'Toole."

"I'm listening."

"You are now on leave with pay," Red continued, "For

up to three months at your discretion."

"That *is* generous," I said, glancing at Avery sidelong. That wicked grin began to play at the corners of her mouth, but she said nothing, focused on the road.

"Not really," Red said flatly, ever the thrifty bean-counter, "Considering she just saved the Department three full agent salaries."

I wondered about Butler, if he had a family. Maybe he could cut a plea deal for giving testimony again Fuego, who I wished a long, painful incarceration.

"Regardless," Red said, "They've also requested Miss O'Toole be the project liaison for the DOJ at TAG."

"What project?" Avery asked. *Here it comes*, I thought, but didn't say.

"The Russian connection to gangs running guns into the United States," Red stated flatly. "Base intel, size of the operation, locations, and key persons."

I decided to cut to the chase.

"Is the contract proposal contingent on Avery representing the DEA?" I asked. That organization was a snake pit I was tired of having in my life. Selfish thought on my part, but still.

"No," Red answered flatly, "And to be completely transparent here, I told the Attorney General we'd rather she wasn't the DEA liaison to TAG."

The tires thumped in awkward silence. Spike barked, as if in silent protest. What the hell? Avery stared at the road.

"I stated that we preferred to have her on *our* team as *our* liaison to the DEA," Red continued. "And they agreed, pending your concurrence in the matter, Miss O'Toole."

"I guess I have a few months to decide."

"Yes," Red answered. "That's just one of many details to be worked out over the next few weeks. The good news is that Faith has made the arrests of Fuego and company back-page news. Once we're past the indictments and arraignments, we'll be finalizing a bill of work and a contract with DOJ."

"How do we know," I asked, "That the DEA won't reverse course and prosecute?"

"Our insurance policy," Red muttered, "Is the transfer data showing seventy-thousand dollars transferred from Fuego's *Colossus* account to the DEA Director's private bank account. Neither the DEA nor the DOJ knows we have that."

"That's some pretty hefty insurance," I said. "Just how big a DOJ contract are you anticipating?"

"Not exactly sure of the total amount," Red said, "But suffice it to say we'll be adding two more budget analysts to our staff next week."

I shook my head. From the brink of disaster to the threshold of prosperity in a matter of days.

"Will they cover the expenses we incurred on this out-of-control operation?" I asked.

"And more," Red said.

"Zagbots for Tu'u," I said. Spike barked.

"Miss O'Toole, your partner," Red continued, "Ducked out of the *Colossus* as soon as we launched our ingress."

"I texted him when we moved in as we all agreed," Avery said. "I also told him to file a whistleblower complaint on Fuego *immediately*."

"He did," Red said. "Looks like he'll either get Fuego's old position, or a reassignment elsewhere. That's an internal DEA matter now, but he's covered. He contributed greatly to Fuego's apprehension, and that's looked on very favorably by the DOJ."

We drove in silence for a long moment, and the thought of everyone going separate directions seemed a little bit sad, in a way. I believed, too, in an unspoken kinship among the tight band of us who'd just walked through the fire together. I believed we all felt a twinge of loss at spreading apart.

"So," Red said finally, "We've all been running at a

hundred and fifty percent for a long time. Let's all go dark for a few days, grab some rest."

I could only agree with that. No need to rush into any decisions after such a period of stress. Budapest could wait a week—or indefinitely.

"Sounds good here," Tu'u said.

Avery glanced my way. I nodded.

"Here too," she said.

"Very well," Red said. "If you need anything, you know how to raise The Maestro. Otherwise, TAG's going dark for now. Good work, everybody."

The comm link went dead. And that was that.

Chapter Thirty-Five

"Where's the monkey?" I asked the bartender with the wonky eye at *Chouette* on Rocheblave Street. The freshwater rinse of Faith that had cleansed the streets hadn't penetrated the tired waterfront hangout, which reeked of spilled beer and cigarette butts.

"Monkey's still busted," the bartender growled, then slammed down before me a piss-looking Chardonnay in a smudged, stemmed glass.

Refreshed from a good rest, I fell back into my professor mode, spinning intelligence relational modeling analytics and savored the comparative irony; Fuego the monkey was busted—still. That I could toast fittingly with a smudged glass and a nasty white wine.

"There he goes again," Avery said to Cassie who perched on a beat-up, wooden bar stool, brooding "Drinking his wussy drinks from a stemmed glass."

"The glass was his idea, not mine," I said. I weighed whether or not to risk the scruffy bartender's ire by requesting a tumbler. Not worth it.

Cassie seemed uncharacteristically distant, and I couldn't be sure if her mood was darkened by worry about Barnabas or the heresy she was about to undertake at *Masperos*. Either way, she pounded down beers faster than most of the dockworkers, idle from the lack of ships due to Faith, raising hell in *The Owl* while they waited. It was time for us to move on.

"After this round," I said, "Let's go visit the devil."

Avery gave me a disapproving frown, nodding at Cassie who crossed herself at the mention of Boucane, or maybe her Catholic perspective on all things Voodoo. Big Lou had always said Boucane was all bullshit, and I only said "devil" in jest. Sort of.

A fight broke out at the dartboard near the back door. Avery glanced over her shoulder as the first smashed barstool flew sideways from the growing brawl. She knocked her tumbler of Scotch back in one gulp.

"You fuckers are going to pay for that," the bartender roared at the mob near the dartboard. "I have your credit cards."

"Probably stolen," I told him with a wink. I took a deep swallow of wine, then another. Swill. It could find its own way to the *Chouette* drain. I slapped another ten on the sticky, worn-smooth bar.

"C'mon, sister girl," Avery said to Cassie, sliding off her barstool. "Better go before the shooting starts."

Cassie nodded and slid off her stool. She followed Avery out the front door as if going to a wake. Poor kid.

An uncommonly dry breeze swept through the nearly deserted French Quarter under a cloudless sky that made the scene look more like a snow globe than typically steamy, bustling Nawlins. Unlike *The Owl* crowded with idle dockworkers waiting for ships to return to the channel,

Masperos was nearly empty. The front doors were wide open, all the lights on and three workers mopped the wet floor—Faith's aftermath?—vigorously with string mops.

Amédée didn't seem surprised to see us. He simply waved us to the small side door next to the broad bar shelf lined with all manner of liquor bottles in a jagged skyline of glass.

We seated ourselves at the lower, silent, drafty bar according to the drinks already set out; Avery in front of a tumbler of whiskey, Cassie before the cool sweating bottle of *Dark Voodoo Dreams* and me, gratefully eying the tumbler of blessed Bourgogne.

Almost immediately, Cassie's eyes grew wide.

"Holy shit," she breathed, crossing herself, staring wide-eyed at the mirror behind the bar.

"That's him," Avery whispered.

I stared at the mirror, then at Avery, then back at the mirror. Nada, at least from where I sat.

"Omigod," Cassie said, nodding.

"What?" I asked quietly. Still, couldn't see or hear anything except the whisper of a breeze and my two companions.

"He said," Cassie murmured, "I don't need to find 'big wings,' they will find me."

Why didn't I hear any of that? I thought back to late night conversations around a kitchen table with Tu'u. Magnetic fields, perceived by one cerebral cortex but not another? Is that why some see an apparition that others did not?

"He says when wings find me, I must take flight," Cassie whispered.

Infrasound? Vibrations in sub-Herz only certain cochlea can detect or even decipher? A voice unheard by most, but definitely heard by some. Or, an equally variable perception of electromagnetic fields? Random ions finding perception on certain neuro-receptors but too subtle—or too heavy—for others?

"Thank Boucane for sending Benjo in Port au Prince," I said cautiously. Whatever the cause, I saw nor heard anything like the legend of smoke I known and seen and heard before, and that last time, Cassie had not.

"He says he didn't do it for you," Avery spoke quietly. "He did it for me. And Audrey."

What the hell?

Both women nodded. Cassie put her hand on mine.

"He says Avery's father gave his life in The Dominican," Cassie whispered, "Saving a young family from rogue US federal agents."

My jaw dropped. Tu'u's revelation to me weeks ago about Avery's past, in Tommy's Gas and Meat's filthy men's room… *their parents were original BNND. Killed on assignment in the Carib. I'm digging, but that's a dead end now. Bureau of Narcotics and Dangerous Drugs—the forerunner of the DEA.* The warning to me about the LaFitte massacre was payback, *but for her*—I just got lucky.

Avery slammed her palm on the bar hard enough to make all of our drinks jump. I did too.

She turned to me, her eyes full of fire. "He says the rest of my story lies with a prophet in the Caribbean. And now he's gone."

I stared at my drink and sighed. Though Boucane had nothing to say to me, *Bondye*, Mama Lucia, *Arará,* Radaloa; we weren't done with each other yet.

"He said Barnabas would find *me*," Cassie whispered, smiling.

The breeze withered, then vanished altogether. We stood; Cassie smiling, Avery with a frown and me, well, just ready to move on.

"I believe we have a plane to catch, Miss O'Toole," I crooned, putting my arm around her. She nodded, her eyes distant. Boucane's revelation about her parents was a lot to take in. And there was so much more of that story to be written. But, not today.

We walked in silence. Cassie led us toward the pier

next to the Aquarium where the *Tub* lay moored. As we drew closer, Cassie's stride picked up.

"Can it be?" she breathed. I squinted at the trawler as she broke into a run.

Finally, Avery spoke.

"Looks like she found her wings," she said. She managed a weak smile.

"Or her wings found her," I said, recalling Boucane's and even Mama Lucia's prophesy; *you don't find your truth—your truth finds you.* "Now let's go find ours."

The *Grub Tub's* hull rail was nearly obscured by the collection Harley's hunched over kickstands on the pier. A group of rough-looking women milled about, some admiring the large, brown feather ball perched on the stern rail, shitting his guts out into the Mississippi. I felt happy for Cassie, sad for the river.

As we drew closer, Gibby pulled on her pink-Mohawk festooned helmet and bellowed, "Mount up, ladies."

Motors roared to life, then revved. Bikes circled and lined up behind Gibby.

"For the record," I said to Avery as she walked towards Gibby's bike. "These aren't the wings I was talking about."

"I know, Perfesser." She flashed that dangerous smile. "But I think we're about to fly just the same."

A throaty, rumbling bike coasted up to me. Cassie jerked a thumb toward the rear. I nodded and climbed aboard. In a crescendo of roaring cycles, we roared out of town, up the freeway, past the shopping centers graveyards, scrapyards, and slanted rooftops till the city gave way to the flatlands and the bayou.

Cassie flew her bike smoothly, artfully, deftly. I surrendered to the ride, to the wind, the curves, the powered movement, to the prophesy, the *Iwa*, *Bondye*; the future, and the story ahead, waiting to be written. To Momma Lucia's bright smile and deep laugh...*you don't find your truth, mon; your truth finds you.* Just enjoy the ride, I decided for myself. All too soon, the end was in sight.

Chapter Thirty-Six

"Just sign here," Tork said, in the hangar office of Callieu Aviation Service. "And here and here."

I scanned the paperwork, verifying that every required overhaul item was complete. Never mind Red and the Maestro, I wanted to be sure Ain't Bee's budget was not squandered. I'd already preflighted the big yellow prop job; she was clean, serviced, and ready to fly. We'd stowed our gear, all that was left was for us to strap in, taxi out, and then claim our own little slice of the sky.

"I can't believe you'll fly that giant banana," Gibby rasped, "But you don't trust a bike."

"As long as she's in front," I said, winking at Cassie, "I have no qualms at all."

I hugged Cassie goodbye; Avery did too. Then we stepped out the door into a partly cloudy day, with winds from the west. I took comfort in the pilot mindset, paying more attention to the sky we'd occupy than the ground we'd leave behind.

Strapped in, with Avery up front, I hit the starter, and the big radial roared to life with a bellow that made the Harleys sound like pups. I taxied slowly, carefully toward the runway.

"So," Avery asked me. "What about this new TAG proposal. One more op?"

"Maybe," I said. "I'm kind of wanting to be done with all this. But maybe."

"Me too. Reluctant, I mean," Avery said as I lined us up just short of the runway, scanning the final approach and downwind for other aircraft.

"Not because of the op," she continued. "But because I'm not sure I want to work for an organization owned by someone like Red."

I laughed, scanning the engine gages one final time.

"Why is that funny?" she asked.

"Red doesn't own TAG," I said. "He runs it, but he doesn't own it."

Avery turned to look at me over her seat back. "Then who does?"

I swung the big bird onto the runway gently, lined up with the centerline, and then held the brakes firmly.

"Tu'u," I said. "And his business partner."

After a moment, she spoke.

"*You*?"

I shrugged, which she couldn't see from up front. "Seemed like a good idea at the time."

"In that case, maybe I could. You?"

I shrugged again.

"I tell you what," I said, easing the throttle forward till the big radial engine roared like a locomotive. I released the brakes, and we leapt forward. I walked the rudder left and right slowly 'til it bit into the air and held us steady. "How about we write another story that would make even

Christopher Sly proud?"

After a short roll, the big bird lifted off, the earth fell away, and we climbed into the blue, unfettered, free, and alone.

"Write another story," Avery mused over the interphone. We climbed gracefully to the north, toward Oxford, and the green haven of Mississippi. "*Our* story. I like that idea, perfesser. I like it a lot."

I said nothing but smiled to myself. This was going to be epic.

Turn the page for
preview
of

East Jesus

by Chris Manno

Chapter One

"The bastard's dead," Momma swore. "And dead is dead, so just leave him lay."

Crammed in the front seat between deaf old Art, who hunkered over the wheel, and my mother, who stared out the side window, Pop cocked his head and worked his jaws. "Dead and buried, but damn well still my brother," he growled, mostly to himself. He'd hardly find sympathy for Uncle Ray in that old wreck.

From the rear seat, I studied the back of my father's neck, the way the thick, sun-cured skin formed a wrinkled "X" crease above his burly shoulders. Try as I might, and God knows I did, in all my seventeen years, I couldn't conjure up an "X," or a "V," or even a halfway "dash" on the back of my neck, no matter how I scrunched and strained. In fact, it seemed I hadn't inherited any of his brawniness or even a touch of his sullen features, although our eyes were the same color. I never could figure that out.

"He's still dead," my mother had to repeat, had to get those words in. Pop's thick silence clotted the stuffy air in the overloaded Chevy, windows rolled up tight against the persistent needle points of rain and sealed closed in deference to Aunt Shirl's hairdo. I could hardly breathe.

We headed east slowly, away from the sinking sun that slunk back toward Dix, away from the weather ahead which raced off to rake the plains with strokes of lightning and a bow wave of red dust. That confounded weather was killing me too, inch by inch. I felt wind-whipped and faded, just like the last Fall's tattered Humphrey-Muskie posters flapping against the row of telephone poles.

And because of the thick, tumbling blue thunderclouds rolling across the plains, ready at any second to blow the sky apart with jagged lightning, the windows would stay shut. They held me prisoner—suffocating—squashed between Shirl and Gram, noosed by one of late Uncle Ray's cast-off string ties. Taking shallow breaths, I picked at my hand-me-down sport coat and worked a finger between the raspy-collared white shirt and my chafed neck.

I sighed. Could have done better; could have inherited his snakeskin boots, or his hat or his vest, maybe looking more like him than I already did, which is what folks who saw us together always said. But then there'd have been nothing much else to bury him in.

While Art dragged us home at a snail's pace, I tried not to fidget. I tried to disappear, actually, to melt into the ripped upholstery, not ready to take a side in the standing feud, a strangling hostage to the lightning and the hail to come. And to Shirl's hair.

Tighter than the windows, I slammed my mouth shut, knowing for the life of me better than to get caught on either side of the battle lines being drawn. Bean sat on my lap in silence, wise enough at age five to do the same.

We'd made it all the way to—and now mostly back—from Dix without a word, much less a cross word, from either Momma or Pop. A careful stalemate, a dangerous stand-off ready to explode, just like the seething sky, and I knew the strained peace was only temporary.

Graveside an hour ago, wind-whipped grit and trash from the Dix Drive-in across the road had swirled and tumbled around our grim cluster, all hunched over Uncle Ray's pine box. A west Texas rain pestered us, splatting one-inch raindrops in dust craters two inches apart, but only now and then, holding the big stuff over your head for all at once, just when you didn't need it.

While Reverend Ruley mumbled flimsy words that fled against a howling west wind, I'd prayed to God for the sky to rip itself apart and dump those lightning shredded clouds full of hail right there on that pink dirt spot. Because I hate those black moments, the heartbeat before the storm when you know what's coming, know it's going to hurt but there's not a damn thing you can do about it. Like the deep breath before a flood of tears, or the shallow gasp before your gut clenches and heaves itself out onto the floor, all you can do is wait until it's darn good and ready. And then hang on for the ride.

But the swollen freight train of inky clouds just teased and rode the gusty wind across the flat red horizon from here to the end of the world, threatening with ragged flashes of blue-green, hollering thunder but moving on just the same while Uncle Ray, the lucky one, lay dead in a box back in Dix.

Pop stared straight ahead, melting the tint clean off of Art's windshield with his dark glare. "He knew how to clean a shotgun," Pop said. "He damn well knew."

True enough. Uncle Ray had shown me how, last year, just after he'd finished his time at Huntsville. "Come here, son," he'd said, unshaven face split by that gap-toothed grin. "You're sixteen. Time you learned how to take care of a shotgun." We'd broke it down to a pile of oily rods and barrel and stock. Ray loved guns, especially handguns. He'd used a bunch.

My mother glared out the side window, jaw set, that

little muscle near her ear beginning to flinch. "Lester said it was an accident. Lester's the law."

My father snorted. "Lester's a horse's ass."

Maybe so. But a horse's ass with a badge, a gun, and unlike Uncle Ray, the okay to use it on people. But more than just the law, Lester Ruley was the judge, the preacher and the junk man too. Because if you were a Ruley in Conroy, somebody with your last name owned just about everything. Rusty-haired Lester wore the badge, his right Reverend Daddy wore the collar and doubled as the Justice of the Peace, and his brother Rooster ran the gas station and scrap yard. Besides the farms, there wasn't much else of Conroy worth mentioning.

"Rusthead," Ray used to call Lester back in high school and after. They'd fight some, back then, but Ray'd always whipped Lester's ass good. So it was natural that Lester, especially being in law enforcement, would get a good laugh about Ray "getting a full scholarship to Huntsville." In fact, he'd laughed real big, until Ray got back in town about ten years earlier than anyone'd figured on. Everyone except me.

Off in her own world, Bean shook her head, letting her pigtails whip my nose. Thunder clouds never scared her. Nor did storms. Bean was an angel, an island of calm, insulated from the furious weather by some power from above.

Art motored on, also unconcerned about the storm gathering in or outside of his hail-damaged sedan. Right behind him, next to me, Gram sat with her lips pursed in pregnant silence, ready to speak but as always, holding back until she finally burst.

Ahead, the sun-bleached standpipe rose into view at the exact moment the smell sliced the air. No one looked, no one remarked on the first turkey farm and the dusty, waddling feather balls strutting uselessly around the hardscrabble yard, heads thrown back, beaks agape, blinking dumbly at the boiling clouds, daring them to open up and drown them outright. And the acrid stink, a rising wave of cutting, shit-smell that floated against the wind, defiant, permanently stationed on that damn spot in the tired blacktop road marking that one scorched patch of packed red dust. Good-bye, Dix. Hello, Conroy.

"Bygones is bygones," Shirl huffed in her tired singsong, mournful even on a good day, much less the day of Uncle Ray's send-off to the hereafter. She'd done her mud-colored hair up in a towering B-52, but Pop had ordered it down out of respect for the dead. Wise direction, because Shirl was a tall girl, much taller than her older sister, and the beehive would have rubbed the droopy headliner in Art's old car.

Shirl and Momma shared the same tired eyes, puffy cheeks, and loose under-chin threatening to go double any day. More than ten years younger, Shirl's hips and waist had held back, barely, where Momma's had given up and let go when she'd come into her thirties. Shirl sat on my mother's side of the car. She had to be careful to stay on Momma's side, her good side, because Shirl needed a roof, our roof, Momma's roof over her head.

"He's in a better place now," Gram promised with uncommon tact. "And you all best pray to sweet baby Jesus nobody in this life finds out how he got there."

Bean brushed my nose again, back and forth, with her red straw pigtails. Like me, she hadn't inherited Pop's "X," nor his pointy nose, drawn face, dark complexion or any other nametag he could have put on her. I never could figure that out either, but Momma's hair might have been a kind of red under the base coat or bleach of the season.

Bean's hair was cut straight, shoulder length, when it wasn't gathered into pigtails, with bangs draped down over her eyebrows like a dark red stage curtain. "Doll" lay on the floor hump, her hair done exactly like Bean's, cut that way by Shirl a couple years back. Bean lived with that toy, never letting it too far from her sight. We'd hoped Bean would name it something; anything, but since she didn't, it became just Doll, which seemed fine with Bean. She'd take no replacement either; I tried two Christmases in a row. Doll's rubber limbs had lost their pink and faded to a pasty grey, and her head fell off all the time, but that never flustered Bea Anne.

In fact now, when things got hectic or dangerous, Bean popped Doll's head from her colorless shoulders before it could fall off, stashing it in the wash-faded pocket of her jumper for safekeeping. For me, that was an omen of doom. Through some sixth sense or guardian angel, Bean saw trouble way ahead of time and set herself and Doll to survive it. So when the head popped off, I took warning.

Still, doom or no, Bean was unflappable. No matter what, she just went quietly about her way, a wall-flower since before she could walk, easygoing as a wagon horse. She didn't even mind sharing her tiny room with Shirl, though Gram said our trailer was "'bout like to explode," even before Shirl came back to Conroy to stay "temporarily" with her big sister. That was three years ago, yet Bean never complained. But then, Bean never spoke.

"Hold still, Bean," I whispered.

Pop's "X" pulled tight and squashed flat as the big head whipped around, showing me the widow's peak. Pop wore his jet black hair in a pompadour and grew his sideburns long. In his meaner, drunker moments, he fancied himself as someone else, so he had to look the part.

His lips pulled back against jagged front teeth. "Not one *goddamn* word outta you, boy. I ain't through with you yet, so don't you go giving me more cause than I got."

I met his black pinpoint eyes with my own matching set. Come hell, come a beating, come whatever, I didn't care anymore. I'd decided what to do. I'd signed and sealed it on the rain-pocked red-dirt near a six-foot hole in the ground in Dix, adding a few drops of my own to those of the teasing rain. Pop could kill me if he wanted; in fact, he'd have to, just to stop me.

Tired of the neck strain, the head turned back toward

the windshield, slowly.

"My two sons, good one dead, bad one snapping like a snarling cur," Gram's lip finally busted loose in a whisper.

Pa snorted again. "Your good son did hard time in prison. Bad son does hard time out and might as well be dead. And that boy next to you will be, soon as I whale his ass for running off."

"Leave Travis be, Jesse. He just run off to see his dying uncle. Nothing you ain't done ten times worse. You just leave him be."

"What are you gonna do, old woman? Call that red haired, fatass preacher's son?" Ignoring Gram, he studied my mother's face as he spat the words but she'd turned to stone, staring out the window.

Not that Pop cared about me running off. Hitchhiking the fifty miles to Lubbock was no big deal. I'd done that before plenty. My unforgivable sin was bumping into him in the Medical Center parking lot, tumbling out of the cab of his rig with The Tramp. The woman none of us ever spoke of. The one who only appeared in Conroy, holed up at the Alamo Cafe, when Pop was in town. When he disappeared, on the road dragging his tractor trailer full of god knows what to who knows where, she vanished too. She was one of the dark things, the many dark things you best leave laying in the closet. Everybody knows they're there, but you just don't talk about them, much less burst right in on them. But I had.

And the whole way east, sitting next to the zombied-out diesel truck long-hauler who'd picked me up mostly to keep himself awake, I'd thought of Pop and the woman, knew they'd be there eventually, but I didn't care. Staring at the sunrise burning through the bug-splattered windshield, I'd practiced my question. "Who, Ray? Just tell me who."

And he'd told me a lot of things. Bandaged, tied down, tubes coming and going but still, he'd told me things.

Art put on his turn signal and began to slow, at least, a

half-mile shy of the only stop light in town. It could have gone through three cycles by the time he got us there, if it worked. Instead, a temporary stop sign, anchored by sandbags, leaned into the wind and managed the intersection until the county could get by to work on the dead light. And we crept along.

Left again, onto Slide Road bordered by rows of scraggly, rotting Dutch Elms, spindly sentinels dying slowly from no other cause I could figure besides the basic poison of life in Conroy. North another mile, past dry pasture land drawn into hopeless plots by rusty barbed wire strung on rough-hewn posts.

Wide-sky country, Uncle Ray would say, because to anyone with open eyes, there was more sky than anything else in the Panhandle. He said if a man fell on his back and looked around, the earth would disappear completely, because there wasn't a hill or valley this side of Palo Duro to get in the way. Lester had no business taking that sky away from Ray.

A mile from the center of Conroy, we trundled by Center Park and its sagging aluminum picnic awning, the hard-packed ball field, and the fifteen-foot sweet gum, "The Tree," the only one in the park to survive a lifetime of lightning, tornadoes, and hail.

A crop of oil wells, pump jacks bobbing and ducking, squatted like blackened steel grasshoppers, siphoning murky liquid gold from the Llano Estacado into some faraway stranger's pocket. In the center of the well-field, a plyboard pump shack with a make-shift TV antenna on the corrugated tin roof sat quietly behind Otis' chopped Harley, squatting out front. The trailer park, an aluminum oasis without a shade tree in sight, drew us closer like the tide.

Art slowed again but the worn tires still shot gravel missiles that clunked against the floorboard as we rocked up the potted road to Rattlesnake Gulch. Scamper, the Masons' scroungy mutt, yapped up the drive with us, dodging the flying gravel, legs scrambling. Shirl sighed, hope expiring as much as breath, and Bean started squirming again, but it didn't matter. Pop could whale my ass, Momma could scream, the trailer could rock and swell and echo like I knew it would, but it wouldn't matter. Because as soon as everyone else had their say, I'd go about my own business. Like the sunset, the moonrise, and the wheeling canopy of pinpoints that dotted the night sky, no matter how ugly the day, everyone had to do what they had to. And I had to kill Lester Ruley.

Lightning Source UK Ltd.
Milton Keynes UK
UKOW01f2258030917
308512UK00018B/429/P

9 781633 632059